The ASHEN HAND of KESSRIN

WAR OF THE TWELVE
BOOK TWO

· ALEX ROBINS ·

Cover and Interior Design by Damonza
Maps by Alex Robins

ISBN 978-2-9576580-2-2 (paperback)
ISBN 978-2-9576580-3-9 (ebook)

Published by Bradypus Publishing
4 rue du vigneau, 49380 Bellevigne en Layon
Dépôt Légal : juin 2021

www.warofthetwelve.com

Pour Ninou

*De toutes les étoiles qui éclairent le ciel de
ma vie, tu es de loin la plus étincelante*

Merci pour tout. Je t'aime

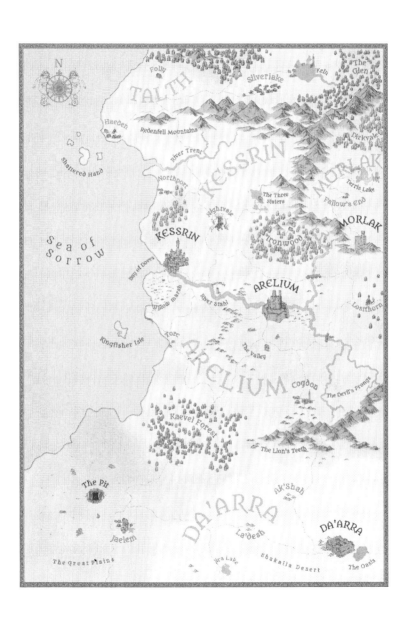

TABLE OF CONTENTS

PROLOGUE

SCRIER

"The Schism was years ago. And yes, at the time we were desperate. Any solution was acceptable, no matter how ludicrous. But it has been over fifty years! Our enemies are routed, our temple has never been stronger! Let us put an end to this despicable practice that continues to taint our bloodline! Let us put an end to the Scrying!"

Sir Caddox, Knight of Brachyura, 417 AT

✍

"**A**GAIN!"

The olive-skinned youth spat out a mouthful of dirt and pulled himself laboriously to his feet. He took a moment to catch his breath, his cold, piercing blue eyes scanning his surroundings. The temple practice yard had been deliberately built on the very edge of the cliff-top. Three sides of the stone-columned square were turned towards the barren, windswept bluffs of Kessrin. The last side looked out over the churning Sea of Sorrow, its foam-flecked waves crashing relentlessly against the jagged rocks hundreds of feet below. No one would survive such a fall, no matter how skilled or resilient he might be. The callous, destructive power of the sea was a constant reminder of man's insignificance.

Dark grey storm clouds boiled angrily overhead, pushed inland by the strong maritime wind. A flash of brilliant white lightning followed by a growling rumble of thunder heralded what was soon to come.

"Aldarin! Again!"

A dozen initiates lined the western side of the square, still as statues, their backs to the desolate sea. They were focused intently on two young men sparring in the grit and dirt of the yard, and the taciturn temple master instructing them.

Aldarin's adversary was different from him in almost every way: squat and broad-shouldered where Aldarin was tall and wiry; blond-haired and pale-skinned where Aldarin was tanned with close-cropped black hair. And, of course, perfect patrician features in contrast to Aldarin's battered, flat nose and scarred visage. His name was Caddox, and Aldarin wanted nothing more than to grind that blond hair and flawless smile into the stinging grit of the practice yard.

"*Aldarin!*" the temple master called again irritably. The wind was picking up, swirling the loose dirt into miniature whirlwinds.

"Yes, Master," Aldarin replied with a sigh. They had been repeating attacks and counter-attacks for the last hour and, despite using everything he had learnt from his time at the temple, he had yet to break through Caddox's defences. His opponent was two years older, stronger, and above all, more experienced.

Aldarin slipped into an offensive stance and edged slowly forwards, seeking some flicker of insight in Caddox's eyes revealing what he would do. But the older youth was cold and unreadable, a slight smile of disdain being the only emotion visible on his face.

Suddenly, Aldarin propelled himself forwards, aiming a quick combination of punches to his enemy's face. As Caddox raised his arms to block the assault, Aldarin swivelled round and sent a sharp roundhouse kick whistling towards his opponent's exposed right knee. At the last moment, Caddox took a half-step backwards and the kick failed to connect. Aldarin stumbled, caught off-balance, and a jab to the shoulder was enough to hurl him crashing to the ground. A kick to the stomach ripped his tunic and sent him rolling backwards.

Caddox laughed, a high-pitched nasal sound half-lost in the wind. He brushed some imaginary dust from his shoulder and winked at the watching initiates. "And so, yet again, the boy does not understand the difference between a dance and a fight! You are trying to hit me, Scrier, not woo me!"

Scrier. Aldarin hated that word. Most of the initiates were born here at the temple, their parents being members of the Order of Brachyura, Fourth of the Twelve, and distant descendants of his bloodline. But, as the population dwindled, it was decided that this was not enough and that if the Order was to survive, it must venture forth from the comfort of the temple walls and search for others whose blood contained traces of the Twelve. This became known as the Scrying, and those brought back from the outside world were quickly labelled as scriers.

Scriers were easy to spot. Those born and raised in the temple spent most of their time in the caves and tunnels cut deep into the cliff face. When necessity forced them outside, they were faced with the damp marshlands surrounding the cliffs, the frequent thunderstorms, and the cold, biting wind. Sun was a rarity, slow to show its face and quick to slip away. Most initiates were pale and thin, their skin bleached white from lack of sunlight.

Scriers, on the other hand, were found throughout the nine Baronies in a myriad of skin tones and sizes. And they were not welcomed with open arms. The opposite in fact. For the most part, scriers were 'half-bloods': only one of their parents was a true son or daughter of Brachyura. They were seen as tainted, inferior. The word *scrier* quickly became derogatory, a symbol of the divide between those born within the temple and its more recent arrivals.

Aldarin's mother had been part of the Order and his father a butcher. His early years were spent slaughtering live-stock, dressing their flesh and selling their meat. These were long, hard days out in the sun with a cleaver or filleting knife, animal blood sluicing down his arms as he worked. His tanned body made him immediately recognisable for what he was and what he would always be. An outsider. A pariah. A *scrier*.

"Well, Scrier? Want another go at it? Or have you had enough for today?" Caddox wandered over to the prostrate form of Aldarin and prodded him with his foot.

"Enough talking," growled Aldarin angrily. He rose

unsteadily to one knee, hand pressed against his aching stomach. "Once more."

"Very well, quickly now, before the storm hits," said the temple master, eyeing the darkening sky warily.

Caddox rolled his shoulders and smiled. "Of course, Master. I don't think it will take more than a minute or two. Scrier? You've eaten a fair amount of dust today. Do you still have some room for a little more?"

I can't beat him, Aldarin thought. *He has had the same training, the same teachers. How can I surprise someone who can guess my every move?*

"Lucky the temple took you in, eh, Scrier?" Caddox continued sardonically. "Heard your mother died from the pox and your father used to beat you with a stick when he'd had a few too many cups of wine."

"Don't talk about my parents."

"Unless you liked it, of course. Did you, Scrier? When your father whipped your back? Did you enjoy it?"

"QUIET!" roared Aldarin. A red haze blurred his vision. He charged forwards, yelling incoherently. Caddox hit him hard across the jaw, but Aldarin barely felt it. Two more strides brought him inside his enemy's guard. His heart pounding, he grabbed Caddox by the shoulders and, with a final cry of rage, slammed his head down in an unstoppable head-butt.

A crack resonated around the enclosed square as Caddox's nose broke in a spray of blood. The older youth reeled backwards with a cry of pain. Aldarin snaked his foot around his opponent's ankle and sent him sprawling. He was down, but it wasn't enough. Aldarin moved forwards, his hands bunched into fists, his breath escaping from his lungs in short, angry gasps.

"That's enough!" came the voice of the temple master, reaching Aldarin beyond a sea of boiling red waves.

"My opponent has not yet yielded, Master," he replied through clenched teeth, drawing on every ounce of self-control he had left.

"You forget yourself."

"But—" The temple master cut him off with a swing of his wooden cudgel, dealing Aldarin a stinging blow across the shoulder.

"I said *enough*, Scrier. I suppose you are pleased with your victory? Do you really believe you fought with honour? With decency? Is this the image you wish to convey to others? Is this how you would represent our Order? If Brachyura was standing here now, he would be ashamed. Though I suppose I shouldn't have expected anything better from a scrier like yourself. You will never be one of us, boy. Not now, not ever. Dismissed."

The temple master's words cut Aldarin far deeper than his cudgel. He turned without a word and walked away from the yard, the initiates, and the approaching storm, back down into the dark tunnels he now called home.

They came for him shortly after supper, as he knew they would.

Caddox was well-liked and his earlier humiliation would not sit well among the other senior initiates. They ambushed him in one of the narrower corridors; two blocking his path, two more impeding his retreat. He managed to land a couple of punches before they slammed him to the ground.

A stray kick knocked a tooth from his mouth. Another cracked a rib. He curled up into a ball on the floor, hands over his head as the blows rained down. One of the stronger assailants stamped on his wrist with a booted heel and Aldarin screamed in agony as the bone shattered. This seemed to satisfy his attackers who ceased their assault and slinked away into the shadows.

He was found a few minutes later and carried to the infirmary where his wrist was splinted and bandaged. He slipped in and out of consciousness as day became night, then night became day. Some time later, he was aware of a robed figure standing at the end of his bed. He struggled to focus his tired eyes.

The figure was a woman, tall and lithe with burnished red hair that spilled down her back like a waterfall of scintillating fire. Her emerald robes, tightly gathered with a simple leather belt, were the same colour as her eyes. The axe icon of Brachyura hung from a silver chain around her neck, nestling snugly between her full breasts. Her sharp, prominent cheekbones and thin nose would have made her seem cold and austere were it not for the mischievous smile that played across her lips.

Aldarin knew her well. Better than most. Her name was Praedora and she was a Priestess of the Twelve. But, more importantly, she was the one who had found him in a squalid village, miles from Kessrin, and brought him home.

"I'm not sure you are doing this right, Aldarin," she said. Her voice was rich and melodious. It flowed over Aldarin like a ray of sunlight on a warm summer's day. "You seem to be spending a disproportionate time in the infirmary compared to out in the practice yard. Surely the more you practise, the less often I should find you here?"

"Yes, my Lady." Aldarin felt a soft flush redden his cheeks. Why did he always feel embarrassed to speak with her?

"And what about your face! Skin as smooth as a baby when I first found you, and now look at you! It looks like you tried to dive off the cliffs into the Sea of Sorrow!"

A pale hand traced the scars that criss-crossed his face. He could see similar white marks cutting through the palm of her own hand. There was only one way to detect the descendants of the Twelve, and that was to mix their blood with that of a priestess, provoking a chain reaction between the two.

Sometimes this was nothing more than a tingling sensation or an electric shock, but occasionally it could be much more, a melding of minds between priestess and initiate. When, two years ago, Praedora had cut open her palm and pressed it against his own, Aldarin had felt the full weight of her strengths, weaknesses, fears, and desires. He glanced up to see her studying him, worry creasing her brow.

"It is nothing, my Lady. A simple jest between initiates." An ebony-skinned patient moaned in the bed to his right. Tall and thin like Aldarin, his face similarly covered in cuts and bruises. Another scrier. In fact, most of the infirmary was full of young men and women who had not been born here.

"I came to talk to you about something," said Praedora. She sat down beside him on the bed and smoothed out the folds of her robe. Aldarin could discern a faint smell of honeysuckle.

"I think you are losing yourself," she continued.

"What?"

"Do you remember when we first met?"

"At the Scrying?"

"No, before that. We had just arrived at your village. It was raining hard and we were exhausted. No one rode out to greet us. We are used to this, of course. It is common for us to be shunned, feared even. And then you arrived. You greeted us courteously. You led us to the nearby inn. Why, one of the knights told me that you had even unsaddled and groomed our horses yourself! And yet you asked for nothing in return. Do you remember?"

"Can't say I do, my Lady. But I always used to greet newcomers to the village. Seemed the right thing to do."

"Exactly. *The right thing to do*. You have great potential, Aldarin. One day, you may be better than all of us. But you must stop wanting to be like those who were born here."

"But they have such an advantage."

"Do they? They have lived here. And only here. They have been raised in safety. In comfort. They know nothing of the outside world and the hardships it can bring. Many are bitter and resentful, unwilling to share this life with others. Why would you want to be like them? Remember the boy who helped me when I was tired and cold two years ago. He did not care who I was, or where I came from."

Aldarin stared into her green eyes and knew she was right. He had forgotten who he was.

"I will try, my Lady."

"I hope you will. Scrier should not be a sign of disgrace but a badge of honour, worn with pride. Maybe if you reached out to others who are suffering as you are," she nodded at the dark-skinned youth in the bed nearby, "you would find it easier to weather the coming storm."

"Yes, my Lady."

"Good." Praedora rose from the bed and made as if to leave. Reaching the doorway, she hesitated, then turned back to Aldarin one last time.

"And Aldarin?"

"Yes, my Lady?"

"If anyone, I mean *anyone*, hurts you like this again, I will find out who it is; I will burn off their shrivelled member with the blue incandescence of Brachyura and throw them from the Cliffs of Kessrin myself."

And, with a swish of silken robes, she departed, leaving behind a startled Aldarin and a lingering scent of honeysuckle.

CHAPTER 1

IRON CHAIRS AND SILVER ANTS

"The tribes had tried to build stone walls without our guidance, but they lacked the patience. Construction is a mix of strength, planning, and ingenuity. Is the land flat or sloping? How deep are the roots of the nearby trees? Are there often high temperatures? Strong winds? All external factors must be considered. A badly-planned wall will last a day. A well-planned wall can last a lifetime."

BRACHYURA, FOURTH OF THE TWELVE, 43 AT

THE GARDEN BEHIND the inner keep had survived the siege of Arelium unscathed.

Its hedges were miraculously untouched by the fire and soot that had claimed so many of the thatched roofs and wooden houses. The plants and herbs that lined the meandering gravel paths were still blooming and colourful.

At its centre, the ornate marble statue stood proudly, arms raised to the sky, water bubbling up from the stone woman's outstretched palms and gushing down into the pool below. The gardeners had scrubbed and polished every inch of the curving sculpture until it gleamed. It had become a shining symbol, embodying the resistance and tenacity of the Arelians, while the garden itself was a place of pilgrimage, a sanctuary for the tired and wounded survivors. They wandered the paths or rested silently on the benches, beginning to heal.

Close to the fountain sat a man in a wheelchair. The chair was an elaborate fusion of wood and iron, with two large spoked metal wheels and plush cushioned armrests. Two handles rose from the back like twisting snakes, allowing some manoeuvrability. The chair's occupant was a man in his early forties with greying hair and a scraggly salt-and-pepper beard. His rugged, careworn face was creased with recent worry-lines and covered with dozens of nicks and bruises. Thick bandages were wrapped tightly around his chest and left shoulder, and a discoloured sheepskin was draped over his legs.

Sir Merad Reed, Captain of the Old Guard, Defender of Arelium, and Commander of the Southern Pit, tilted his head back and closed his eyes. Somewhere overhead, a pair of larks were twittering cheerfully as they flitted from tree to tree. The water in the fountain swirled and gurgled, its lazy current dislodging a croaking green frog from its lily pad. If Reed concentrated hard enough, he could almost hear the rocking of a hide boat and the splashing of a silvery fish.

A grunt of effort broke his absorption and the images faded. He looked up to see a young man on crutches circling the fountain slowly and sweating profusely. The man's left leg ended just below the knee. Reed watched him sit down awkwardly on the fountain's stone edge and cup some of the cool water in his hands. *We have lost so much,* he thought. *Arelium is saved, but what a terrible price we have paid.*

More memories returned unbidden. The pitch black of the tunnel entrance. The sour taste of bile in his throat. The threshers bursting out of the darkness to tear apart his spear-wall. Ferris sacrificing himself to save him. His men crushed, pummelled, beaten, and broken.

Reed had learnt that of the several hundred valorous conscripts — farmers, traders, and family men trained to defend the town — only fifteen now remained, Orkam among them.

It was the indomitable willpower and courage of those few men that had bought enough time for the Knights of the Twelve to arrive, and for Praxis, the new Regent *in tempera* of Arelium, to turn the tide. And it was thanks to Reed's brave spearmen that the garden where he now sat had been saved.

A crunch of booted feet on gravel told him that Jeffson had arrived. The stooped, balding manservant turned personal secretary had barely left his side since Reed had awakened from his coma, tutting over him like an elderly matron and force-feeding him one of the foul concoctions prepared daily by the healer, or one of his own, equally foul, vegetable broths. Jeffson was outstanding at many things, but cooking was not one of them.

"Good morning, my Lord," said Jeffson in his dry,

monotone voice. Reed had never heard him raise or lower it. The man seemed unfazed by the world in general, maybe just slightly put out that the last few weeks had forced him to change his schedule somewhat. He was wearing his typical nondescript, faded clothes and smelt faintly of moth balls.

"Jeffson, I do remember telling you several times that I am not your Lord. It was bad enough having the others call me 'Sunny'. Reed or 'Sir' is fine."

"Of course, my Lord," the manservant replied blithely. "As the weather is quite fine today, I thought my Lord would like to travel down to the barbican to inspect the repairs being made by the Knights of the Twelve? It would be more productive, I would think, than sitting around here moping."

"I am not moping."

"Quite, my Lord. My mistake, I am sure. Shall we? I believe it may be pertinent to remind you that the Baron's funeral is set for this afternoon, and his Lord Regent has asked to see you afterwards."

"Well, considering that the healer has forbidden me to walk in order to conserve my strength, and that you have already placed your hands on the handles of my wheelchair, I would conclude that I have little choice in the matter?"

"Astute, as always, my Lord." Jeffson paused, his eyes flickering to a pair of tortoiseshell butterflies weaving in and out of the purple passionflowers. The gleaming marble woman smiled down at them both, a distant twinkle in her stone gaze. Laughter was carried to them on the breeze: two men on the far side of the garden enjoying a joke told by a third.

"I do not think I ever said thank you, my Lord," he said softly, his voice barely audible over the sound of the fountain.

"Thank you?"

"Yes. Thank you for saving this place. And for everything else."

Reed felt his wheelchair shake as the handles trembled. Then Jeffson turned the heavy chair away from the forgotten goddess and out into the town.

Reed sat in stunned silence, enraptured by the sight of the Knights of Brachyura swarming over the ruined gatehouse like an army of silver ants. Some had removed their burnished argent plate, but most were still fully armoured, carrying great chunks of fallen masonry, wooden beams, and metal bars with little visible effort. Reed had been unconscious for only three days, but the progress made in such a short time was staggering.

The bulk of the broken stone and mortar had already been used to fill the tunnel exit. Several hundred yards away, in the shadow of the dilapidated mansion out in the valley, more knights were working with picks and shovels to block the tunnel's entrance. Once finished, the remains of the hard granite used to build the gatehouse would be much more difficult to dig through than the soft dirt. The greylings would not be able to collapse the barbican again.

Twenty yards from where Reed sat, space had been cleared for the new foundations, with four large roped-off squares demarcating the location of the corner towers. Here the knights had dug trenches and filled them with more compacted rubble. All they needed now was stone for the walls, and it looked like this was starting to arrive.

To the west, down by the river, three heavily-laden barges were moored at a makeshift dock, their wooden hulls straining against the weight of dozens of blocks of chiselled stone. Knights were offloading the stone onto sledges pulled by their own warhorses. Two of the enormous beasts were harnessed to each sledge, powerful enough to move them easily from the dock to the construction site.

The repairs were being supervised by a bald, grizzled knight with a white, drooping moustache that hung like snowy icicles from his prominent nose. He was in his six-ties, maybe older, but still radiated the same strength and assurance commonplace among the Knights of the Twelve. Seeing Reed, he barked a few orders to his men and strode over, towering over the metal wheelchair.

"Sir Reed," he said, bowing stiffly. "Greetings. My name is Sir Manfeld and I have the honour of commanding here. It gives me great pleasure to see you out of the infirmary. Have you come to inspect our efforts? I took some small liberties in laying out the foundations, but now that you have returned to us, it would perhaps be auspicious for me to relinquish command to you once more?"

Reed let the knight's eloquent words and archaic way of speaking sweep over him, hiding a smile. He thought back to meeting Aldarin for the first time, remembering how he used to speak in a similar fashion before slowly losing his anachronistic wording as they spent more time together.

"Sir Knight, I am in turn honoured to count you among our friends and allies. I convey my most profound thanks for all you have done, and for all you continue to do for Arelium."

The older man seemed uncomfortable at hearing this. "I

must confess, Sir Reed, there is still a modicum of guilt that clouds the minds of my comrades. For too long, we have been distant from the affairs of the nine Baronies. In our selfishness, we chose to look inwards at the petty problems surrounding our Order rather than outwards at the greater threats preying on those we had sworn to defend." He turned and stared out towards the western edge of the valley and the green, undulating hills beyond.

"One of the greatest of our Order, a priestess, is strong in her connection to the Twelve. She can feel things, flashes, pieces of broken memories. Visions of the past, but also of things to come. They are nothing more than shattered shards, a jumble of conflicting emotions, indecipherable for the most part. And yet … in some rare cases, these random threads can be woven into something more coherent. Several months ago, she was blessed with one of these … visions. She told us of a dark crater, stone weathered by biting winds, feelings of anger, longing, and anticipation. The Southern Pit, obviously."

Sir Manfeld paused as some of his fellow knights poured more rubble into the trenches, the sound echoing off the curtain wall.

"It was then that we were too complacent in our actions," he continued. "We should have acted decisively, mustered our Order and travelled in force to the Pit. Had we done so, many lives might have been saved. Praedora, our priestess, urged us to do just that, but I and others of my Order refused. We argued that this would leave our temple open to attack from the fallen—" he caught himself, "I mean from other enemies. We placed greater value on our own lives than the lives of others. Brachyura would not be pleased."

"Many of us have made mistakes," said Reed softly. "I spent a long time questioning my choices and my actions. I wondered how my life would have differed if I had trodden a different path. We should not waste the present by dwelling on the past. I believe our previous actions should help define us, but they should not control us. I do not hold you responsible, any more than the Baron for his decisions, or Aldarin for his. What matters to me is that when Aldarin asked you to come, you did."

"My thanks, Sir Reed. It does me good to hear these wise words. As you may have surmised, we decided to choose one of us to travel to Arelium and from there to the Pit to see if there was any truth in our priestess's visions. And to send for us if there was great need."

"That is how you managed to arrive so quickly."

One of the warhorses whinnied, shaking its mane and pawing the ground. A knight caught the reins and stroked the beast's neck, murmuring soft words of comfort.

"Indeed," Manfeld said. "We began to prepare not long after Aldarin's departure. When we received his message, we were ready. And we have fought well. But we have always been builders first, warriors second. Now we can put our expertise to good use. I have men rebuilding the gatehouse here; more in the valley rebuilding the holdings and farmsteads. The Barony will be reborn, stronger and more resilient than ever before. This I promise."

Reed looked on as the knights began to manoeuvre the huge stone blocks into place, filling the gaps between them with mortar. They applied the same precision as Aldarin used on the battlefield: economical, measured gestures. Further away, a pair of knights were splitting logs of wood with their battle-axes, the sharpened blades cutting through the bark effortlessly.

"How did you get the stone so fast?" Reed said, pointing at the ponderous barges buoyed by the River Stahl.

Jeffson gave an embarrassed cough. "I may be able to answer that question, my Lord," he said. "You may remember the Baron telling you that he received regular reports from the Pit? Captain Yusifel asking for men and supplies? Well, after that last request came in, the Baron decided to order some stone from the quarries up in Morlak to repair the damaged towers. Praxis was against it, arguing something about extravagant and unnecessary expenses, but he was overruled. This is the first shipment. I believe there are more to come. We thought it would be put to better use here than at the Pit."

"Of course," Reed replied. To his right, an unarmoured knight was scrubbing furiously at a dark stain on the cobbles. A patch of dry blood. Could that have been where Ferris fell? Where Reed himself nearly lost his life? It was all a blur. He shuddered, feeling a sudden chill as if a cloud had passed over the sun.

"The Pit is empty," he said. "There is … nothing there now. Nothing and no one. Let the stone be used here where it can benefit the living. Oh, and Sir Manfeld? One thing I have learnt in my short time as a captain is that you should surround yourself with people better at doing things than you are, and know when to admit it. I have no experience in any sort of repair work apart from filling in a few cracks and replacing rotten wood in the towers around the Pit. You are far better qualified. I would be most grateful if you would continue to supervise the work here."

"It would be a great honour and pleasure," Manfeld said, bowing again. "I will not betray the trust you have placed in me." The knight turned his gaze to the scorched and blackened earth that covered the valley floor. His expression grew troubled. "Rebuilding the town and outlying buildings is well within my expertise. It is the land I weep for. Acres of charred soil, such a terrible loss. I wish we could do more. I have spoken to Lord del Conte on the subject; I believe you know of him?"

Reed nodded, thinking of the disfigured one-eyed man who had been there to greet him when he awoke. "We have met briefly, yes."

"He is quite knowledgeable on the subject. It appears that although the temperatures at surface level can be very high, just below they can be quite normal. In fact, some root systems will have remained intact and will regenerate on their own come spring. For the rest, we will need seed, fertiliser, and a great deal of hard work."

"What of the refugees?"

"Lord Regent Praxis sent messengers west soon after our victory over the greylings. Baron Derello del Kessrin must be well appraised of the situation by now. I imagine we will start to see the women and children of Arelium returning to us in a few days' time. I only hope they will be prepared for what they will find here. Many of the women will now be widows, and some of those children will have lost their fathers. They will need courage and fortitude to survive the days ahead."

"I entrusted the riders with a list of the deceased," said Jeffson. The knight glanced at the manservant as if seeing him for the first time.

"I thank you. That was well thought of indeed." He inclined his head. "You must be Jeffson. I would like to take the opportunity to thank you for watching over Sir Reed here during his, ah, convalescence as it were. Praxis tells me that you barely left his side for three days and nights."

"What?" interjected Reed, thinking he must have misheard.

Jeffson looked almost uncomfortable. "Um, yes, my Lord, it was no trouble, I had no other tasks, you see—"

"… Changed his clothes, washed him, had the healer sew up a cut on his arm …" Manfeld continued.

"Ahem. Yes, thank you, Sir Manfeld, I don't think my Lord Reed needs to know—"

He was cut off mid-sentence as the bronze bell set in the highest tower of the inner keep began to toll mournfully. Five long peals, then silence, then five more long peals.

"What does that mean?" asked Manfeld.

"Five tolls of the bell. The Baron is dead," said Reed sadly. "They are calling us to his funeral."

CHAPTER 2

THE BLACK ARMBAND

"Kessrin. The sparkling jewel of the Bay of Doves, the undisputed maritime capital of the nine Baronies. And it is indeed a wonderful, magical place. The view from the top of the central tower is breathtaking! Why, on a clear day, you can see halfway to Arelium! I just wish it didn't smell so much of raw seaweed and rotten fish."

XANDRIS, HEALER'S APPRENTICE, 426 AT

❧

"MY LADY?"

Jelaïa groaned and rolled over onto her stomach. Why was this mattress so hard? It felt like someone had removed all the soft, downy feathers and replaced them with a sack of gravel. She would have to talk to Mava about it in the morning.

Then, as her mind pushed through the last clinging

tendrils of sleep, she remembered where she was. Miles away
from Arelium and her comfortable four-poster bed, lying on
a patch of dry ground twenty yards from the banks of the
River Stahl with only her travelling cloak between her and
the cold, hard earth.

"My Lady, it is time."

She boldly raised an eyelid just a crack. It was enough
to make out the imposing figure of Aldarin, Knight of the
Twelve, staring down at her with a concerned expression on
his face. He truly was an impressive sight. Over seven feet
of tanned, muscular physique, from his scarred and battered
face down to his powerful thighs and calves. Jelaïa could read
nothing in his calm features and piercing ocean-blue eyes,
but she knew he was coiled like a spring, ready to explode
into action at the slightest hint of danger.

It was one of the many things she knew about Aldarin.
Since their blood had mixed in the soggy marshlands east of
Arelium, she had shared his memories, his thoughts, and his
fears. She had seen him hold the hand of his dying mother
as the light left her eyes, watched him climb the sheer cliffs
of Kessrin, and felt the tremors running down his arms as
he forged the massive double-bladed axe that never left his
side. Years of suffering and hardship compressed into a single
burst of energy that had set her veins on fire. An agonising
wave of pain rippling through her body, more intense than
anything she had ever felt before.

And yet … she had sensed something else too, at the
very moment the burning fire reached its paroxysm, a feeling
of unbridled, limitless potential. Fleeting, yet intoxicating.
It would perhaps be worth a little pain to experience that
sensation again.

She rubbed her itching eyes and stifled a yawn. "I'm awake," she mumbled groggily, patting at her mop of chestnut-brown hair. The humid river air had curled and twisted her shoulder-length locks, making them writhe like a nest of angry serpents. Thank the Twelve she had at least had the sense to dress correctly. Her leather trousers and crimson doublet were muddy and stained but otherwise intact. Anything more lady-like would have already been torn to shreds on the sharp stones that littered the river bank.

Aldarin looked as tired as she felt. The ugly welts and bruises on his face, the direct result of him jumping off a collapsing gatehouse and fighting two fallen Knights of the Twelve, were slowly waning from a dark shade of purple to a brownish-yellow. Jelaïa was more worried about the puncture wound in his shoulder. The opposing knight's blade had cut deep and wide. Aldarin would need stitches for the muscle to heal properly. She had packed the wound with mud to reduce the risk of infection and bandaged it as best she could, but she knew it was still causing him some pain.

The worst injury, however, was not to the tall knight's body but to his spirit. As an initiate, Aldarin had been told the story of the great Schism that had divided the Knights of the Twelve, a day of bloodshed followed by years of infighting and betrayals that had led to the decline of his Order and the creation of the Scrying. It was a terrible, unforgettable scar on the temple's history, but only its oldest members had actually raised arms against their brothers. Until now. Aldarin had faced off against two fallen Knights of Mithuna.

And he had lost.

Jelaïa glanced past the knight to where his cracked helm lay by the glowing embers of the campfire. The symbolism was obvious. She only wished she could do more to help, but he had been mostly silent since they had left Arelium behind and, after a few fruitless attempts at conversation, she had given up. Aldarin was staring at her expectantly and she realised she had missed what he had been saying.

"I am sorry, Sir Knight, my mind was elsewhere."

"We are close to Kessrin now, my Lady," he repeated patiently. "I would estimate that if we set off now, we should reach the port by early afternoon. I have prepared some sustenance."

The River Stahl was the main source of fresh drinking water for animals living in the hills: rabbits, mice, and other small rodents. Aldarin had set up traps whenever they stopped to rest. While he hunted, Jelaïa had scoured the riverbank for fruits and berries, using her rudimentary knowledge of medicine to avoid the deadlier varieties.

Aldarin had wrapped the remains of last night's rabbit in dock leaves and placed it over the dying fire. The rich, juicy smell of cooked meat wafted over her and made her mouth water in anticipation. She speared the steaming packet with the dagger that she kept belted to her waist and sliced off a long strip of flesh.

"Have you ever met Baron del Kessrin?" she said through a mouthful of rabbit. "I saw him a few times when he came to visit my father, but we never really spoke, apart from the necessary pleasantries."

"I have met him several times." Aldarin had seated himself on a nearby log and was sharpening his double-bladed axe with a whetstone. Jelaïa knew he did this not only to keep his weapon sharp but also because the rhythmic gesture calmed him.

"What do you think of him?" she asked.

"He is a difficult man to describe. Very different from your father. Listus is, at heart, an open, straightforward man who wears his intentions clearly on his sleeve. He is a man who speaks his mind, sometimes rather impulsively I might add. It is one of the things I like about him. Both Listus and Reed have a tendency to be quite undiplomatic when they feel like it. It is very refreshing."

Jelaïa suppressed a smile as she remembered her father ordering Aldarin to take her to Kessrin, no matter the cost. The knight had responded by destroying the bedroom wall with his axe. By the Twelve, it would be good to see her family again.

"Derello del Kessrin is much better at hiding his true intentions. He has neither the martial prowess nor the imposing presence of your father, yet he manages to turn this weakness into an advantage. Every time I see him, his clothes are more opulent, his manners more extravagant. It is all a lure. Many have underestimated him, and have woken up the next morning to find themselves swindled out of a trade deal or bound by some contract or other to serve the Baron's interests."

"The next morning?"

"Indeed. It appears that Derello also has a voracious sexual appetite. Something to watch out for, methinks."

"But I am the Baron's daughter!"

"Exactly, you would be a fine prize, I am sure. Now, if you have finished, I would suggest we proceed? We do not want to keep the Baron waiting."

᠊ᡧ᠊

Kessrin was an imposing sight. It straddled the estuary where the River Stahl met the Bay of Doves; countless wharves, jetties, piers, and quays weaving forth from its base like an entanglement of intertwining roots. A crenellated wall of ashen-grey stone separated the ports from the town itself, much like at Arelium, although no guards manned the ramparts. In lieu of a defensive barbican, there were five wide gates allowing the hundreds of sailors, traders, and other visitors passage into the town centre, where a magnificent feat of architecture awaited them.

Four cylindrical towers with conical, blue-tiled roofs encircled a fifth central tower, higher and wider than the rest, perfectly positioned to dominate the estuary, the Bay of Doves, and the raging tides of the Sea of Sorrow beyond. It was from the top of the central tower that Baron Derello del Kessrin surveyed his domain. The surrounding towers were linked to one another by elevated stone walkways, no more than four feet wide. They were closed off at night or during particularly bad weather but remained no less treacherous to the untrained or incautious.

Jelaïa and Aldarin reached the outer jetties in the early afternoon. They refused to pay the exorbitant mooring fees and set their battered boat adrift to float downstream and out to sea.

The jetties were packed with boats of all shapes and sizes: flat cargo barges from Morlak or Arelium, bigger merchant ships from up the coast near Talth or further north, and even a few carracks — massive, multi-decked monstrosities employed to patrol the waters around Kessrin or act as an escort for some of the more dangerous trade routes. Their decks bristled with ballistae; large crossbow-like weapons that could propel six-foot-long iron-tipped bolts hundreds of yards across the water.

These ships of war were financed by the noble houses of Kessrin and all sported various shields, pennants, and banners proclaiming their patronage. One coat-of-arms stood out from all the others, a white, winged sea serpent on a field of dark blue: the personal heraldry of Baron del Kessrin.

After days of near silence, the vibrant thrum of civilisation was deafening. Jelaïa had barely stepped off the quay before she bumped into a barrel of fresh fish, spilling its slippery contents all over the boardwalk. The irate owner swaggered over and seemed ready to throw her back into the water until Aldarin calmly intervened. The temple of Brachyura was only a day or two's ride away from the provincial capital, and the men and women of Kessrin were used to seeing the initiates and priestesses of the Order. The boat captain bowed respectfully to the knight and, with a final dark look at Jelaïa, returned to join his crew.

"Stay close," said Aldarin, and began to thread his way through the throng of sailors and merchants towards the closest gate. They were waved in by a pair of bored town guards wearing boiled leather breastplates and wide blue knee-length breeches and stockings. The narrow, cobbled street on the other side was packed with people and wound up past houses and shops to the circle of tall towers overlooking the town.

Humidity, sea salt, and harsh winds determined the style and shape of the buildings. Residences were squat, angular structures of granite or fieldstone with thin, glassless windows and flat roofs. Some of the more elaborate houses had blue-tiled coverings or wooden struts, a clear sign of wealth considering the cost of maintaining such fragile materials.

Jelaïa managed to advance a few hundred yards before she was accosted by a band of grubby orphans, their hollow cheeks and weathered faces making them look far older than they really were. She gave them the last few bits of meat and cheese from her satchel of supplies, and their leader tugged his forelock before cartwheeling away with a gap-toothed smile. It made her think of the refugees from Arelium who must still be here somewhere. She hoped they were being well looked after.

After what seemed like an eternity, they reached the base of one of the towers and it was now apparent that all five towers rose from a single, rounded stone base three storeys high, like the skeletal fingers and thumb of an enormous hand. A lowered portcullis blocked further progress. Next to it, a bronze bell set into the wall allowed visitors to announce themselves.

Aldarin rang the bell and a moment later a round, tonsured head popped out of one of the openings on the second floor. "Yes?" the head enquired.

"Aldarin, Knight of Brachyura, and Lady Jelaïa del Arelium. We would like to speak to the Baron immediately."

The guardsman squinted down at Jelaïa, taking in her travel-worn clothes and straggly hair. "Pardon me, my Lady, but you don't look much like a Baron's daughter."

"Yes, I hear that a lot," said Jelaïa in exasperation. "Now, would you please give me your name and rank so that I can convey to his Lord Baron exactly who delayed us from meeting with him?"

The head withdrew and after a muffled conversation reappeared again, looking suitably chastised.

"My most humble apologies, Lady del Arelium. Once the portcullis is raised, please proceed directly through the courtyard to the central tower. I will send a messenger to inform the Baron of your presence."

With a squeal of rusty gears, the portcullis trundled upwards and the pair of travellers entered the Baron's keep. They were greeted by an open courtyard, surrounded on all sides by marble columns. Multiple corridors branched out from the square towards the other towers. Floral archways covered a slate pathway that led from the gatehouse to a pair of reinforced doors on the far side. In the centre, a nine-foot-high granite statue of a writhing sea snake spiralled up into the air, the creature's stone eyes fixed on the central tower.

As they reached the double doors, the latter were pulled open from the inside by two vigilant soldiers. Jelaïa gasped as she stepped into the Great Hall of Kessrin. It took up almost the entire ground floor of the central tower, its circular walls lined with the colourful heraldry of the vassals who had pledged their allegiance to the Baron. A series of columns placed strategically around the room held up its vaulted ceiling.

Opposite where Jelaïa now stood was what had made her gasp: an enormous stained-glass window dominated the hall, vibrant hues of red, blue, green, and yellow illuminating the walls and dappling the stone floor with multi-coloured patches of light.

The window depicted a golden-armoured woman with flowing auburn hair battling a dark green, tentacled creature resembling a large squid or octopus complete with angry, beady eyes and a gaping maw filled with pointed teeth. The woman wore an expression of almost religious zeal, stabbing down triumphantly with a two-handed sword, impaling the monster through one eye.

In front of this striking image, on a raised dais, stood four high-backed chairs and a long oaken table. Three of the chairs were occupied. Baron Derello del Kessrin lounged nonchalantly in the middle seat, one leg hooked over an armrest. His short black hair was expertly styled, slick and greased with some kind of natural gel. He was wearing heavy amounts of dense black eyeliner and a slender trace of dark red lipstick. More make-up darkened his features, giving him a slight tan and making it difficult for Jelaïa to guess his age; he could be anything from thirty to fifty. A tiny diamond earring pierced his left ear, sparkling in the light of the stained-glass window. He looked bored.

To the Baron's left, a tall, thin woman with square-cut grey hair sat up straight and stiff, her spine pressed against the wooden back of her chair as if glued there. She wore a simple black dress and bodice with a starched collar fastened tightly around her neck. She was staring thoughtfully at Jelaïa over steepled fingers, her brow creased and lips pursed.

The last of the Great Hall's occupants was a short, pudgy, sandy-haired man with a cropped goatee doing little to hide his generous chin and jaw. A pair of wire-framed glasses hung on a frayed cord around his neck, and various scrolls and parchments were scattered over the table in front of him.

The Baron's eyes lit up when he caught sight of Jelaïa. He bounded out of his chair and leapt down from the dais to stand before her. Derello bowed deeply, extending his arm and wrist in a gentlemanly flourish. Before Jelaïa could react, he grabbed her hand and pressed it fervently to his lips. He smelt strongly of flowers and southern spices.

"My Lady," he murmured.

Jelaïa made to curtsy in return, remembered she was wearing trousers, and gave an awkward bow instead.

"Lord Baron, it is so good to see you," she replied. There was something odd about the Baron, a strange look in his eye that she could not quite place. Something about his attire too. He was wearing a black doublet and shirt, black trousers, and black doeskin boots. Hadn't Aldarin told her that Derello was an extravagant over-dresser?

Her eyes flickered to the other two seated figures, the woman in her dark dress and the bespectacled man. He had shifted in his chair, fiddling with one of the scrolls on the table, and Jelaïa could see now that he wore a black armband on his right side. A feeling of insufferable dread began to seep through her body. She inhaled sharply as her hands started to shake.

She turned to Aldarin and saw the grief written on his face.

"My Lady, I have terrible news," said the Baron softly. Then Jelaïa's world came crashing down and she heard no more.

CHAPTER 3

THE LAST LEAVES OF AUTUMN

"I detest these immutable definitions of good and evil. Murder, for example, is considered morally unacceptable. But what if the victim is a rapist? A child molester? A man responsible for the deaths of thousands? Surely, if life is a canvas, then it is not each individual brush stroke that should be judged but the final, magnificent painting."

ZYGOS, SEVENTH OF THE TWELVE, 16 AT

⌁

PRAXIS, LORD REGENT of Arelium, stood in front of the polished silver mirror practising his half-smile. It was not an easy thing to fake. Too wide and it would seem mocking. Too tight and it could be insincere. Too lopsided and it would seem foolish.

The smile was part of his persona, an expertly crafted

package of mimics and gestures which, when paired with his keen intellect, had allowed him to insert himself into the life of one of the most powerful men in the nine Baronies, Listus del Arelium. It had all been set in motion by poisoning the Baron's previous steward — a doddering geriatric who drank gallons of tea a day without ever checking the contents of his mug — and then taking his place.

For over ten years, he had played his part perfectly, befriending the Baron's daughter and wife, doing what he could to weaken relations between Arelium and the neighbouring Baronies, and sowing the seeds of discord among the greedy nobles.

Then, at long last, the momentous event his Order had been preparing for finally arrived: the greylings returned. All Praxis had to do was watch as they destroyed Arelium. Unfortunately, it was at that point that his plans had started to unravel.

It had been easy enough to send the brash, headstrong Loré del Conte to his death but, against all odds, the man had survived. A meticulously planned assassination attempt against the Baron had failed, and the old veteran's incredible determination and charisma had done much to bolster the defenders' morale, drawing out the siege for far too long. Even so, the town would have fallen if not for Aldarin, that Pit-spawned Knight of Brachyura.

Praxis hated the knight, a deep kernel of hatred that had festered within him ever since he was a child listening to his mother tell him how they were driven out of their temple and left to starve for no other crime than following the teachings of their Order. The Knights of Brachyura who refused to follow the signs, who refused to honour the simple tasks that had been asked of them, deserved no pity, and no redemption.

He remembered being forced to stand by and let that silver-plated hypocrite lecture the Baron on temperance and virtue. How despicable. He had clenched his fists and dug his fingernails so hard into the palms of his hands that his flesh had bled.

Aldarin had survived the Pit, survived the ambush in Kaevel Forest, and survived the siege of Arelium, but hopefully he had not escaped two fully-armoured Knights of Mithuna. Praxis had sent men into the marshlands every day after the battle and, so far, they had returned empty-handed. It mattered little. Either Verona had had the good sense to dump the body in the river or Aldarin had survived. If the latter were true, he was on his way to Kessrin with Jelaïa, and Praxis had already taken steps to ensure that neither of them would survive the night.

Moving closer to the mirror, he ran his fingers through his immaculate beard, frowning as he felt the puckered skin of an all-too-recent scar that formed a line down his handsome face from below his left eye to his chin. Another unforeseen divergence from his carefully laid plans.

Still, his quick thinking had given him control of Arelium, and, if he played his remaining cards right, Kessrin and Arelium would grind each other to dust without him needing to call on the greylings at all. There were just a few final loose ends to tie up.

A tentative knock on the bedroom door pulled him out of his introspection.

"Who is it?"

"The healer, my Lord Regent."

And speaking of loose ends. "Ah yes, just one minute!" shouted Praxis. He gave himself one last admiring glance before buttoning up his high-necked black leather coat and sheathing his long stiletto dagger in the scabbard strapped to his thigh. His silver-scales medallion had been hidden away during the siege, and he had chosen to replace it with a snarling wolf's head, officially as part of his change in status from steward to Lord Regent, but also because the scales were rather too close to the heraldry of the Order of Zygos, Seventh of the Twelve.

Right, now to deal with this bumbling idiot.

"Enter!"

The door creaked open and the healer bustled in, his round face red and sweating from the climb up the narrow stairs leading from the Great Hall to the Regent's quarters. He still wore a leather surgical apron stuffed with an assortment of scalpels, bone-saws, and other tools of the trade.

"Lord Regent, I have finished my study of the, um, late Baron's body. He is being prepared for the last rites as we speak, but I believe you asked me to report my findings as soon as I had finished?"

"You came straight here?"

"Yes, my Lord."

"You brought the weapon?"

"Yes, yes." The healer removed the dagger from one of the pockets sewn into his apron. It was unmistakeably Kessrin, the blade curved like a claw. The hilt was engraved with a coiled serpent and a long-beaked bird with triangular wings, a kingfisher perhaps.

"Very good. What did you find?"

"That you are lying."

Interesting. The man has found a spark of courage some-where deep in his dumpy belly.

"Really? That is quite an accusation. Please elaborate. Oh, and it's 'my Lord', or 'my Lord Regent' if you would."

"Yes, um, quite. I was already bothered by the lack of arterial spray. And, of course, no bloodstains on the floor. Then I examined the Baron's body. I have determined three things. Firstly, the cut on his throat was made from left to right, clearly the work of a right-handed man. But you were wounded on the, um, left-hand side of your face."

"Yes?"

"And if I recall correctly, you told us the assassin leapt towards you? Well, as the cut is straight and vertical, that would mean that the assailant was holding his weapon in his left hand. Why would he switch hands before cutting the Baron's throat?"

Maybe not such an idiot after all.

"Clearly, either I misremember or he was ambidextrous. You are not making much of a case, healer. What else?"

"Well, secondly, the throat wound was made after the Baron died, not before. Why would the assailant do that?"

"To be absolutely certain he had completed his contract?"

"Perhaps. But you told us he attacked the Baron and yourself, then jumped out of the window. A victim of a belly wound takes some time to die. The person who cut his throat would have had to have waited, um, minutes at least."

Praxis's eyes grew hard. "And thirdly, healer?"

"Well, after examining the body closely, it appears I was correct in my initial hypothesis concerning the stab wound. The puncture is long, straight, and narrow; utterly inconsistent with a curved Kessrin dagger. In fact, I believe there is only one style of weapon that would leave such a lesion, and that is a stiletto knife like your own, um, my Lord."

"Really?" said Praxis, drawing his dagger from its jewelled sheath. The light from the blade reflected in his dark eyes. "You have been most thorough, healer. A little too thorough, unfortunately."

The healer licked his lips and swallowed nervously. A glance around the room told him that the bedroom door was his only way out. He took a step back towards it. "I, um, took the liberty of informing Captain Orkam and Lord del Conte I was coming to see you, my Lord," he stammered. "They would find it very strange for me to enter your quarters and never come out."

"Never come out? What are you talking about, man? Do you think I am going to kill you? What a ludicrous notion!" Praxis smiled benignly, although the smile never reached his eyes. "Your arguments are fairly convincing, I suppose, but enough to discredit the saviour of Arelium? That's what they are calling me now. Apparently, I single-handedly turned the tide of battle in our favour. Rather amusing, don't you think?"

He took a step forwards and grasped the healer's shoulder. The rotund man shivered at his touch. "Let us speak of other things," Praxis continued amiably. "How fare your two apprentices? One was conscripted to the town guard, and the other was one of those chosen to help the refugees reach Kessrin safely, am I right?"

"Ye ... yes, my Lord."

"What was his name — Xandris, I think it was? Intelligent man, very erudite like yourself. The Baron chose well." Praxis's hand never left the healer's shoulder, his grip tightening. "He must be *very* dedicated to his apprentice-ship, young Xandris. I was told he rarely left your dispensary. Slept there most nights, even. All in the name of science, I am sure."

"It's not like that—"

"He has been given a nice place in Kessrin, I've heard. Not too far from the keep, with a great view of the north-western shores. Unfortunately, it's not in the safest neighbourhood; a bit close to the slums and some of the seedier alehouses. Why, not two days ago, a bloated corpse was washed ashore less than a hundred yards from his house. Murdered, appar-ently. They never caught the man who did it. We can but hope young Xandris doesn't suffer a similar fate."

The healer was staring at Praxis with wide, bulging eyes. With a clatter, the Kessrin dagger he was holding fell from his limp fingers. Praxis leant forwards and fixed the shorter man with a viper-like stare. "I will be praying to the Twelve every day for your apprentice's safe return," he said, his voice low and hard. "And I suggest you do the same."

The healer opened his mouth to reply, then shut it again and nodded miserably.

"Excellent!" said the Lord Regent, bending to pick up the dagger from the floor. "I'll keep hold of this. Thank you again for your concise and detailed report, healer. You may leave me now, I must prepare for the funeral. Please have the body brought out into the courtyard and ask the watchmen to sound the bell."

Praxis flashed one of his well-practised half-smiles and, sheathing his dagger, turned back to his mirror.

The healer, after a moment's hesitation, fled the room.

⋙

The inner courtyard was packed with the men and women of Arelium, come to pay their final respects to their liege lord. Autumn continued its relentless crawl towards winter, and the air was crisp and chill despite the warming rays of the noonday sun. Amber-hued fallen leaves swirled around Praxis's booted feet as he walked solemnly through the crowd of mourners to the centre of the square where the Baron lay on a simple wooden bier, surrounded by garlands of white chrysanthemums.

His golden armour had been repaired and buffed to a fine sheen, the aureate glow softening his pale, careworn features. The elegant bastard sword with its wolf's-head hilt had been placed carefully on his embossed breastplate while his one remaining hand rested lightly on the crosspiece. The morticians had done exceptional work. Listus looked as if he was in the midst of a deep, peaceful slumber, the worries of the world never to trouble him again.

Two figures stood at the foot of the raised bier, their heads bowed in reverence. The Baroness, a thick veil hiding her face, had lost weight. Her black mourning dress was far too big and hung loosely off her diminished frame. She was grasping the hand of the second figure, a tall man in his late fifties with short blond hair. He had once been exceptionally good-looking until a greyling ambush had taken his eye and left one side of his face a mass of disfigured scar tissue. He wore a black doublet with silver buttons and leant heavily on a wooden cane topped with an ivory eagle. His leg was fitted with an ornate metallic brace that whirred and clicked when he walked.

"Loré. My Lady." Praxis nodded to each of them in turn.

"Lord Regent. So good of you to join us. We were starting to wonder if you would come," Loré del Conte replied in a rasping voice.

"Apologies. I was detained by urgent news from the healer. News that needs to be shared."

Praxis looked around at the groups of soldiers, knights, nurses, nobles, and servants. Many were weeping openly. The Baron had always been well-liked. Short-tempered and stubborn but just and honourable. He had believed in people and their capacity to overcome tragedy and hardship. And he had known how best to leverage the resources at his disposal; using Aldarin to strengthen the curtain wall, the barges to evacuate the non-combatants, and Merad Reed to train the conscripts. All these tactics had bought them precious time. Enough time for the Knights of Brachyura to arrive.

He could see Reed near the entrance to the inner keep, deep in conversation with Orkam, the gruff, bald captain of the town guard. Beside them, his head lowered respectfully, was Sir Manfeld, the leader of the delegation of knights sent to break the siege. *Another problem to deal with.*

Praxis cleared his throat and raised his hands for silence. "Brave people of Arelium. Knights of the Twelve. We are gathered here to bid a final, fond farewell to Listus del Arelium. I have known the Baron for ten years, much less than some of you, and yet, for those ten years, I was with him nearly every day. I saw him at his best, and at his worst. I do not think he liked me much at first. He used to take me out on horse rides to the most remote corners of the Barony, then gallop away laughing, leaving me there alone."

Nervous laughter rippled through the throng of onlookers.

"I think he hoped I would get lost or just give up and go home. One of those times, my horse sprained a leg and I had to walk back to Arelium on foot. It took me three days and I had blisters the size of pomegranates by the time I hobbled into the Great Hall. I remember that, instead of apologising, the Baron began chastising me for leaving my horse behind!"

More laughter, genuine this time. Even Loré had the shadow of a smile on his ruined lips. "He was strong, wilful, and determined; and he respected those whose qualities matched his own. He was a ruler, a friend, a husband, and a father. He excelled at all of these, but I believe I never saw him happier than when he was with his daughter. Jelaïa was his shining star, and it is only fitting that she should continue her father's legacy."

"Hear, hear!" shouted Orkam and his cry was met with a smattering of applause.

"Some of you may be wondering where the future Baroness is now. Listus felt it right to send her to Kessrin under the escort of Aldarin, a Knight of the Twelve. She should have arrived there by now, but we have yet to hear from Derello del Kessrin, and this is most troubling.

"Perhaps you have all heard the rumours surrounding our liege lord's demise. I am here today, on the day of his funeral, to put those rumours to rest and to share with you all, the survivors of the siege of Arelium, the sad but indisputable truth. The Baron was murdered, assassinated before my very eyes at the exact same moment that the Knights of the Twelve were riding to our salvation."

Horrified gasps of shock and angry shouts of disbelief

broke the respectful silence as those present reacted to the news. Captain Reed sat up straight in his wheelchair, mouth agape, hearing the story for the first time.

Grief is such an interesting emotion, thought Praxis. *Sadness, anger, hope, and denial pushing and pulling against one another for dominance. All I must do is lure that feeling of rage closer to the surface.*

"Friends!" he said, raising his arms again. "Friends! There is more. I was there when the assassin slit the Baron's throat. I was there when his life's blood stained my hands and face. I fought for your Lord's life, but I was too weak." He traced his scarred cheek. "The murderer escaped. But I saw his face. The man was from Kessrin. And he dropped this." Pulling the curved dagger from a pouch on his belt, he held it up for all to see. Sunlight flashed along the crescent blade, and there was no mistaking the weapon's origin.

"Friends! There is something evil brewing in the Barony of Kessrin. A delegation attempts to kill the Baron days before the greylings arrive. Jelaïa, our Baroness, is missing since she left our borders. A Kessrin assassin succeeds in entering our Lord's private chambers. This is no coincidence. And we owe it to Listus to find the source of this infestation and eradicate it.

"I have thought much on this; I have looked to the Twelve for guidance and I have reached a decision. I will travel to Kessrin and I will find the answers you deserve, even if I must tear the place apart piece by piece. Are you with me on this?"

"Praxis!" came a cry from the crowd, then another. "Praxis, we are with you!" came a third shout from further away, quickly echoed by others.

The men he had paid and carefully briefed this very morning were carrying out their instructions to the letter. "Praxis!" chanted a dozen more, until the name was picked up by hundreds of grief-stricken voices. A cry for justice, a cry for vengeance.

A cry for war.

I have you now, thought Praxis, and with one last lingering look at the cold corpse of his fallen liege lord, he left the bier behind to prepare for the long journey west to Kessrin.

CHAPTER 4

THE ALMOND BOUQUET

"We still have not found them, my Lord. I've sent ships south as far as Torc, and north as far as Haeden. I've even sent men to search the villages along the coast. All have returned empty-handed. I am sorry, Derello, but there is nothing more we can do. I think it is time to make it known that your parents have been lost at sea. And for you to become Baron."

HIRKUIN, CAPTAIN OF THE KESSRIN GUARD, 421 AT

I T HAD BEEN two days and Jelaïa could still not believe that her father was dead. She vaguely remembered Aldarin carrying her from the Great Hall and up a wide stairwell leading to spacious guest quarters on the second floor. There he had left her to grieve.

Why did you leave me, Father? she thought. It was not supposed to happen this way. She needed him. It would be impossible for her to avoid the inevitable plotting and scheming of the Arelian nobles without his guidance. And what about her suitors? How could she bring herself to make the right choice? And what then? Her father would never see her married. He would never see his grandchildren. In all her dreams of the future, he had been there, standing next to her. And now he was gone.

At the end of the first day, Aldarin had entered her chambers with a tray of shellfish soup and flatbread. He had placed the food on her bedside table before returning to stand silently in the open doorway. Jelaïa had refused to acknowledge him, and after a few minutes he had left, quietly closing the door behind him. She had left the food untouched.

And now he returned, unarmoured and clean-shaven, his muscular arms pressing against the tight fabric of his tunic. She watched from the depths of a padded armchair as he set another tray of food down beside the first; a freshly-grilled haddock with crisp, brown skin, and a slice of lemon.

"It would do you good to eat, my Lady." His deep, soothing voice enveloped her like a warm blanket, and for the first time since learning of her father's death, she felt a little comfort.

When she did not reply, he moved closer, the varnished floorboards creaking under his sandalled feet. He dropped to one knee and she found herself tumbling into his swirling blue eyes, deep and mysterious as the ocean. She saw no shame there, no anger, only a deep sorrow.

"Aldarin, he has left me! My father has left me, and I am alone." A terrible sob wracked her body. Then she felt the knight's powerful arms wrap around her, and she buried her face in his chest, releasing days of pent-up emotion in a torrent of tears. They stayed locked together for some time until, finally, he released her.

"My mother died when I was barely more than a child," he said gently. "A terrible plague that took many from our village. Her death was neither quick nor painless. You saw it, and you felt it, or a part of it, when my blood was shared with your own. When she was gone, I cursed the Twelve for taking her from me. Food lost its taste. Flowers lost their scent. I was locked in a prison of my own making. Listless and dissatisfied. Then the First Priestess of the Twelve found me. Praedora was her name. She gave me purpose, something worth living for. She brought me to the temple, and there I found new friends, a new life."

"It is too hard, Aldarin, there is an emptiness inside me. I can feel it gnawing at my very soul. What I have lost can never be replaced."

"And it never will be. Loss is like a deep wound, Jelaïa. Raw and burning at first, causing constant pain. Then, after a time, with help and courage, the wound closes and the pain subsides. But the scar it leaves never fades. It remains a visible part of you until the day you die. And some days you will forget it is even there; other days you will feel it burn and itch, making it difficult to focus on anything else. Such is loss. Faded but never forgotten."

With a calloused thumb, he wiped away the wetness from under her eyes. "One thing I can tell you is that you will never be alone. We will travel to my temple, to meet with Praedora. Then, when you wish to return to Arelium, I will accompany you. You will have me by your side as long as you need me."

"Aldarin, I do not know what I have done to deserve you, but thank the Twelve for the day you entered my life."

"It is an honour," the tall knight replied, rising to his feet and bowing gracefully. "Now try the fish. It is excellent. And maybe tomorrow you will feel ready to come and eat with us."

Jelaïa waited until he was gone then pushed herself out of the chair and over to the bedside table. She opened up the grilled fish and sampled a morsel of white flesh. Aldarin was right. It was divine.

For the first time in days, she smiled.

The next morning, she sent word that she would be joining the Baron for lunch and then set aside the next few hours to prepare. Kessrin keep had an ingenious plumbing system that allowed servants to draw seawater up from the bay through a series of buckets and pulleys, then heat it by running it through fifty feet of corrugated metal pipes. The hot water could be diverted for cooking, showering, and, most importantly, bathing. Jelaïa spent far too long in one of the ornate ceramic baths, scrubbing her skin until it turned a healthy shade of pink and enjoying the warm salt water.

She was not alone for long, however. The moment she stepped from the bath, she was ambushed by an army of servants. Her brown hair was straightened and braided, her nails trimmed, the salt scraped from her skin, her body oiled and perfumed. No sooner had she recovered from this first assault than she was whisked off to a walk-in closet filled to the ceiling with corsets, hose, underwear, hats, and shoes. Then there were the dresses — hundreds of them. Jelaïa had the impression she wasn't the first woman to be restyled before meeting the Baron.

She settled on a plain pea-green dress, not unlike the one she had torn to pieces during the siege of Arelium, although rather more revealing. This was unavoidable. All the clothes were low-necked, some of them to such an extent that they showed off far more cleavage than they hid.

The search for underclothes was even worse. By the time she had found something larger than a napkin, the luncheon gong was ringing. She quickly added a dab of light blue eye shadow and a touch of lipstick before heading down to the Great Hall to join the others.

The dais at the end of the hall had been removed and replaced with a large u-shaped oaken table. Dozens of chairs and benches surrounded the table, packed with nobles of all shapes and sizes. Servants bobbed and weaved among the guests, deftly distributing great steaming platters of mussels and boiled potatoes from the kitchens.

The Baron was seated directly below the magnificent stained-glass window, toying with a glass of white wine. His jaded expression dissolved into one of pleasure when he caught sight of her. He shot to his feet, revealing a daring combination of a pale pink puff-sleeved shirt and wide marine-blue breeches.

"My Lady!" he called, winking and beckoning her over. "My heart soars to see you up and about. And may I compliment you on your choice of attire; the green of the dress brings out the colour of those captivating eyes of yours."

Aldarin was seated next to the Baron and Jelaïa was sure she saw him roll his eyes. It was the most uncharacteristic thing he had ever done. She covered her mouth with her hand to hide her smile, then graced the Baron with an elaborate curtsy.

"Thank you, my Lord."

"Of course, my dear. May I present to you my steward, Lady Arkile? She was most grieved to hear of your loss."

"Indeed," said the stiff-necked, grey-haired woman, not seeming especially perturbed. She sniffed and looked down her nose at Jelaïa as if she was studying a new species of insect.

"Lady Arkile," said Jelaïa, her voice dripping honey. "Such a delight."

"I am blessed by the Twelve to be graced by two such beautiful women," the Baron continued, unfazed. "And you have also met Xandris? One of your own, of course. Part of the group of refugees we so generously allowed into our fine city."

"My Lady," said the sandy-haired, overweight man sitting to the Baron's left.

"Of course! Xandris! Apprentice to the healer! I thought I knew that face. It is good to see you!"

"Thank you, my Lady. If I may, I have compiled some financial information about our food and lodgings here. The refugees—"

"All in good time, dear Xandris. Jelaïa, please, come sit with me, have some wine. I have great things planned for this afternoon. A tour of our magnificent walls. Our lighthouse! The five towers! The markets! The docks! So much to do! And then, this evening, a light meal in my quarters. I have an unparalleled view of all of western Kessrin. There is no better place to see the stars. And who knows where the night will take us?" He smiled broadly, flashing two rows of immaculate white teeth.

Jelaïa took a deep breath. *Right,* she thought. *Time to start acting like my father.*

"Derello?"

"Yes, my beauty?"

"SHUT UP." The words came out louder than she had intended and the hubbub of the surrounding guests died down to a glacial silence.

"I'm sorry?" said the Baron. He didn't seem annoyed, just slightly bemused.

"No, it is I who am sorry, for you seem to be mistaking me for someone else. I am not one of your courtesans to be toyed with, or one of your subjects to be ordered about. I am not your *beauty*, your *dear*, or even 'Jelaïa'. My father is dead. I am Baroness Jelaïa del Arelium, your equal. The food you are eating has arrived here because I allowed it passage through my lands. The stone used to build the walls you are so desperate to show me came down the river through my valley."

The Baron was staring at her, his expression indecipherable.

"All you have done by attempting, rather pathetically, to flirt with me is endanger the already fraught relations between your Barony and my own. And you disrespected one of my subjects. I will have you apologise to Xandris for interrupting him or I will go and eat my meal elsewhere."

Jelaïa was aware of twenty pairs of eyes staring at her in astonishment. She felt a blush creep slowly up her body and, with an effort of will, she forced it back down.

"Out!" shrieked the Baron, red-faced. "All of you out!" The nobles looked at each other, confused.

"NOW!" he screamed, throwing his half-empty wine-glass onto the floor where it shattered.

The sound was enough to jolt the nobles into action. With a clatter of plates and cutlery, the Great Hall was emptied of its occupants until only the Baron, Aldarin, Arkile, and Xandris remained. The heavy double doors were closed with a clang.

The Baron's lips twitched, then he grinned. Not the fake, toothy rictus from before but a genuine smile that made his eyes twinkle. It transformed his features, and Jelaïa realised she was privy to a hidden secret: another man was hiding in the shadow of the first.

"Thank the Twelve, you aren't an idiot, Jelaïa," he said happily. "I do so hate playing the arrogant, insufferable fool. The prancing about, the garish clothes, the constant flirting, the permanent bored expression, the air of naivety … but the advantages of being underestimated are undeniable."

"You don't hate the constant flirting, my Lord," Lady Arkile interjected.

"Well, I—"

"Or the clothes."

"Fine. Perhaps not. What can I say, I like silk. Anyway, I believe I owe you an explanation. When my parents were lost at sea five years ago, the Barony was in political turmoil. The only way I could find to protect myself was to convince the nobles that I wasn't a threat. Weak, superficial, easily manipulated. Much to my chagrin, it was easier than I anticipated."

"Maybe that's because you really *are* weak, superfi—"

"Lady Arkile. If you keep interrupting me, I'll never finish. I have kept up the charade ever since. The nobles believe me to be a malleable puppet. And I have to balance pretending to be a despicable womaniser with the slow and subtle remodelling of their agendas to better fit my own. It is quite exhausting. Lady Arkile was steward to my father and has been invaluable to me in navigating these treacherous legislative waters. Quite an astounding woman."

A fleeting smile flickered across the steward's face, gone so soon Jelaïa almost thought she had imagined it.

"Luckily, your angry tirade has given us the perfect excuse to dine in relative peace for once." He rang a small silver bell and a servant materialised from behind one of the stone pillars.

"Wine, if you would? The bottle I chose this morning, please."

The man nodded and disappeared for a moment, returning with a decanter filled with a dark purple liquid, and a set of bulb-shaped crystal glasses.

"We have much to discuss," said the Baron, pouring five generous measures of wine. "But let us begin with a toast! To Listus del Arelium!" He swirled the liquid round in his glass and held it up to the light. "Just look at the colour! Please, take a moment to breathe in the floral bouquet! Delightful! An excellent year!"

Jelaïa was unconvinced; nevertheless, she brought the glass to her nose and took a tentative sniff. There was indeed a faint floral scent, mixed with ripe fruit and nuts. She shrugged and opened her mouth to take a sip.

"WAIT!" cried Xandris. His round nose was still hovering over his glass of wine and he was inhaling rapidly. "There is something strange about the smell, something unnatural. It's bringing back memories of my medical studies. A smell the healer warned me about."

He sent the wine spinning round the glass and breathed

in the aroma. "Almonds!" he sputtered, his eyes widening in recognition. "It's almonds! Prussic acid! Poison!"

Jelaïa threw the glass away from her. It hit the wooden table and shattered, showering the half-eaten food with wine and pieces of broken crystal. "Watch out!" she heard the Baron shout. Aldarin leapt forwards and tackled her to the ground. As she fell, something short and sharp buzzed past her ear and thudded into the back of a chair next to her.

Raising her head cautiously, she saw the servant who had brought the decanter inserting another bolt into a miniature crossbow barely wider than his hand. He finished reloading his weapon and raised it with a snarl. Derello, without a second thought, snatched a silver plate from the table and threw it at the man like a discus. It hit him in the shoulder and the bow discharged, the bolt spinning harmlessly away into the rafters.

With a curse, the assassin turned heel and ran from the room.

"We cannot let him get away!" yelled Jelaïa angrily and, without waiting to see if the others were following, she set off in pursuit. Bursting through the side door, she found herself in the keep's kitchens. Cauldrons of shellfish and vegetables boiled and bubbled in preparation for the noonday meal, but the kitchens were otherwise empty.

Out of the corner of her eye, she caught a flash of black as the traitor stepped out from behind one of the pots and fired. She threw herself sideways and felt the bolt graze her cheek, close enough to draw blood.

"Damn you to the Pit!" she cursed. Aldarin and Derello crashed through the door behind her. The knight was an impressive figure despite his lack of armour and weapon.

The assassin spat and retreated yet again, running along the line of pots and out into a small courtyard beyond.

"Aldarin, after him!" Jelaïa urged. Derello caught her arm.

"Wait a minute, my Lady. The courtyard leads to the south-eastern tower. The tower has no other exits. Once inside, he will have to either come back down the way he went up or cross over to one of the other towers using the upper walkways. I'll send my men to the adjacent towers and we will trap him between us."

"Agreed," said Jelaïa. She grabbed a large kitchen knife from a nearby table and cut a long slit in the fabric of her dress from ankle to thigh. She put the knife back down, hesitated, then picked it up again and stuck it into the belt around her waist.

"Aldarin, let's go!"

"My Lady, I believe it would be prudent if you stayed—"

"He may know who killed my father, Aldarin. I am *not* letting him get away."

The tall knight nodded and they picked up the pace, running out across the courtyard and into the tower on the far side. A central staircase spiralled up as far as the eye could see, branching off towards rooms and galleries. They could make out the unmistakeable dark shape of the assassin a few storeys above them.

"Come on, Aldarin, we are losing him!"

Aldarin accelerated, taking the stairs two at a time. Jelaïa dragged herself after him, willing her tired legs to carry her up just a little further. They followed the fugitive floor after floor, slowly closing the gap. When he reached the fifth floor, they were less than ten feet behind. The man risked a glance at his pursuers. Seeing how close they were, he swerved away from the stairwell and pushed open a thick wooden door leading to one of the narrow stone walkways linking the towers.

With a final burst of effort, Aldarin dived through the open doorway and caught the tip of the man's heel. The two men tumbled to the ground in a tangle of flailing arms and legs. Jelaïa stepped out onto the walkway and was immediately hit by a gust of biting cold wind. The bridge linking one tower to the next was just wide enough for two people to pass each other without touching. It was bordered on either side by a four-foot-high stone rampart, not nearly high enough to protect them from the treacherous winds.

Far down below her, piers and jetties spread out in all directions like a box of overturned matchsticks, the miniature ships moored there no bigger than the palm of her hand. To her left, the estuary opened out into the Bay of Doves and beyond that the Sea of Sorrow. She could make out the fishing boats bobbing on the water, pulled to and fro by the tide. To her right, the River Stahl twisted and turned across the plains before being lost in the low-lying hills that served as a natural border between Arelium and Kessrin.

She heard a cry from Aldarin and saw that the assassin had managed to tear away the bandage protecting the knight's injured shoulder. The wound was bleeding again, thin rivulets of blood running down his tanned arm, staining his tunic. His other arm was gripped around his assailant's neck, trying to lock him in a chokehold.

Jelaïa hesitated, unsure of what to do. Then Aldarin's bloody sleeve jogged her memory; a memory of pale blue flames exploding from her fingertips, that feeling of unbridled power.

"Aldarin! Give me your arm! Release the fires of Brachyura!" she shouted above the whistling wind.

"No, my Lady! The price is too great! I can handle this!"

The assassin drew a bolt from the folds of his cloak and tried to stab Aldarin with it. The knight batted it away, sending it flying over the edge of the ramparts.

"Aldarin!" she pleaded. She needed it now, she had to have that strength back, that feeling of fire running through her veins bringing such a delicious mixture of ecstasy and pain.

"Aldarin! I am your Baroness! I order you to do this! Give me your blood. Give me my gift. GIVE IT TO ME!"

"NO, I WILL NOT!" yelled Aldarin, and with a cry of anger he lashed out at the assassin with a powerful kick to the stomach. The man staggered backwards, hit the top of the rampart wall, and toppled over the edge. For a fleeting instant, his hands scrabbled for purchase on the crumbling stone, then he fell screaming, smacking into the cobbled courtyard fifty feet below.

The door at the far end of the walkway slammed open and Derello rushed through, a curved scimitar flashing in his right hand.

"Where is he? Where's the assassin?"

Jelaïa slumped to the ground and put her head in her hands.

"Oh, Aldarin," she said miserably. "What have I become?"

There was no reply.

CHAPTER 5

RIPPLES AND REPERCUSSIONS

"Two things must be considered when treating a wounded patient. The first is his or her physical condition: broken bones, torn muscles, and the like. The second is the patient's mental state: how the injury has impacted their emotional, psychological, and social well-being. And I would argue that the second is more important than the first. The patient will never fully recover if he or she is not of sound mind."

KUMBHA, ELEVENTH OF THE TWELVE, 42 AT

REED SAT IN his iron wheelchair near the crackling fire of the Great Hall and picked idly at the hem of his vermilion cloak. The cloak had been his constant companion for almost twenty years: on the walls above the Pit, during the harrowing journey from Jaelem to Arelium, and more recently on the cold, dusty streets in front of the ruined gatehouse. It was almost as much a part of him now as his own arm or leg.

When Reed had been brought to the infirmary, his dirt-stained clothes had been cut from his body and thrown into one of the wicker baskets to be burned. Jeffson had, for the second time, rescued the cloak from its untimely demise, washed out the worst of the grime, and patched up the numerous rips and tears. The emblazoned surcoat had been beyond saving, replaced by a plain dark blue shirt, and matching trousers. A pair of golden crossed swords had been stitched onto the right shoulder to denote Reed's rank of captain.

The newly-repaired cloak was held in place by an embossed wolf's-head clasp, a gift from Listus. Reed had been surprised at how much the Baron's death had affected him. He had only known him for a scant few days yet, in that time, he had come to admire the old veteran's way of thinking and unshakeable principles that were so often in line with his own. His absence would be keenly felt for a long time to come.

"Ah, a fellow cripple," came a rasping voice, startling him from his melancholy thoughts. Loré del Conte had appeared at the end of the hall, his carved cane tap-tap-tapping on the paving slabs as he limped closer to the fire. "Broken but not yet defeated!" He sank gratefully into one of the comfortable armchairs.

Loré had changed since his injuries. Abandoned by his family, shunned by his extra-marital concubines, and deserted by his noble lackeys, he had in just a few short days lost his looks, his wealth, and his political influence. A lesser man would have given in to despair but, after a moment of doubt, Loré had risen to the challenge, exploiting his shrewd intellect and vast knowledge of the workings of the Barony to begin to regain what had been lost.

"The healer says I only have to stay a few more days in this contraption," Reed said with a weary smile. "There's nothing wrong with my legs, it's my chest that took the worst of it. Four broken ribs. I'm told one of the shards of bone punctured my lung. Healer managed to get it out, but it still hurts like the Pit."

"Oh, please. Four broken ribs? Child's play. I beat you hands-down, Sir Reed! You'll have to do better than that!"

Reed gave a short chuckle. It felt good to laugh again. "I think I must have done something to annoy the healer, though. He's forcing me to do these breathing exercises every morning, supposedly to hasten my recovery, but I get the impression he likes to see me suffer. And this Pit-spawned chair. No physical effort for a week! It's driving me mad!"

"Exercises! Pah! Take a whiff of this!" Loré removed a metal flask from the depths of his dark robes, unscrewed the top and passed it over. Reed inhaled briefly and his eyes immediately began to water. The viscous liquid smelt of mouldy earth and rat's urine.

"Ugh. What is that?"

"That, my friend, is my new drink of choice for as long as I live." He took a deep swig and grimaced at the acrid taste. "I think the healer hates us both."

The great double doors at the end of the hall swung open to reveal a bedraggled Praxis, flanked by Captain Orkam and Sir Manfeld, their cloaks and armour soaked by the pouring rain that battered against the walls of the inner keep. Pools of water and fallen leaves spread over the entranceway as the men struggled out of their soggy coats.

"Ah, Sir Reed, Sir Loré, I see you have set up camp near the fire. An excellent idea. I believe we will join you." Praxis shook the last of the mud from his boots. The scar running down his cheek looked swollen and inflamed.

"We have returned from our tour of the valley," said Sir Manfeld. He had removed his helm and drops of water were beginning to form at the tips of his drooping moustache. "I am pleased to say that there are no traces of greyling activity. Kaevel Forest will have to be patrolled frequently for the next few years, but I am confident we have routed the majority of the enemy stragglers."

"Any news of Nidore? Jelaïa?" asked Loré hopefully.

Manfeld shook his head. "Sorry, my Lord. Nothing yet. We are still searching."

Loré gave an exasperated sigh. "Damn that boy. Where has he run off to?" He dabbed at the corner of his mouth with a silk handkerchief. "It is not the first time he has disappeared like this. It is of no matter, I'm sure he'll turn up eventually. Did you visit my holdings? How are the fields?"

"I have men tilling the soil. The surface is completely dead but, as I was saying to Sir Reed, I believe the deeper layers are unharmed. You will have crops again in Arelium, given time."

"It is just as Listus told us," said Praxis. "The most valuable asset in Arelium is its people. Once the refugees have returned to our Barony, we can start nursing our land back to full health. And it is for that same reason I have brought you here. You heard my promise to my subjects—"

"Lady Jelaïa's subjects," corrected Loré.

"Of course," continued Praxis smoothly. "My promise to the men and women of Arelium. Someone must answer for the Baron's death. I am not one to point a finger, but all the evidence indicates Kessrin's involvement, whether it be Derello pulling the strings himself or not. I intend to travel there myself. I will be leaving tomorrow morning at first light. Orkam will come with me along with as many of the town guard as can be spared. It will not be enough to take the city if Kessrin has turned against us but, hopefully, it will be a sufficient display of force to dissuade them from attacking us outright."

"I fear you are letting your emotions get the better of you, Lord Regent," murmured Loré, his coarse voice grating like paper on sand. "You have only been Regent for a week and already you abandon us. Who will govern Arelium in your absence?"

"Why, you, of course, Sir Loré."

"I beg your pardon?"

"With Orkam coming with me and Jelaïa still missing, you are the next logical choice. I spoke to the Baroness about it this morning, and she couldn't agree more. She is still unable to leave her room, poor thing, distraught with grief. But she gave me her blessing."

"Well, I suppose that might work," Loré conceded. "I will do my best to continue what Sir Manfeld has started."

"Indeed," said the scarred old knight. "For I will be accompanying his Lord Regent to Kessrin. Derello has not held the position long, but I have already met with him several times and, despite his ... eccentric tendencies, I believe him to be an honourable man. I will leave some of my knights with you to finish the more delicate restoration work, Sir Loré. They will return to the temple directly in a month or so."

"So, we are in agreement?" asked Praxis. The men nodded, apart from Reed who was looking confused.

"Sir, I mean, Regent, my Lord—"

"I think you have earned the right to call me Praxis, Reed."

"Right, yes, sorry. I haven't heard my name mentioned in all of this. Am I to accompany you to Kessrin or stay here with Loré in Arelium?"

"Neither, I'm afraid," said Praxis. "The barges from Morlak brought us not only stone but also unsettling news from the Barony. They have lost contact with the Morlakian Pit, Reed. A contingent of the Old Guard, hundreds strong. I am sending you up there as a representative of Arelium. I need you to find out what's going on. I can't spare any of the town guard for an escort, so if you find yourself out of your depth, get back here as quickly as you can, or look for asylum in Morlak."

"Fair enough. The Baron had planned to send me to one of the other Pits at some point. I am happy to go," said Reed, and realised that he meant it. "But what about my condition? I cannot ride a horse, not for the next few days at least. In fact, I'm supposed to be lying down until my lung is stronger."

"Yes, so the healer tells me. For every problem, a solution! I have already arranged for a cart to be prepared; you will be travelling in style! You can leave as soon as this afternoon."

"A cart is fine, but I can't lie in the back and drive it, can I?"

"No, that is why I have found you the perfect travel companion."

A stooped, balding figure detached itself from the shadows where it had been waiting patiently and unnoticed.

"I am honoured to serve, my Lord," said Jeffson blandly, bowing stiffly.

Reed groaned.

✺

My own manservant is trying to kill me, thought Reed as the rickety cart hit another pothole, sending a jolt of pain through his chest. It was their second day on the road. They had left the valley of Arelium by the eastern path, a paved but poorly maintained stretch that skirted around the impassable outlying marshlands to cross the River Stahl at Southbank. Once on the other side, they would be in Morlak.

It had been raining since mid-morning, and Reed could hear its soft patter on the tarpaulin cover, the fabric stretched outwards at the front and back to protect the driver's seat where Jeffson held the reins loosely in one hand and a slim red-covered book in the other. He was wearing a wide-brimmed black straw hat and a dark riding cloak, a similar attire to that worn by the self-proclaimed 'priests of the Twelve', those who believed the ancient warriors were closer to gods than men.

The priests of the Twelve did not hold much power in the southern Baronies, reduced to travelling from village to village as missionaries, living off the sale of amulets, trinkets, and other such accoutrements. Further north, over the Redenfell Mountains, things were quite different. The priests had permanent places of worship, and in Klief the head priest was an advisor to the Baron himself.

Reed raised himself onto his elbows. The view from the back of the cart had changed little in the last few hours. Once they had left the scorched earth of the valley floor, the terrain had become flat, unremarkable grasslands, a never-ending series of verdant fields punctuated by the occasional herd of cows or flock of sodden sheep, huddled together in the afternoon drizzle.

The light was dimming when they reached Southbank, a small, drab village amounting to little more than a half-dozen houses clustered around a broad stone bridge. One of the buildings, larger than the others, had a creaky wooden sign of a painted beer tankard hanging from one corner.

"I would suggest we stop here for the night, my Lord," said Jeffson over the drumming of the rain. "If memory serves, this is the last village of note before Morlak; our last chance for a cooked meal and a good night's sleep." Reed agreed without hesitation, remembering their first night spent together on the hard, flat bed of the cart, Jeffson's snores ringing in his ears.

They left the wet and miserable piebald shire horse in the hands of the stable boy just as the sun was vanishing below the horizon, and entered the inn. The interior was lit by fat, stubby candles set on a few greasy tables. A fire burned in a stone pit taking up one corner of the room. Despite the early hour, the place was more than half-full of small isolated groups of dour patrons nursing a pint of beer or a cup of red wine.

"What can I do for 'ya, Milords?" grunted the round-bellied innkeeper, his bristly eyebrows raised inquisitively.

"Two rooms for the night, if you would, good man," said Jeffson. "Oh, and a couple of plates of whatever you have stewing in the kitchen, with a pitcher of your finest Arelian red."

"Aye, can do that. Cost 'ya a couple of silver Barons." The innkeeper spat into one of the beer glasses on the counter and began to dry it with a grimy, threadbare towel. Reed wasn't quite sure whether he was actually cleaning the glass or making it dirtier.

"Here's a gold Baron for the food, lodgings, and horses," said Jeffson, fishing a small coin with Listus del Arelium's head stamped on one side from the pouch on his belt and setting it down on the counter. The innkeeper's eyes widened at the glinting gold. The coin disappeared into the folds of his apron in the blink of an eye and a pudgy hand waved the two travellers over to an empty table by the fire.

Reed made his way carefully across the room. It felt liberating to be standing and walking again after so long, but his atrophied leg muscles cried out in protest at each halting step he took. The ten or so yards felt more like a hundred and he was sweating by the time he got to the table.

"We are making good progress, my Lord," said Jeffson, removing his wide-brimmed hat and cloak.

"I'll take your word for it," Reed replied. "Everything looks the same out here. What were you reading, if I may ask?"

Jeffson held up the little red book.

"*Morlak, a political conundrum,*" Reed read slowly. "Any good?"

"Fascinating."

"I'm sure it is. Ah! Food."

The innkeeper sauntered over and set down two steaming plates of roast meat and pumpkins covered in thick chestnut gravy. The smell of cooked meat made Reed's mouth water. He attacked his meal with gusto, barely noticing when the man returned with two pewter cups of wine and a half-empty decanter.

The simple meal was delicious, the piping hot sauce sliding down Reed's parched throat and warming his aching limbs. He mopped up the greasy remains with a hunk of dry bread and belched contentedly.

"My Lord, I wish you would adhere more closely to the *noblesse oblige*, as it were," said Jeffson with a resigned sigh.

"Knobless what?"

"*Noblesse oblige*. It means to comport oneself in the manner of a noble of Arelium."

"Well, we're stuck in the middle of nowhere, no one here knows who the Pit we are or where we're going. I think we can let decorum slide for once."

"My Lord, is it not the, ahem, manners that maketh the man? We must at all times—"

"So, you're nobles from Arelium, then?" interrupted a slurred voice. Its owner was an enormous barrel-chested man with thick, hairy arms as wide as tree trunks. Dark, close-set eyes glimmered dangerously in a heavy-jowled porcine face. The man wiped his nose on the sleeve of his dirty tunic and spat a wad of something viscous at Reed's feet.

"So my travelling companion keeps reminding me," Reed replied amiably. "How can we help you, friend?"

"Friend? You here that, Baxon? Never thought I'd be friends with a noble!" A second man set down his half-finished chicken leg and came to stand behind the first. He was short and spindly where his companion was tall and wide, with pockmarked cheeks and a long, pointed nose.

"Is there some sort of problem here, gentlemen?" said Jeffson. He was as calm and unflappable as ever, although Reed noticed that he had put down his book and cup of wine so that both his hands were free.

"Problem?" sneered rat-faced Baxon. "Have you been hiding under a rock for the last few weeks? Your Baron burned down half the valley! I lost a whole acre of corn to that man's folly."

"He did what he thought was right to defend the Barony—" began Reed hotly.

"Oh, what *he* thought was right, eh? I suppose that's all right then, isn't it? So next month, when the nights get colder and I don't have any coin to buy wood for the fire on account of me losing my harvest, I'll just tell my wife the Baron did what he thought was right? I'm sure that'll warm her heart more than a blazing fire would, eh, Ernst?" The second man said nothing, his eyes narrowing.

Reed rose unsteadily to his feet, wincing at the pain in his aching legs. "I am sorry for the loss of your crops. I believe some of the fields in the valley were harvested before the attack; a portion of your corn may have been saved. I would be happy to relay your grievances to Lord Praxis."

"Yeah, either that or your servant there could hand over his money pouch," snorted Ernst, his prominent brow creasing into an angry frown.

"Excellent idea, Ernst," said Baxon. "Cut out the middle-man. Manservant! Hand it over."

"That is quite impossible, I'm afraid," said Jeffson. "We need these funds to pay for food and lodging."

"What a coincidence, so do we." A chair scraped noisily and a third man ambled over, his face flushed from too much wine.

"'Nough in that pouch for three of us, Baxon," said the new arrival. "You weren't the only one to lose everything to that Pit-spawned old man. 'Eard 'e spent most of the battle hiding like a little girl in his chambers, probably crying and wetting the bed, wallowing in his own piss—"

"Excuse me?" interjected Reed politely.

The man turned towards him just in time to catch Reed's fist on his lower jaw. The force of the blow spun him around and he fell crashing into one of the tables, flipping it over. Clay mugs shattered as they hit the floor, soaking the grimy floorboards with wine and ale.

A firm hand on Reed's shoulder pushed him back into his chair. "I think it best if you allow me to deal with this rather unfortunate situation, my Lord," said Jeffson placidly, rolling up his sleeves. "Gentlemen," he continued, addressing the two irate farmers still upright. "Let us leave things as they are, shall we?"

Ernst snarled and leapt at the balding manservant, arms outstretched. Jeffson grabbed his chair and sent it spinning into the charging man's legs. He went down with a strangled cry, head hitting the floorboards with a crack. Baxon chose this moment to come to his friend's aid, aiming a clumsy punch at Jeffson's expressionless face.

The manservant seemed to sense the punch coming, and he swayed backwards, avoiding the blow. Momentum carried Baxon forwards into Jeffson's return swing, a low jab to the stomach. The breath exploded from the pock-faced man's lungs with a whoosh and he collapsed, groaning.

Ernst, rising groggily to his knees, received a kick to the face and fell back down again.

Reed stared at Jeffson in astonishment. The man was barely even winded!

"I suggest we retire for the evening, my Lord," the man-servant said, running a critical eye over the broken table and chairs. He plucked a silver coin from his pouch and flicked it to the innkeeper who caught it deftly, inclining his head in thanks.

"I believe you have been hiding things from me, Jeffson," said Reed. The two farmers had regained their senses and were unsuccessfully trying to revive the third, who still lay sprawled unconscious in a puddle of spilt beer.

"We all have a past, my Lord. Forty years is a long time. I did not spend all of it as a servant to the Baron."

"But—"

"Another time, I think, my Lord. The men's anger was not entirely unfounded. We will continue to see the conse-quences of our actions; the siege of Arelium has left its mark on us all, even men like these who were miles and miles away. Ripples expanding slowly outwards from a sunken stone. Something to ponder upon during our long trip north to Morlak."

Reed nodded, wheezing, and fumbled his way wearily to the guest rooms behind the inn, shrugging off his clothes and falling into bed.

Yet, despite his throbbing head and heavy eyes, sleep would not come. He lay awake in the dark, staring at the ceiling, thinking of Hode, Yusifel, Ferris, Listus, and all the others who had given their lives to defend the Barony. So much pain, loss, and sacrifice. And it was only the beginning.

Winter was on its way. Harsh, glacial, uncaring winter. There would be no escape for those who had lost their homes, those who no longer had the means to buy food or supplies, those who had lost brothers, husbands, and fathers, and must now face the icy cold alone.

So much pain and loss.

And so much more to come.

CHAPTER 6

STICK FIGURES

"Courage comes to us in many forms. I have seen astounding acts of bravery among my initiates. And yet, beyond the temple walls, I have borne witness to even greater things. A mother defending her child against an abusive husband. A brother giving his clothes to his sister to keep her warm. These are the things I will remember. These are the things that remind me that humanity is worth fighting for."

BRACHYURA, FOURTH OF THE TWELVE, 72 AT

⁂

WHERE WAS SHE?

Felq's mother had left their sparse little campsite over an hour ago to find some food for the evening meal and had still not returned.

Things had started out reasonably well. They had arrived at the southern edge of Kaevel Forest in the late afternoon, setting up the flimsy tent close enough to the tall pine trees to be sheltered from the worst of the wind that blew up from the Great Plains.

For the first time ever, his mother had let him use the tinderbox to light the fire himself. It had been difficult, striking the steel just right with the sharp piece of flint, but he had managed it, sending glowing sparks dancing into the dry leaves and kindling. His mother had smiled down at him and ruffled his brown hair so he knew he had done well; she always did that when she was especially pleased.

They had plenty of water in the canteens but nothing of substance to put in the iron pot. With no food or game in the immediate vicinity, his mother had tied back her hair, taken up her sling, and ventured into the thick line of trees to find something to eat.

He had waited patiently for a while, drawing stick figures in the dirt by the fire. He was used to being alone. His father was long gone, killed in a logging accident three years ago when Felq was five. His mother kept telling him that his father was with the Twelve now, up in the sky among the stars, fighting to defend the realms of men. One of the stick figures was always his father, fearlessly wielding his spear, axe, or sword against the enemies of humanity.

The shadows lengthened and there was still no sign of his mother. It would soon be too dark to see, and she had taken nothing to light her way back to the camp. It was time for him to be brave. He searched around the clearing for a thick branch of wood and plunged the tip into the heart of the fire to set it alight. With his makeshift torch held high, he pushed his way past the wall of pine needles and into the forest.

"Mother?" he called out tentatively. Tall trunks spread out in all directions as far as the eye could see. An owl hooted somewhere in the leafy canopy far above his head. He tried to clear his mind and remember everything his mother had told him about tracking a wild animal. Squatting down on his haunches, he started to look for imprints on the ground, scratches on the bark, broken leaves; anything that would indicate which way she had gone.

After a few minutes of searching, his patience was rewarded: a soft bootprint in the mud of the forest floor, the toe pointing north. He laughed with relief, his voice sounding too loud in the relative quiet of his surroundings. Keeping his torch low to the ground, he started following the trail, spotting more footprints and trampled leaves that confirmed he was going the right way.

He did not know for how long he followed the muddy tracks, but his torch was burning low when he heard something grunting not far ahead. After a moment's hesitation, he stamped on the torch to put it out and crept slowly towards the source of the sound, trying to keep his steps as light and quiet as possible. The trees were thinning, and patches of clear night sky appeared overhead.

He reached the edge of a small clearing and saw what was causing all the noise. A dead deer lay on its side in the middle of the glade, its belly slashed open. It had been killed recently, ropes of still-warm intestines and internal organs steaming in the night air.

Four creatures were crouched around the dead animal, bickering among one another in a series of guttural chitters and shrieks. From a distance, they could almost be confused with children; small, hairless, grey-skinned children with spindly arms and bulbous yellow eyes. One of the creatures raised its hand, and Felq could see that instead of fingers the thing had three claws; two long and straight with a third shorter and hooked.

With a cry, the creature slashed down, separating the deer's head from its body. It cackled as fresh, warm blood spattered over its companions. A black tongue darted out from behind serrated teeth to lick the claws clean.

Felq stood rooted to the spot, his knees trembling. He tried to force himself to move, but his body wouldn't respond. *Do something!* he pleaded to his motionless legs. Cold fear writhed inside his belly, pushing down on his bladder. He felt a spray of hot urine run down his thighs.

Suddenly, a hand clamped tight around his mouth, smothering his cry of alarm. He turned to see his mother behind him, her hair loose, the thick woolskin travelling cloak she always wore covered in mud and leaves. She brought a finger to her lips. He nodded, and she released her grip.

"They're everywhere," she whispered, her eyes darting around the clearing. "Dozens of 'em, maybe more. And bigger ones too, bigger than ya' Dad. Great hulking beasts. We've got to get away from here, back to the camp." They retreated slowly from the creatures, inch by careful inch.

Then Felq stepped on his fallen torch and the dry wood split with a loud snap.

One of the creatures raised its wrinkled head and, for an instant, its evil yellow eyes met Felq's. It let out a shriek of rage and scampered in his direction, closely followed by its companions.

"RUN!" screamed Felq's mother and they fled back the

way they had come, swerving round tree trunks and jumping over treacherous roots. Felq didn't dare turn to look behind them, but he could feel the creatures closing in on them, chittering wildly as they converged on their prey.

A massive shape appeared to their right and Felq's mother was suddenly sent flying through the air. She hit a low-hanging branch and crumpled to the ground.

"MOTHER!" Felq cried out in panic. *She isn't moving! Why isn't she moving? What have they done to her?*

His way forward was blocked by two enormous monsters, nearly twice as tall as his pursuers. They had darker skin and sunken eyes glittering with malice. Thick veins crisscrossed their muscular arms and legs. One had a crude, rusty iron breastplate that was little more than two thick plates of metal strapped together. The other was bare-chested, holding a gnarled wooden cudgel almost as large as Felq himself.

Felq whirled around, searching for a way out. The four smaller creatures emerged from the darkness, spreading out and cutting off all avenues of retreat.

I am going to die here, he thought. A solitary tear wet his cheek. *At least I will try to die with dignity.* He stared defiantly at the creatures as they approached unhurriedly. *Father, you will no longer be alone. I am coming. I will join you among the stars.*

Something ferocious burst from the undergrowth and one of the creatures ceased to exist.

There was no other way to describe it: one moment the thing was standing there, the next moment it was gone, leaving behind a severed arm and a pool of dark black ichor. In its place stood a human male, the biggest living human Felq had ever seen. He must have been at least ten feet tall, dark-skinned and hairless. He was bare-footed and wearing what looked like a faded flag or banner with holes cut for his head, arms, and legs; it was tied around his waist with an old piece of rope. The fabric was pulled tight against his chest and arms as if struggling to contain the muscles beneath.

The man turned slowly and Felq gasped to see that there was no whiteness in his eyes, only two hollows of darkness, as deep and as empty as the starless night sky. He felt drawn towards those eyes, compelled to stare into their abyssal depths. Then something inside him recoiled at the idea, and he forced himself to look away.

One of the creatures scuttled forwards and was met by a casual backhanded slap that ripped its head from its shoulders. The headless body stayed upright for a moment, fountaining black blood before collapsing.

The man's hands moved again, faster than Felq could follow, and two more creatures were torn apart in a spray of ichor. Only the two hulking beasts remained. They seemed less intimidating now, barely reaching the man's chest. They grunted to each other in their alien tongue before moving cautiously forwards, one of the two circling slowly round to hit their enemy from the rear.

Without a word of warning, the cudgel-wielding beast attacked, bringing its weapon down in a powerful two-handed swing. The man caught the blow on his right forearm and, with a resonant crack, the cudgel exploded in a shower of splinters. The man's left fist hammered forwards and punched clean through the thing's stomach, exploding out of its back in a fountain of gore and broken bone. It screamed in agony and fell. The man spun around to catch the second creature coming at him from behind. Hauling the brute up into the air, he held it aloft for a moment before bringing it down onto his raised knee, snapping its back like a twig.

Silence returned to the forest. The man strode over to Felq and kneeled. His lips twitched and Felq realised he was trying to smile.

"Good 'morrow, little one," said the giant in a deep, cavernous voice. His hairless scalp gleamed in the moonlight.

"M ... m ... mother," Felq stammered through trembling lips. The man frowned and strode over to the comatose form nearby. He put his ear to her chest, then lifted her with one arm, nestling her unconscious body close to his chest.

"She lives. Show me to your camp."

Felq pointed south with a shaking hand and the behemoth set off, the little boy running behind him to keep up. They soon reached the campsite and the man laid Felq's mother carefully down by the fire, checking her for broken bones or other wounds.

"She is lucky, little one. A bang on the head, methinks, nothing more. You must care for her this night."

"You cannot stay?"

The man turned his gaze north and a great sadness overcame his features. "No, little one. I am needed elsewhere. It is the beginning of the end, and I must be there to see it through."

"Could you at least tell me who you are? My mother will want to know the name of the man who saved us."

"My name? I was once called Brachyura, Fourth of the Twelve."

He bowed his head respectfully and walked away, his great strides carrying him swiftly back into the forest and out of sight.

CHAPTER 7

A TROUBLED REUNION

*"We are much alike, my city and I. From a distance, the high
walls seem impregnable, the five gates unbreakable. But if you
were to look closer, you would see that the illustrious sheen hides
flaking mortar and cracked stone worn thin from erosion. We
are both frauds, hiding our true selves behind a painted façade."*

BARON DERELLO DEL KESSRIN, 423 AT

J ELAÏA STOOD ALONE in the Great Hall of Kessrin, staring
up at the stained-glass window that filled the far wall.
The armoured woman with the long, flowing hair
looked so confident, so in control. What she would give to
feel like that again.

They had found what was left of the assassin scattered
all over one of the cobbled alleyways beneath the walkway.
He had hit the ground face first, his head cracking like a ripe

melon. Little remained to identify him, even his fingers had been mangled beyond all recognition.

He had been wearing black, nondescript clothes with nothing in the pockets, no jewellery, and no tattoos or scars. If only they had managed to capture him alive, they would have been one step closer to finding her father's murderer. Instead, they were no nearer to the truth than before.

Aldarin had been angry; angry at himself for losing his temper. She knew from their shared memories that he prided himself on his self-control, bottling up his choler deep inside. She had seen him suffer his father's beatings, the hardships of his training, the scapegoating and mockery of the other initiates, all without succumbing to his rage. And now, for the second time since they had met, she had caused him pain.

"We call it a kraken," came the accented voice of Derello from behind her.

He had come straight from his morning swim, his black hair slick and wet from the salt water of the bay. It was strange to see him without make-up. His lightly-tanned face looked younger, immature even. It made her remember that he wasn't much older than her; it was just that the painted mask he wore was carefully tailored to alter his features, to make him less like an innocent young man and more like a Baron.

"Like what you see?" he said. Jelaïa realised she had been staring at him, and she turned away, blushing.

"Apologies, my Lord. Seeing you like this reminded me how close in age we actually are."

Derello touched his face. "Ah, yes. You see me now as an empty canvas. Lady Arkile will be here soon, she's the only one I trust to get the make-up just right. May I give you some advice, Jelaïa? Remember those treacherous political waters? Self-confidence is the key to keeping yourself from drowning."

He drew level with her, tightening the belt of his striped red and blue trousers.

"For some of us that confidence comes naturally. Men like your father, or my own. Warriors. Others need a crutch, a buoy to keep them afloat. When I am wearing my painted mask, I can hold the gaze of my vassals. I can stare at my reflection without fear or doubt. Maybe all you need is to find your own pillar of support, something to give you that little extra bit of strength that you need to excel."

"But relinquishing that support would make us vulnerable."

"Yes, exactly."

"Yet you are here without your jewels or make-up."

Derello spread his hands and smiled ruefully. "Yes, I suppose I am. I didn't really think of it that way. I suppose that means I trust you. You are the first woman to see me naked in a long time. Well, naked like this I mean. There are plenty who have seen me without my clothes on. Why, last night I—"

"Derello!"

"Right. Sorry."

They stood side-by-side admiring the stained glass. "Who is the woman fighting the tentacled octopus-thing?" Jelaïa asked.

"The creature is a kraken. Much bigger than an octopus, though I've never seen one. My father told me they prowled the Sea of Sorrow hundreds of years ago. Body as big as a carrack, and tentacles wider than a ship's mast. Long gone now."

"And the woman?"

"Not sure who she is. One of the Twelve probably. We still know so little of what they looked like. Feisty-looking, isn't she? I've spent many years staring at her face. Sometimes, when I'm bored, I think about what she would look like with her armour off."

"*Derello!*"

"Right, right, sorry. Now and again, a bit of the old persona slips through the cracks."

"Do women really fall for all that?"

"Of course! Well, some of them do. Those attracted to power, youth, or eccentricity. I barely have to do more than glance in their direction. You don't want to be spending much time with them the morning after though; minds as empty as a fish."

Jelaïa laughed, feeling the last mists of her depression fade away.

"Think like a fish, and talk like a fish too," Derello continued. He put his hands behind his ears, flapped his palms like makeshift fins, and made popping sounds with his mouth.

Jelaïa laughed even harder, and was still laughing when Lady Arkile arrived, a make-up bag slung over one shoulder and a scowl on her face.

"Duty calls," said Derello dejectedly, and allowed himself to be transformed into Baron del Kessrin.

❦

An hour later, they reconvened in the Great Hall to discuss the state of affairs between the two Baronies, each represented by three delegates.

Lady Arkile and Derello were joined by a ginger-haired guard captain with impressive side whiskers that wrapped around his cheeks and upper lip like a fox's brush. On the opposite side of the table, Jelaïa sat flanked by Aldarin and Xandris. The Knight of Brachyura was helmless but otherwise fully-armoured, his battle-axe propped against his chair within easy reach.

"Gentlemen and Baroness," said Lady Arkile crisply. "This meeting is long overdue, and we have much to talk about. I have asked Captain Hirkuin to join us. The captain oversees our military operations up and down the coast. As such, he may have some insight into the imminent greyling threat."

Hirkuin tapped two fingers to his round forehead in an unofficial salute. He had the rough hands of a sailor, the tips of his nails stained yellow from too much tobacco.

"I believe the first item of business should be the refugees," Lady Arkile continued. "His Lord Baron has most graciously granted asylum to thousands of women and children from Arelium. They have been lodged at our own expense inside the town for weeks now. It is time for them to return home."

"I could not agree more, steward," said Jelaïa. "And I would like to take the opportunity on behalf of all Arelium to thank you for your kindness, generosity, and patience in the matter. As you may have heard, we have lost a great deal to fire and war, but if you would draw up a list of expenses, I promise you we will do everything we can to repay you in full."

"No need for that," Derello replied affably.

Lady Arkile arched a grey eyebrow. "Are you sure, my Lord? The cost was quite substantial—"

"Quite sure, thank you, steward. I believe you are forgetting that, in halting the greyling tide, Arelium not only saved itself but also denied the enemy passage through its lands to Kessrin and Morlak. Our inhabitants are safe due to the valiant efforts of Listus and his men. We should be thanking them, not taxing them."

The steward's expression softened. "You are right, Derello. My focus on the Barony's finances seems to have made me forget more important things."

"You are forgiven, my dear." The term of affection earned the Baron a sharp look, which he ignored completely. "Our guests are free to return to Arelium whenever they are ready. The barges will have to stay here, of course. Some of the merchants were most, ahem, *peeved* to give up their boats and cargo for the evacuation. I will spare what men I can to escort the refugees back home via the main roads."

"Thank you, Baron," said Jelaïa. "Xandris, you were our liaison here. Anything to add?"

"No, my Lady." He stroked his forked goatee thoughtfully. "In fact, it would perhaps be best for me to leave you now? I can get started on the necessary preparations right away."

"Of course."

The little man bobbed his head and gathered up his satchel of scrolls.

"Now, what of the greylings?" said the Baron, turning to Hirkuin.

"Well, that's just the thing, my Lord," said the ginger-haired captain. He unrolled a vellum scroll map of Kessrin and placed it on the table before him. "We've been up and down the coast these past few weeks, and no sign of 'em. Torc and Northport are safe. I've sent riders inland to Ironwood and Three Sisters Lake but they won't return for another week at least."

Lady Arkile pursed her lips. "It is not as strange as you may think, Captain. Kessrin has no caves, no craters, nowhere the greylings can return to the surface, save perhaps our northern borders and the lower peaks of the Redenfell Mountains. We have no Pits and no Old Guard."

"Agreed," said Aldarin, speaking for the first time. "My fellow knights and I have neither seen nor heard anything of note here in Kessrin. But what of our neighbours? There is a Pit across the eastern mountains in Morlak, and another to the north in Talth. Have we news from our distant allies?"

"No," Derello replied, his eyes wandering over the map. "And we have not looked to contact them either. That is a mistake. Hirkuin, send a ship up to Haeden if you would, and riders east to Morlak. Our neighbours may be in trouble. And recall any of the carracks still on patrol. I would not want us to be caught unawares if the enemy decides to show its face."

"Yes, my Lord. And what of the town itself?"

"You know as well as I do that Kessrin has become nigh undefendable. You could hit our walls with a wooden stick and they would come crumbling down. Too much erosion and humidity have weakened the mortar. And don't get me started on the piers. Did you know there are nearly a hundred now? Once I'm through the gates, I have to walk for ten minutes just to get down to the water! We'll have to hope it doesn't come to that."

A blue-clad servant slipped through one of the side doors and bent to whisper something in Lady Arkile's ear. She frowned and waved the man away.

"It seems steward Praxis is on his way to see us, Lord Baron," she said, and Jelaïa could detect a tone of annoyance in her voice. "He has concluded his investigation into Listus's murder and his findings do not paint us in a very favourable light."

"What do you mean?"

"He pulled out a Kessrin dagger at the funeral, claiming it was the murder weapon."

Derello tapped a finger against his bottom lip.

"Interesting. Well, I think I would remember if I had ordered the assassination of one of our closest allies, so I'm fairly sure it wasn't me. It's more likely that whoever hired the man to do the job is looking to stir the pot between Kessrin and Arelium. I'm surprised Praxis got hooked so easily. I've met him a few times and he gave the impression of being an intelligent man."

"He most surely is," said Jelaïa, louder than she had intended.

Pull yourself together! Stupid girl!

She cleared her throat. "What I mean to say is that he has been a good friend to my father and me, and has never shown any undue animosity to Kessrin. I'm sure there is a logical explanation for all of this."

"I hope so," said Derello. "I sparred with him once or twice when he last visited; the man knows his way around a weapon. I wouldn't want to get on his bad side." He pulled a face. "Now we know each other a little better, maybe you could put in a few good words? An allied *tour de force*, as it were?"

"I … I'm afraid I cannot." Jelaïa shuffled uneasily in her chair. "I will not be here. I am leaving tomorrow for the temple of Brachyura with Aldarin."

"What? Why? Your people have a new Baroness. They will want to meet with you, to seek your guidance. Can you not postpone your journey?"

"If only I could. I am … unwell, my Lord. There is something wrong with me, and Aldarin believes there is a priestess at the temple who can help. We spoke earlier of self-confidence. This is what I need to do to regain my own. This is what I need to do to be fit to rule. Praxis will be fine without me for a little longer."

Something in her tone of voice must have convinced the Baron, as he didn't press the matter further. "Very well," he said. "I will have horses and supplies prepared for your trip to the Cliffs of Kessrin. May the Twelve guide you both."

We can but hope, thought Jelaïa and looked across at Aldarin, but the knight refused to meet her gaze.

They left early the following morning. Derello, true to his word, had provided them with two sturdy horses, their saddlebags filled to the brim with food for the journey. A thin, sickly-looking sailor ferried them across the estuary in exchange for a few copper Barons and they were soon deep in the coastal marshlands south of the city.

Expansive wooden boardwalks cut through the mud, surrounded by shrubbery and stagnant pools of water.

Aldarin rode in silence, his face lost in the shadows of a deep-blue hooded riding cloak, a gift from the Baron. They stopped briefly for lunch, the tall knight barely touching his food, morose and lost in thought. A heron soared overhead, using the warm updrafts to circle the larger ponds effortlessly in search of fish and frogs.

Towards the end of the afternoon, the fading light and cooling air began to draw out the mosquitoes. Jelaïa was bitten a half-dozen times before capitulating and raising her own hood over her head. They found a dry patch of ground just off the main path as the sun was setting and stopped to make camp. Jelaïa slid wearily down from her saddle and massaged her aching thighs. She was cold, tired, damp, and itching all over.

And she had had enough of the silent treatment.

"How long are you going to be angry with me, Aldarin?" she said finally, pulling her bedroll off her horse's back. "Because if you no longer desire my company, I relieve you of your duty. You may return to Arelium, or to Kessrin, or wherever you want to go."

"My Lady?" the knight replied. He looked genuinely surprised. "I thought it was you who was angry with me?"

"Whatever for?"

"I failed you, my Lady. I let my temper get the better of me and cut short any chance of us gaining a lead on the Baron's murder. First Listus, then you. Someone is trying to end the bloodline of del Arelium. And because of me, we are no closer to finding out who."

"You are not vexed that I tried to get you to give me your blood?"

"Vexed? Of course not! I am well versed in the way the azure fire can cause certain … cravings. Praedora, the priestess who brought me to the temple, told us that she once chased after a Knight of the Twelve with a kitchen knife."

"Well, that's not too bad."

"In her undergarments," said Aldarin seriously. "It was most unbecoming for one of her status."

Jelaïa gave a relieved laugh and threw herself at the startled knight, wrapping her arms around him and kissing him on one scarred cheek.

"I don't know what I'd do without you, Aldarin. Friends?"

"Always, my Lady."

"Then let us move on to better things, like the treasure trove of interesting and embarrassing stories from your time at the temple I'm sure you are keeping from me."

"Indeed, there were many humorous incidents," Aldarin replied, visibly relieved. "I will tell you some over supper. I think I spied a couple of eggs and a leg of mutton at the bottom of my saddlebags. Let me find my tinderbox and we can get started. And Jelaïa?"

"Yes?" she said, realising the knight had used her actual name after what felt like a long time.

"Stop scratching, you'll only make it worse. Stay close to the fire once I get it going, the insects don't like the smoke. Oh, and thank the Twelve we are not travelling during the summer."

They laughed and joked throughout the evening, settling down close to the guttering flames as the stars came out.

The sun rose bright and early. In a few short hours, they had left the marshlands behind, the path taking them back towards the coast and the rugged cliffs overlooking the Sea of Sorrow. The wind was stronger here, swirling around the two travellers and tugging at the horses as they struggled valiantly uphill.

As they reached the top of a steep incline, the temple of Brachyura came into view. There was not much to see at their level. A stone gatehouse, two storeys high and topped with a crenellated rampart, protected a narrow passageway that led into a square, columned courtyard, and from there to a set of stairs winding down into numerous rooms and corridors hollowed out of the very bedrock of the cliffs.

Despite the simple entrance, there was no mistaking that they were in the right place, for in front of the gatehouse stood an enormous bronze statue of Brachyura, ten feet high, a double-bladed axe raised in triumph over his smooth head. The sculptor had dressed the statue in the same style of plate armour worn by Aldarin. A cloak flowed out behind him; the metal expertly styled to make it seem as if the fabric was billowing in the wind.

Before the statue stood a middle-aged woman in an emerald-green dress and cloak. She was wearing an irritated expression, her arms crossed in displeasure. Aldarin barely had time to dismount before she strode up to him and slapped him hard across the face.

"Two weeks, you said you'd be gone. Two weeks! It's been two *months*, Aldarin. I was worried sick. Manfeld said you were missing. Presumed dead even. I was so worried!"

Aldarin opened his mouth to reply, but the woman silenced him with a gesture and turned beaming to Jelaïa.

"Baroness! We meet at last! My name is Praedora, First Priestess of the temple of Brachyura. Welcome home."

And with a sound like rolling thunder, the heavy portcullis barring the way rumbled open, inviting them inside.

CHAPTER 8

FALLOW'S END

"Why is fighting alone and unaided seen as a sign of strength? It is easy to be a lone wolf. It requires no effort, no dedication. Now think of a pack of wolves, working together, the weak protecting the strong, generations of knowledge and culture shared among them. Which is stronger? Which would you rather face?"

KRIARI, FIRST OF THE TWELVE, 11 AT

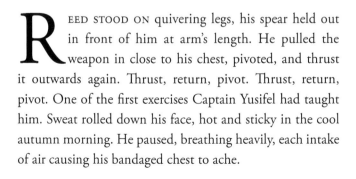

REED STOOD ON quivering legs, his spear held out in front of him at arm's length. He pulled the weapon in close to his chest, pivoted, and thrust it outwards again. Thrust, return, pivot. Thrust, return, pivot. One of the first exercises Captain Yusifel had taught him. Sweat rolled down his face, hot and sticky in the cool autumn morning. He paused, breathing heavily, each intake of air causing his bandaged chest to ache.

I'm getting old, he thought. *An ageing member of a dying regiment.* The Old Guard had never been a more appropriate name.

Thrust, return, pivot.

He twisted too slowly and his tired legs collapsed under him. He tumbled into the mud, dropping the spear.

"Overdoing it a bit, my Lord?" The stooped shape of Reed's manservant blocked out the sun, his voice somehow managing to be both completely devoid of sarcasm and a tad reproachful.

Reed rolled onto his back but made no move to get up. "I don't like having other people fight my battles for me, Jeffson. Next time we run into trouble, I'll be ready."

"Not if you tear your stitches or break your ankle, my Lord. No need to overexert yourself. I must confess it did me some good to work up a bit of a sweat."

Except you didn't sweat. At all, Reed thought.

"You still haven't told me how you learnt to fight like that," he said, pulling himself up into a sitting position and wiping the mud from his hands.

"There is not much to tell, my Lord. I was born into poverty, an orphan by the time I was five. The only means of survival was to associate myself with groups of older boys, boys of disreputable character. I spent much of my early life executing a plethora of menial tasks, many of them on the wrong side of the law."

"That's where you learnt to fight like that?"

"Among other things, my Lord. I would stay in one of the Baronies until it became too dangerous, then move on to the next. I am ... well-travelled, to say the least."

"But how—"

"Enough for the moment, I think, my Lord. We are still a few days travel from Morlak keep. We should return to the road."

"Oh, what joy, another day being bounced around in the back of a wagon."

"Quite, my Lord. But first, your medicine." He brandished an iron kettle filled to the brim with water. "If you would allow me a few minutes to prepare your concoction?"

Reed rubbed his aching chest. "You are enjoying this, aren't you, Jeffson, watching me suffer?"

"I'm sure you are in agony, my Lord," the manservant replied mildly, hanging the pot over the campfire to boil the water.

Reed grunted and went to pick up his spear. The dirt path they were travelling along stretched away from their campsite, cutting a straight line across the grasslands to the northern horizon where the sky met the jagged peaks of the Redenfell Mountains. And beyond the mountains, the Pit. It was there he would finally meet others like him, watchers of the Old Guard.

The herbal tea was just as disgusting as Reed had imagined. He gulped it down so fast he nearly burnt his tongue, then helped Jeffson roll up the two small canvas tents and pack them onto the bed of the wagon. They were soon back on the road, the shire horse stubbornly covering the miles with its slow, steady pace.

From his cushioned seat in the back of the cart, Reed studied his companion. Once again, Jeffson was deep in the pages of his little red book, completely absorbed by its contents, his nondescript features shadowed by the wide brim of his straw hat. It seemed far-fetched that this plain, unassuming, middle-aged man had once been wanted in half the nine Baronies. Or was it? Reed vowed to keep a closer eye on his manservant from now on.

Just after midday, four black dots appeared in the distance; hazy figures as still as statues spread across the width of the road. As the cart drew closer, the shapes became four armoured riders on barded warhorses.

"A welcome committee, perhaps?" wondered Jeffson. "But then what are they doing so far from Morlak?"

"Let us find out," Reed replied, straightening his vermilion cloak and patting down his greying black hair in an attempt to make himself presentable.

The riders remained motionless, still blocking the road, as the cart approached. Jeffson pulled hard on the reins to stop the horse a few yards short and Reed stepped down from the back of the cart to meet them.

The four men were wearing half-plate armour: a shaped metal breastplate, greaves, and vambraces tied with leather straps to a thick, padded under-tunic; a good compromise between protection and freedom of movement. None of the men had helmets, instead each wore a black or grey fur mantle draped over their armoured shoulders. Their hair was styled in a manner Reed had never seen before: the sides of their heads were shaved to a thin stubble, leaving only a narrow strip of long, thick hair on the top, which was pleated or braided down their backs.

The four riders were armed with short swords, and each carried an enormous rectangular curved shield of canvas and wood, at least five feet high, with a metal boss set in the centre. Three of the shields were black and unadorned whereas the fourth was more ornate; the central boss was reworked into a ram's head with painted horns spiralling out to cover the wooden canvas.

The warrior holding the shield dismounted with a clink of metal and stamped over to the cart. He had a braided beard the colour of autumn corn that put Reed's facial hair to shame. Silver rings and beads had been added for decoration, while another ring pierced his left nostril. His brow furrowed as he took in the captain of the Old Guard and his manservant.

"Greetings," he said finally, lowering his shield and letting it rest against his leg. "My name is Sir Vohanen, Knight of the Twelve." He proffered a gloved hand and Reed stepped forwards to grasp his wrist. Vohanen's forearm was as hard as tempered steel.

"Greetings, Sir Knight. I am Sir Merad Reed, Captain of the Old Guard. I am here at the behest of Regent Praxis to investigate the disturbing news that has reached us concerning my fellow watchmen stationed at the Morlakian Pit."

"I surmised as much. I would imagine that you are an advance party of some sort? When will the Arelian infantry and cavalry arrive to assist us?"

Reed shared a look with Jeffson.

"Well … never," he said. "We are the entirety of the aid Praxis deemed fit to send. Arelium has already suffered grievous losses and those still fit to fight have followed the Lord Regent west to Kessrin."

"By the Pit!" snapped Vohanen. "Foolish man, this Praxis! Did he not understand our message? The Barony of Morlak is crumbling as we speak. If we do not act soon, there will be nothing left! I described the urgency of the matter most emphatically in my missive. Why does he not listen?"

"I am sorry, Sir Knight. None of us was privy to the contents of the letter save Praxis himself."

"Ah, 'tis no matter. Lad! Picket the horses and find us a skin of wine, would you? My throat is parched and it looks like I'm going to have to do a bit of talking!"

One of the other knights, a clean-shaven man in his early twenties, nodded with a scowl.

"Avor, my eldest!" said Vohanen. "We're really scraping the bottom of the barrel to find initiates nowadays. Hates it when I call him 'lad'. Shall we?" He gestured at a nearby fallen tree trunk a few feet from the road.

"I will see to the cart, my Lord," said Jeffson with a curt bow.

Sir Vohanen settled himself on one end of the tree trunk, the wood creaking under his considerable weight. "Ah, at last, a bit of relief for my tired backside. We've been waiting since dawn out on the road for you, Sir Reed. My buttocks feel like my wife has hit them repeatedly with a broom handle."

"Well, I—"

"Don't ask me how I know what that feels like," Vohanen continued with a wink. "Ah, thank you, lad." Avor passed a leather wineskin to the older knight who took a deep swig and smacked his lips. "Exquisite! Nothing like a Morlakian red. It's all this mountain air, you see. Does wonders for the grapes."

He offered the skin to Reed, who raised a hand to decline. "Another time, perhaps. I am recovering from a recent injury and the healer thinks I should avoid alcohol for another week or two."

"No alcohol? Doesn't sound like much of a healer to me."

Avor coughed politely.

"That's my son telling me to get on with it," said Vohanen. "Do you have children, Sir Reed?"

"No."

"Well, don't. Avoid all women like the plague. Nothing good can come of it. Now, on to more important things." He took another drink of wine and leant forwards, his expression grave. "What do you know of the Twelve, and of our Order?"

"Quite a bit, actually. I was fortunate to meet one of your brothers, Aldarin, a Knight of Brachyura. He told me much of your history, and of the Twelve themselves."

"I see. That will make things easier. Before I talk of Morlak, I believe you are owed an explanation as to who we are. We are Knights of Kriari, First of the Twelve." He pointed to the embossed metal ram's head on his shield. "The sign of our Order. Just as Brachyura was a builder, Kriari was a warrior and tactician. During the first war with the greylings, he used his leadership and authority to merge the scattered tribes into a cohesive whole. The concepts of brotherhood and camaraderie fascinated him, and he looked to strengthen the bonds between men to the best of his ability.

"The tactics he developed were built upon the foundations of this creed. Before the Twelve appeared, our ancestors fought alone, each man being an individual unit, spread out from the others and unprotected. One of the first things Kriari sought to do was change this. The primal nature of the greylings meant that they were always aggressive and impatient. They would always attack first. We had but to wait for them to come to us.

"And thus, the concept of the shieldwall was formed. Oval, overlapping shields, with each man protecting his neighbour. When locked together they would form an impenetrable barrier against the enemy."

"Like at the Battle of the Northern Plains," said Reed, remembering the sunny afternoon spent with Aldarin in the gardens of Arelium.

"Yes, precisely. That was where it was used on such a large scale for the first time. Our own shields are based on this tactic. We are, ahem, bigger and stronger than the average man, allowing us to use much broader and thicker shields. These don't lock or overlap, but what we lose in protection, we gain in flexibility." Vohanen patted the rim of his shield affectionately.

"As part of our training, we are all taught to make our own shields. Cut down the tree, glue the wooden planks, stretch out the canvas, add the rivets, the handle, the metal rim. A work of art. As much a part of me as my own son."

"Father!" said Avor impatiently. "Stop blathering! They don't want to hear about your shield. Time is of the essence!"

"Yes, my lad, calm yourself. Ah, the impetuosity of youth! So, Kriari built our temple in what is now northern Morlak, in the depths of a pine forest called Dirkvale. Then, just like all the others of his kind, he disappeared. We have done our best to follow his teachings in his absence. Our temple is located just a day's short ride from the Pit, and we are on good terms with the Old Guard stationed there. We meet with some of them several times a year. Hardy folk, proud of the work they do.

"Two months ago, something changed. A couple of things, actually. We had planned to rendezvous with a company of Old Guard up by Terris Lake. They never arrived. My fellow knights and I waited for a whole day, then turned back to Dirkvale. One of us volunteered to travel on to the Pit to make sure everything was all right. He has still not returned."

Reed shivered as the image of Hode, his throat cut by a greyling claw, came unbidden to the forefront of his mind. "That is worrying indeed, Sir Knight, for the Southern Pit was attacked at roughly the same time."

"Yes," continued Vohanen, his expression darkening. "That brings me to the second thing. When we returned to the temple, we were surprised to find the entirety of the Morlakian garrison waiting for us. Fifty of our Order, forced to leave the capital, on the orders of the Baroness herself."

"The Baroness?"

"Aye, Syrella del Morlak, one of the most power-ful women in the nine Baronies. Been ruler of Morlak for nigh on fifteen years now, still unmarried. It is said she has never even laid with a man. We call her the White Rose of Morlak, on account of her being, ahem, pure. Lovely-looking woman, must be in her forties but looks ten years younger. Long, braided black hair. Strangely coloured eyes: one blue, one green. Makes her look all the prettier if you ask me."

"Father ..." interjected Avor wearily. Reed was starting to feel sorry for the young man.

"Yes, yes. Anyway, we were perplexed, to say the least. Relations with the Baroness have always been a bit strained but never hostile. The knights stationed in Morlak were there not only to bolster the town's defences but also to train the Baroness's men in the use of the shieldwall.

"I decided to go there myself, see what the problem was, and ask for help dealing with whatever is going on up near the Pit. And guess what I found?" He leant closer, and Reed could smell the red wine on his breath.

"I entered the outer town all right, but the gates to Morlak keep were closed! Shut tight! No one in sight save for a gaggle of travellers and merchants milling round the base of the gatehouse like lost puppies. I went and banged on the door for a while without much success.

"Luckily, I had my ram's horn with me. I blew long and hard, enough to get a guard to poke his head over the ramparts, and I sent him scurrying to get the Baroness. She appeared on the wall of the keep for all of five minutes. Told me the Knights of Kriari were no longer welcome in Morlak. I asked about the Pit, but the only answer I got was to stay away from the internal affairs of the Barony.

"Now that's all well and good, but I had some good friends among the men of the Old Guard. My Order would not risk intervening for fear of further degrading my temple's standing with the Baroness, but I couldn't just sit there and do nothing. Comradeship and unity, two of the most important things taught to us by Kriari himself. The very cornerstone of our identity fading away as our Order loses its memory and purpose. As no help would come from within, I sent word to Arelium and called in what few favours I had left. Four knights against the dark."

Vohanen's voice trailed off and he stared down glumly at his steel-shod boots, the beads of his plaited beard jingling as he moved. Despite the man's boisterous good humour,

Reed could plainly see an inner turmoil churning below the surface. The events of the last month had left the knight deeply troubled.

"I have never seen so skilled a warrior as Sir Aldarin," Reed said, breaking the uncomfortable silence. "Nothing could resist that man and his axe; he is practically an army all by himself! And now, before me, I see *four* Knights of the Twelve? No matter what we find at the Pit, I think we are well-equipped enough to deal with it."

Vohanen smiled at this and clapped Reed on the shoulder with one meaty hand, strong enough to make the guard captain wince. "Agreed, Sir Reed! Our numbers do not change our objective! Let us proceed as planned! The sun is yet high in the sky, giving us ample time to reach Fallow's End. 'Tis the closest village to the Pit itself. We will stay overnight and head up to the Old Guard garrison on the morrow."

They returned to the main road and followed it north, avoiding the eastern turnoff to the Barony's capital. Reed used the time to get acquainted with the other two knights joining the expedition: Taleck, an older knight with a bushy grey beard and a missing right ear; and Krelbe, a dour-faced, bony man with two silver rings piercing each eyebrow. He had lost rather badly against Vohanen at cards a few months ago, and had only agreed to join the others in the hope of seeing his slate wiped clean.

Fallow's End appeared on the path before them as the day was drawing to a close. An inn and a few shops lined the road, hoping to attract passing travellers with the promise of fine clothes or a hearty meal. Behind the first line of houses, a dirt square gave access to the village hall and a conical granary.

"It's quiet," remarked Jeffson. The door to the inn was shut tight. Reed peered through the glazed windows but could see only vague shapes in the room beyond.

"Hello?" he shouted. The only reply was the whistling wind and the far-off screech of a bird of prey.

"Let's try the town hall," said Taleck. As they crossed the village square to the hall, they could already tell something was wrong. Dark patches on the ground, overturned barrels, and splashes of maroon red on the stone steps leading to the main entrance.

There was a crack as Vohanen stepped on the broken haft of a pitchfork. "There has been violence here," he said softly, shrugging his embossed tower shield from his back and slipping his hand through the handle. "Let us be wary." He drew his short sword. Jeffson said nothing but stepped in front of Reed, positioning himself between the guard captain and the closed door at the top of the steps.

Avor, after a nod from his father, pushed lightly on the wooden door. It swung ponderously open on creaky hinges, revealing the carnage within. Dozens of men and women lay in the middle of the hall, piled high in a chaotic heap of rent skin and broken bones. They all bore great gashes along their chests and backs. Claw marks. Many were missing limbs, hacked off to be carried away as grisly trophies.

One of the bodies near the edge of the pile was a boy no older than eight, his back torn to shreds, his dead eyes rolled into the back of his head. Reed blanched and looked away.

"A massacre," spat Vohanen. "Defenceless farmers, women, and children. No honour."

"It was greylings," Reed replied. He could taste bile in his mouth.

"Aye. So, it's not just the Southern Pit. They are here too. But this can only be half the village. Where are the others?"

"Father, look!" cried Avor. He had reached the far end of the hall and opened a second set of doors. A trail of upturned soil and dried blood led away from the village, heading steadily north.

"Some of the villagers are still alive," said Vohanen grimly. "The greylings have taken them back to the Pit."

CHAPTER 9

THE EMERALD QUEEN

*"You are not listening! Your little fishing boats with overlapping
hull planks and single sails are seaworthy enough, but do you
never dream of leaving the safety of the coast behind? Of seeing
what lies beyond the horizon? For that, you will need a vessel
big enough and strong enough to resist the ferocious storms and
treacherous currents of the ocean. And I will teach you how to
build it."*

MINA, LAST OF THE TWELVE, 17 AT

PRAXIS LOOKED DOWN at the sprawling port of Kessrin
in disgust. It was everything he despised. There was
no order, no logic, just a formless mass of wood
and stone, sagging under the weight of its own greed and
opulence.

He raised a scented handkerchief to his nose as the

Arelian delegation approached the main gate. The flowery smell was not enough to smother the sickening odours of seaweed and fresh fish, or the sting of the raw, salty air that made his eyes water. He glanced across at Orkam to see the disgruntled guard captain was not affected in the slightest.

His senses are probably numbed by years of patrolling the shantytown of Arelium, he thought. Now *that* was something that would not be getting rebuilt. The docks were bad enough.

Kessrin. A slowly crumbling symbol of decadence, from the rotten planks of its docks to the cracked walls of its towers. Of course, the greylings would burn it all to the ground. He just had to make that job a little easier.

His force of Arelian infantry and temple knights had set up camp a couple of miles down the road, close enough to be called upon if needed but not too close as to appear threatening. He had left Sir Manfeld to oversee the camp construction, partly because he didn't want him upsetting his future plans with Derello del Kessrin, and partly because the knight's insufferable, flowery speech and holier-than-thou attitude had become increasingly difficult for Praxis to handle the more time he spent in his company.

The guards at the gate threw him a hurried salute as he passed by on his snow-white mare. Orkam and the dismal remains of the Arelian cavalry followed behind. Loré's disastrous cavalry charge had reduced the one hundred riders to fewer than twenty; lesser vassals and their squires carrying the heraldry and banners of their deceased masters.

The procession rode slowly through the cobbled streets to the circular keep that served as a base for Kessrin's five towers. Shutters banged open as the town's inhabitants gazed curiously out of their squat stone houses at the delegation from Arelium. The road was full of people, and most stood respectfully to the side to let them pass, removing their caps or bowing with respect. Praxis kept his half-smile firmly in place, giving the occasional wave.

As they approached the keep, the inner gates were thrown wide open and a horde of servants rushed out to take care of the horses. The company of nobles was politely asked to wait in the courtyard, while Praxis and Orkam were ushered into the Great Hall to meet with the Baron himself.

Derello del Kessrin greeted the new arrivals with a tired yawn. He was seated on a gilded throne below the stained-glass window, playing with a bowl of dates. The Baron was wearing a frilled green shirt patterned with yellow stripes, in stark contrast to Praxis's usual high-collared black leather coat. A curved scimitar was belted to his waist, its glittering emerald pommel complimenting his pair of jewelled earrings. Thick mascara ringed his eyes. With a laconic gesture, he sent two town guards forwards to relieve the visitors of their weapons.

"Praxis," said the Baron in a voice filled with tedium. "How good of you to come and see us." He flicked a date up into the air and caught it in his mouth.

"It's 'Lord Regent', now, Baron," Praxis replied sharply.

"Of course, of course. I meant no offence." A small smile played across the man's lips.

Ah, thought Praxis, *it seems I am not the only one skilled in the art of deception. This will be interesting.*

"I believe you have already met Lady Arkile, and Hirkuin, my guard captain?" the Baron continued, gesturing vaguely at his advisors.

"Once or twice, yes."

"Lady Arkile was quite taken with you if I recall correctly."

The Kessrin steward glared at Derello with undisguised anger.

"That was told to you in confidence, *my Lord*," she hissed, her eyes flashing dangerously.

"Oh, my dear, you know full well you should never tell me anything in confidence. Can't keep a secret for the life of me! Now, shall we move on? Apologies for the brusque welcome, by the way. Things have been a bit hectic these last few days. An assassination attempt, in fact, on none other than the future Baroness of Arelium, Lady Jelaïa."

Orkam gasped in surprise. Praxis did his best to follow suit, hiding his disappointment. *Attempt. Damn the Pit! His man had failed! That woman was as slippery as a fish! First Verona missed her chance, and now this!* He struggled to fix an expression of concern on his face.

"My Lord Baron, this is terrible news. How fares Lady Jelaïa?"

If she is injured, I'll make sure she never leaves the infirmary.

"The Baroness is in excellent health, thank the Twelve."

Damn.

"Thank the Twelve indeed. Is there a reason she is not here to greet us?" Praxis glanced around the room as if expecting her to appear from behind one of the stone columns.

"Lady Jelaïa is no longer with us. Urgent matters called her south, to the temple of Brachyura."

"I … what?"

"I am as flummoxed as you, my dear fellow, but she told

us it couldn't wait. You have her utmost trust and confidence to continue as Lord Regent until her return."

This changes things, Praxis thought. *She has gone to one of the only places where the Knights of Zygos can't touch her. None of us would be foolish enough to try and breach the sanctity of our brother's temple. And even if we got past the knights, their priestesses have a nasty habit of picking up on things that others miss. No. I will have to wait a little longer to eradicate the last vestige of the line of del Arelium.*

"It is a most unusual way to begin her reign as Baroness," he said with a nonchalant shrug. "But we will abide by her wishes, of course. I will attempt to explain her choices to her subjects as best I can."

"Yes, you seem to be quite calm about the whole thing, Praxis."

"A steward must always keep a level head, my Lord, it is what we are trained for. Ask Lady Arkile."

"I'd rather not. I think she is still angry with me. Let us discuss the purpose of your visit. I have been informed that there is a large force gathered a few miles from the city gates. I conclude that you are not here simply to enquire after Lady Jelaïa's health?"

Captain Hirkuin leant forwards and crossed his arms. "I have several hundred of our own men ready to *dismantle* Lord Praxis's camp if the need arises, my Lord," he said, his ginger eyebrows creasing like a pair of angry caterpillars.

"Oh, let us hope that will not be necessary. I'm sure there's a logical explanation for all this, don't you think, Praxis?"

There was a sound of booted feet as the Kessrin guard stationed around the Great Hall moved a step closer.

"Naturally, my Lord," Praxis replied, licking his dry lips. He pulled the Kessrin dagger from his coat pocket and held it up for all to see. "Behold the weapon that murdered Listus, Baron of Arelium!"

"Hmm, looks like my guardsmen still need to learn a thing or two about searching visitors," said the Baron. He rose suddenly and came to stand before Praxis, hand outstretched. "May I see the dagger, please?" He took the weapon without waiting for a reply, turning it over and over, examining the curved blade, the engravings, the leather-bound pommel.

"You are right, Praxis. This is a Kessrin dagger. No mistake."

Excellent.

"The serpent engraving proves without a doubt that the weapon is not only Kessrin in origin but belonged to one of my subjects. If this is truly the dagger that murdered your liege lord, then someone in Kessrin wanted him dead. Unless, of course, the weapon was planted on the murderer in an attempt to blame Kessrin for the deed."

"I saw the assassin myself, my Lord. This was the weapon he used."

"Very well. It is the second engraving that troubles me. The kingfisher. There is only one place in all of Kessrin that this dagger could have come from, and that is Kingfisher Isle, a small, remote island off the south-western coast of our Barony."

Damn the Pit! What is he going on about? Diacrosa was to bring me a dagger. Any dagger, as long as it was Kessrin. Praxis's scar began to itch.

"Kingfisher Isle is more or less deserted apart from a

tiny fishing village. I do not see why the killer would use a knife coming specifically from the island, but it is the only lead we have."

Praxis clenched his jaw and said nothing.

"I hope Kessrin has already proved to you that we are staunch allies of Arelium. We gave your refugees safe passage, food, and lodgings in our city. We offered the same hospitality to Lady Jelaïa and sent her on her way with horses and supplies. This is, I would think, enough to attest that we have only the best intentions towards your Barony and your subjects."

Orkam nodded silently.

"Nonetheless, this is troubling. A Baron assassinated, his heir attacked. We cannot be complacent. This is what we will do. Tomorrow, at first light, we will set sail for Kingfisher Isle. You will accompany us, with an escort if you wish. Twenty of your best men. And Sir Manfeld will join us. Agreed?"

"Agreed," Praxis replied, gears turning in his mind, parsing, analysing, trying to see how he could transform this new turn of events to his advantage.

"Have you heard of the parable of the two wolves, Lord Regent?" said Derello suddenly. He was studying Praxis intently.

"The parable of … no, my Lord."

"It is said that within us all live two wolves, locked in combat, claws and teeth ripping and tearing at each other's fur. One wolf represents how we are perceived by others, the carefully constructed image we choose to let them see; the other represents our true selves, whatever is hiding behind the smoke and mirrors, free and unburdened."

Praxis felt a chill run through his body. *Why is he telling me this? What does he know?* He searched Derello's eyes for an answer but could see nothing but his own reflection.

"And which wolf will win, my Lord?" he said tentatively.

"The answer is simple, Praxis. The one you feed the most. Now, which one would that be I wonder?"

"Neither, I fear, my Lord; they are both equally well-nourished."

"An excellent answer," said Derello with a laugh, clapping his hands together in satisfaction. Praxis felt like he had just passed some sort of test. "Now I must insist you stay and eat with us; the menu is particularly exquisite today." He reached for a silver bell and rang it. Servants arrived with oval platters covered with metal cloches.

Praxis took a seat next to Lady Arkile and lifted the cloche to reveal an entire eel wrapped around a pile of rice and shrimp. The head of the dead fish stared at Praxis. The whole thing stank of seaweed and brine. He swallowed and poked hesitantly at the scaly skin with his fork.

"A toast! For Kessrin! For Arelium!" said Derello, raising a glass of dry white wine.

Praxis sighed and forced himself to eat a small shrimp. Things were not going according to plan.

The *Emerald Queen*, the Baron's personal carrack, was a thing of beauty. Nearly one hundred and fifty feet long, carrying eighty sailors and soldiers, she was the pride of the Kessrin navy. Her hull was wide and deep, with three central masts. The middle and foremasts were rigged with square sails;

the lower mizzen mast with a smaller, triangular lateen sail. Once unfurled in open water, the ocean-blue fabric proudly displayed the white serpent of Kessrin. Her sterncastle, with its small glazed windows and carved wooden beams, housed the Baron's private cabin and the officer quarters. The even larger forecastle protruded out over the bow, stocked with weapons, armour, and supplies.

A total of eight ballistae filled the deck, four on either side. Each of the massive, crossbow-like siege weapons was mounted on pivots allowing it to swivel forty-five degrees to the left or right. Tarpaulin covers protected the intricate firing mechanism from the elements. At the carrack's prow, a magnificent golden figurehead gave the ship its name: a stern-faced woman with long, flowing hair, staring fiercely out at the open sea.

The *Emerald Queen* rocked gently at the end of Derello's private pier. Sailors swarmed over the rigging, checking everything was in place before casting off. Blue-uniformed guards moved up the gangplank and down into the crew quarters below decks. An occasional splash of crimson red was visible among the sea of blue; the twenty Arelian soldiers of the Lord Regent's honour guard.

Praxis watched the proceedings impatiently, clenching his hands into fists and fighting to keep his annoyance from showing on his face. *Another wild goose chase,* he thought, fuming. *We are losing valuable time.* He had eschewed his high-necked coat for his set of fitted black leather armour, including the twin stiletto blades. The knife cut on his face was still itching terribly as it healed.

Sir Manfeld appeared at the end of the pier, surrounded by knights in full plate. Each helmet was slightly different, the horns or pincers twisting in various ways, closer or further apart, ridged, funnelled, indented; a mix of styles and shapes. Praxis knew the Order of Brachyura forged their own axes, maybe it was the same for the helmets. A stupid tradition, in any case. The Knights of Zygos used whatever weapon was best-suited to the task at hand, as long as it was well-balanced, as all things should be.

Sir Manfeld was instantly recognisable. His horns were simple, straight spikes of metal. *A simple decoration for a simple man,* thought Praxis.

"We are ready to embark, my Lord," said the veteran knight, bowing courteously.

"Please do so, Sir Knight. I hope Derello will be arriving promptly, the day is not getting any longer."

Manfeld nodded and beckoned to the five knights he had chosen to accompany him. More than enough to deal with a bunch of disgruntled island villagers. The remaining members of his Order had stayed with the Arelian infantry.

Derello del Kessrin finally arrived. He wore a plumed tricorne hat, extravagantly decorated with gold lace trimming. The fluffy green feather matched his shirt and earrings. An emerald cloak billowed out behind him, caught by the maritime wind.

"Praxis!" he said, twirling. "What do you think? An emerald Baron for an *Emerald Queen*! We will remind these islanders to whom they owe their allegiance and get to the bottom of Listus's murder. Two birds with one stone, or rather two fish with the same hook as we like to say here in Kessrin!"

"I'm sure they will be most impressed, Lord Baron," said Praxis as convincingly as he could muster. "Are we ready to set sail?"

"Just about. Lady Arkile has been briefed. Hirkuin will command our naval forces for the trip south. The *Emerald Queen* will not be alone. He has requisitioned the caravels *Sapphire Night* and *Latent Folly* to escort us. Smaller ships but more manoeuvrable. They will be able to scout ahead and protect our flanks if we encounter any trouble."

"Are you expecting some?"

Derello shook his head. "The waters around Kessrin have been free of pirates for some time. One of the first things I did upon becoming Baron was to scour the trade corridors clean." He paused. "My … parents were taken by the sea. They were travelling in a carrack like this one, fully crewed. None survived. We searched for the remains of their ship for months, up and down the coast. Nothing. Even today, I'm not sure whether they were sunk by marauders or victims of some violent storm. In any case, in recent years there has been the occasional attack on some of the merchants' convoy, but it is now *always* answered with the swift vengeance of Kessrin. And the penalty for piracy is death." The Baron spoke the last few words in anger, before remembering himself. He blinked his painted eyes and strode on past Praxis up the gangplank.

Careful, Praxis thought. *Your mask slipped for a moment there.*

The *Emerald Queen* sailed out of the Bay of Doves and waited patiently for its escort. The two smaller caravels skipped towards them from the lower docks, their blue lateen sails turning to catch the gusts of wind blowing onto the coast from the Sea of Sorrow.

"Signal for them to spread out, loose escort position, speed five knots," Hirkuin shouted to a nearby sailor, who nodded and relayed the message up to the watchman stationed in the crow's nest eighty feet above deck. He unfurled his coloured signal flags and flashed a short series of precise gestures at the approaching vessels. Moments later, both caravels signalled back and moved to flank the larger ship. The convoy turned south, the reinforced hull of the carrack cutting through the waves with ease.

Praxis stood on the poop deck, his hands gripping the rail tightly enough to show the whiteness of his knuckles through the skin. He forced himself to inhale and exhale slowly, his eyes fixed on the horizon as the towers of Kessrin slowly faded from sight behind him. His first boat trip a few years ago had ended in disaster and he was determined not to make the same mistake twice. Besides, it had taken days to scrub the vomit from his boots.

Further down the deck, Orkam and Hirkuin were huddled together under the mainmast. The ginger-haired Kessrin captain was showing Orkam how to fill a pipe with tobacco using the thumb and forefinger of one hand, leaving his other hand free to hold a torch or weapon. Sailors clambered over the rigging above them, checking the ropes and cables holding the sails in place, communicating with whistles and short, chopping hand movements.

Sir Manfeld, his body swaying in time with the bobbing of the ship, climbed laboriously up the sterncastle stairs to reach Praxis. "My fellow knights are bunked and ready," he said. The sea wind was pulling his long moustache up around his cheeks, making it look like he was sporting a set of cat's whiskers. "Kingfisher Isle is close to the temple of Brachyura. If you allow it, we will petition the Baron to take us there once our mission is finished."

Praxis opened his mouth to reply, felt his stomach heave unnaturally, and clamped his lips shut. He nodded, walked unsteadily down the steps leading to the main deck, and pushed open the door to the Baron's quarters.

Fragrant aromas assailed his senses. Derello was standing next to a round oaken table, a glass of red wine in one hand, poring over a map of the island. He looked up as Praxis entered. "Lord Regent, how good of you to join me! I was going quite mad from lack of company. Maybe we should have brought a few courtesans along for the ride, eh?"

Praxis stared blankly at him.

"Ahem. Anyway, you'll have to do. Come join me!" The pencil-drawn illustration of Kingfisher Isle showed it to be an empty, desolate place. The lone village was sited on a horseshoe-shaped beach on the northern peninsula, with pathways snaking inland towards a few sparse hills and woodlands. The southern side was inhospitable, nothing more than a series of razor-sharp rocks and steep cliffs.

"We will land to the north," the Baron said, a slender, manicured finger pointing at a spot near the village. "The water will be too shallow for the carrack, but we can bring the caravels closer and lower the rowboats."

"How many men?"

"About ten per boat. Should be enough to deter any violence from the villagers. We'll start there, then move further inland if our initial search is unsuccessful."

Praxis was only half-listening. The dagger supposedly used to kill Listus was lying on the table next to the map, the engraved kingfisher mocking him. Another mistake. The masters at the temple of Zygos would be furious. Every plan must be studied, from every angle. All possible outcomes must be explored and accounted for, with nothing left to chance. He should never have trusted Diacrosa to find him that knife, the arrogant fool. One loose thread was unravelling the entire tapestry of lies that he had worked so hard to maintain.

"Land!" came the cry from the crow's nest. Praxis and Derello hurried outside. The northern coastline had appeared: a long stretch of shining, golden sand, empty save for a tiny ramshackle pier stretching out into the water. A wooden boardwalk led away from the pier up to a handful of thatched huts.

"Drop anchor. Lower the rowboats," barked Hirkuin, buckling on his curved officer's sword. Sir Manfeld was standing next to him, his pronged helmet in the crook of his arm.

"Maybe it would be best if you stayed aboard the *Emerald Queen*, Sir Knight," said the Baron with an apologetic smile. "They are but fishermen. A seven-foot-tall armoured knight with a double-bladed axe may be a bit too … intimidating."

"As you wish, Lord Baron. Might I suggest the following? Leave one of the rowboats. My fellow knights and I will remain here, vigilant and ready. Take the signal flags and call us if you need us."

"A sound plan!" said Derello, adjusting his ornate tricorne jauntily. "Praxis, Orkam, Hirkuin — with me. Bring six of your best men. Scimitars and crossbows. Oh, and take the tarpaulins off the ballistae. Just in case."

The ship's captain had brought the *Emerald Queen* as close to the shore as possible, and the rowboats only took a few short minutes to reach the pier. Praxis was the first ashore. It felt good to be standing on something that wasn't in perpetual motion.

The group of armed men made their way slowly up the path to the huts. As they got closer, they were hit by the rank smell of rotting fish. Nets full of stinking flesh, days old. More fish lay on racks, half-gutted, their innards desiccating in the sun.

In the middle of the village square, a tall, slender figure sat on an overturned cart awaiting the men of Kessrin. He wore bronze-plated armour with bladed shoulder plates; vicious, curved sheets of metal that rose as high as his neck. His skin was pale and wrinkled, loose skin sagging from his chin and neck in folds as if he had recently lost weight. His head was bare save for a few wispy strands of hair. An enormous two-handed broadsword was strapped to his back. The man was eating a raw fish, chewing through the flesh and bone with a sickening crunching sound.

He looked up, wiped his mouth with the back of a gauntleted hand and threw the remains of his meal into the sand. "Greetings!" he said in a thin, reedy voice. "My name is Sir Ghelsin. Welcome to Kingfisher Isle."

Derello was staring at the man in amazement.

"But you are—"

"An initiate of the Order of Mina. I am a Knight of the Twelve."

CHAPTER 10

FOUR SPLINTERED SHARDS

"One of my children was brought to me, clawing at his face and screaming incomprehensibly. He was plagued with constant visions of fire and darkness. Two days later, his hut collapsed with his wife and daughter still inside. I do not think this to be a coincidence but an unforeseen consequence of our increasingly frequent interspecies relationships. If my theory proves to be true, there will soon be others cursed with the same affliction."

KUMBHA, ELEVENTH OF THE TWELVE, 52 AT

T HE TEMPLE OF Brachyura reminded Jelaïa of a rabbit warren, a seemingly unending maze of winding underground corridors and tunnels. Upon her arrival, one of the younger temple initiates had volunteered to lead her to her quarters and, despite trying to keep her bearings, she was soon hopelessly lost. All the tunnels looked the same: hewn directly into the granite rock of the cliff, lit by flickering torches on metal poles spaced at regular intervals along the walls with no signs or markings to distinguish one from another.

There were no stairs. The tunnels occasionally sloped downwards giving some indication that they were descending towards the sea but nothing more. At times, she passed by doors or openings in the rock giving tantalising glimpses into the lives of the initiates.

She saw training rooms, barracks, storerooms filled with crates and barrels of supplies, a mess hall, what looked like a mushroom farm, a pantry stocked with salted fish and meat, an arsenal, a granary, leather workshops, meeting halls, and much more. It was clear that the temple was not self-sufficient; they had plenty of fish and dried grain but no fresh fruit, crops or livestock. These must be brought in from the outside world.

Once or twice, the tunnel they were walking along opened out suddenly onto a balcony or columned gallery overlooking the churning waves of the Sea of Sorrow. Seagulls circled the cliffs, some nesting close to the temple itself. Far down below, half-hidden among the saw-toothed rocks and grinding tides, Jelaïa could just make out a stone jetty leading down to the water from a cave mouth that looked big enough to house a couple of small boats. It would take a courageous man indeed to brave the treacherous currents and take one of those boats out to sea.

After some time, they finally reached Jelaïa's quarters. The initiate opened the wooden door and then took his leave with a bob of his head, the sound of his flapping sandalled feet slowly receding as the young man disappeared back into the labyrinth of corridors.

"I suppose I'll just wait here then, shall I?" she called after him, not expecting a reply. She took stock of her new accommodation. The room was barely larger than her lavatory back in Arelium; four bare stone walls just wide enough to squeeze in a single bed and a rickety-looking desk and stool. The only source of light was a tiny arched window set high in the far wall. A plain white tunic and a pair of leather slippers had been laid out on the bed. She sat down on the mattress, as hard and unyielding as a block of marble.

The screeching cry of a seagull and the rhythmic pounding of the waves against the cliffs filtered in through the window. A stray lock of chestnut-brown hair had managed to escape the restrictive confines of her ponytail and hung across her face. Absent-mindedly, she began chewing on one of the loose tips, something she always did when pensive or anxious. Mava, her maid, had tried for a year or so to make her break the habit but, after meeting fierce resistance and a couple of tantrums, she had given up.

She waited patiently for a while, her index finger tapping distractedly against the mattress. It looked like no one was coming to get her. Her mind began to wander, back to the windswept sky bridges linking the tall towers of Kessrin, the falling assassin, the aching hunger in the depths of her stomach. The feeling started to return, calling out to her. Who was Aldarin to refuse her such power? She was the Baroness of Arelium, not some useless farm girl. If she asked him to do something, he should do it without question and without hesitation!

"Shut up," she said aloud, pushing the whispering voices

back into the darker recesses of her mind. She stood up and squared her shoulders resolutely. She was wasting valuable time sitting here in this gloomy, dank room. She returned to the corridor and set off back the way she had come, trying to remember the right path. After a few minutes, she was forced to admit she was lost again. *I am going about this the wrong way,* she thought.

Stopping at one of the many junctions, she closed her eyes and concentrated. Her ears could just pick up distant voices echoing from the rightmost branch. Following the sound, she soon arrived at the entrance to one of the underground training halls. Inside, a group of young initiates, no older than fifteen or sixteen, were sparring with wooden poles, each as thick as an axe haft. An older man with thinning hair and hooded eyes was watching the group intently.

Stepping into the room, she cleared her throat. "Hello?" she said tentatively. Her voice was lost in the cracking of wood on wood and the grunts of exertion uttered by the sweating initiates. She sighed.

Time to be a Baroness.

"Initiates, heed me!" she yelled, attempting to look suitably displeased. The sound of combat bled away as the surprised trainees jolted round to see her standing in the doorway. One of the boys dropped his pole and it rolled along the floor, coming to a stop near her mud-spattered leather boot.

"Good day, my Lady," said the older man, bowing deeply. "How may we be of assistance?"

"I wish to speak with Lady Praedora, pl …" she caught herself before saying 'please', "… right away!"

"Of course. Do you perhaps have an appointment with the priestess?"

"I am Baroness Jelaïa del Arelium," she said haughtily.

"Of course, of course," the knight repeated. He seemed embarrassed. "One of my young initiates will take you there at once." He beckoned to one of the taller youths, long-limbed with bony knees and elbows, who bowed clumsily.

"If my Lady would follow me?" he crooned in a soprano voice. They moved silently through the tunnels, the initiate taking her slowly back towards the surface without hesitating. "How do you never get lost?" she asked curiously.

"Oh, we do, my Lady," the young man replied, tapping a knowing finger to a nose covered in red spots. "It took me at least three weeks to memorise the layout of the temple, and I still lose my way from time to time. When I first arrived here, I once missed the evening meal after taking a wrong turn. Master tells us it is one of the many trials we must pass on the long road to knighthood."

He stopped so suddenly that Jelaïa nearly ran into him. "Sorry, my Lady." He gestured to a door decorated with gold leaf. "We have arrived. I'll leave you to go in alone. Master'll have my hide if I'm gone too long." He flashed a nervous smile and set off back the way they had come.

Jelaïa tentatively pushed the door open to find herself in a haven of warmth and comfort. A fireplace was set into the opposite wall, the crackling flames suffusing the room with a yellow-tinged glow. The heat from the fire seeped into her tired bones, making her realise how cold she had become while wandering the temple tunnels.

The remaining walls and floor were covered in decorative woven rugs, dyed in hues of pastel orange and green. In fact, so much of the stone was hidden that it was easy for Jelaïa to forget that she was still underground.

In the centre of the room, three comfortable armchairs surrounded a round table upon which had been placed a decanter of wine and three crystal glasses. All the chairs were occupied. Aldarin was sitting closest to the fire, wearing a simple blue tunic. He had washed and combed his cropped black hair and, despite his fading bumps and bruises, he looked rejuvenated. He was smiling.

Lady Praedora sat close by, her hand resting lightly on his arm. Her curly red hair spilled down her shoulders, shining like embers in the light of the fire. She had changed little from the image that Jelaïa had seen in Aldarin's memories; a few more lines around her eyes, a few streaks of grey in her hair.

The last member of the trio was someone Jelaïa had never seen before; a handsome, muscular figure with coal-black skin. He had coarse sable hair that had been styled in braided rows from his hairline to the back of his head. Like many of the knights, his face bore several scars, the white lines sharply visible against the darker tones of his skin.

Aldarin's smile widened when he saw Jelaïa. "My Lady! We were going to send for you. Come, take my place by the fire, I have been resting for long enough."

Jelaïa slipped gratefully into the warm cushioned chair and accepted a glass of white wine.

"May I introduce one of my closest friends, Ka'arka."

"My Lady," said the ebony-skinned knight, inclining his head respectfully.

"Ka'arka is somewhat of an exception here in the temple. The only initiate ever recruited from Da'arra. We believe it is because Brachyura didn't venture as far south as the Great Desert. Few of his bloodline are to be found there."

Ka'arka laughed. "I am perhaps also the only one to have suffered more beatings and insults than Aldarin! We probably spent more time in the infirmary cots than in our own beds!"

"And yet, you are now among the most trusted advisors of the First Priestess of Brachyura," said Praedora in a dulcet, soothing voice, "Is it not strange how the wheel turns?"

"What is strange, my Lady, is that you still pretend you didn't know all of this was going to happen," said the Da'arran teasingly.

"I've already told you a thousand times, Ka'arka, my visions don't work like that. I get flashes, nothing more. If I had known that Arelium was going to be under siege, do you not think I would have done something about it?"

She leant close, smelling faintly of honeysuckle, and patted Jelaïa's hand sympathetically. "I must offer my condolences for your loss, Lady Baroness. Aldarin has been telling me of the twists and turns of the last few weeks and I am filled with admiration at how you have handled such a difficult situation."

"It was nothing, my Lady. Aldarin did most of it, I mainly just followed his lead."

"Nonsense. Besides, Aldarin has spent over half of his life training for this. You have not. And yet you have conducted yourself admirably. I am most proud. Would you allow us to dispense with the formalities? I have not been anyone's lady for a long time."

"Of course, Praedora," Jelaïa replied. Maybe it was the wine, the fire, or the plush chair, but she was overwhelmed with warmth and friendship, as if she had known the priestess all her life.

"Excellent!" said Praedora, her green eyes sparkling. She drained her glass with a flourish. "Now, if you would all be kind enough to follow me?" She set off at a brisk pace, her emerald robes making a swishing sound as she crossed the carpeted floor. Jelaïa stumbled to her feet and half-ran to catch up, feeling the chill of the cold bedrock as they left the comfort of the fire behind.

A short way further down the corridor, they came to a set of double doors that opened into another chamber. Three women stood silently waiting for them to arrive, hands clasped together and heads bowed. They wore the same emerald-green dress as Praedora, their necks adorned with the same axe-shaped silver necklace.

"Ladies," Praedora said affectionately. "May I present to you Baroness Jelaïa del Arelium."

The three young women curtsied in perfect harmony with a chorus of "My Lady", averting their eyes.

"Right, I think that's enough decorum. Let us tell Lady Jelaïa and these ruggedly handsome knights what we have seen."

Aldarin coughed uncomfortably. "I think—"

"Oh, do be quiet, Aldarin. Now, as you know, several months ago I was plagued with images of the Southern Pit, images that I believe we interpreted correctly because, despite the reservations of the temple Conclave, we managed to avoid the total destruction of Arelium. What you do *not* know is that since you left, the visions have continued.

"Not only that, but my fellow priestesses are affected too. This has *never* happened, not in the entire history of our Order. Each of us is habitually blessed once a year by a sign from the Twelve. Once a year *at the most*. In the last few months, we have been having visions simultaneously. It is worrying, to say the least."

"Are the visions similar?" asked Ka'arka, eyeing one of the priestesses with interest.

"No, that is the other thing. They are completely different, which is why I brought you here to hear them from my sisters directly."

The three girls raised their heads, and Jelaïa was shocked to see that they were blind, their sightless eyes clouded with a creamy-white mist. The first girl began to speak in a dull voice, as if reciting a phrase committed to memory.

"*Crater. Darkness. Scratching claws. Golden sands. Forgotten depths. Misery.*"

"The Da'arran Pit," said Ka'arka, frowning.

"Yes, easy enough. Niane, if you would?"

The second girl began. "*Water. Snow. An unlit tunnel. A crimson sun. A bloody rose.*"

"Tunnels, snow ... Morlak, perhaps?" said Aldarin, rubbing his jaw thoughtfully.

"It is possible. The Morlakian Pit, maybe. It merits investigation."

The last girl uttered the segmented description of her vision in the same monotone. "*A bird with broken wings. A headless serpent. An ashen hand.*"

"The serpent? Is that not the heraldry of Kessrin?" asked Jelaïa. "Could the Baron be in danger?"

"The Baron is always in danger," Praedora replied with a faint smile. "I'm not sure. And a bird? A hand? The interpretation eludes me ... And finally, I will tell you mine. More mysteries, I'm afraid."

She closed her eyes and furrowed her brow in

concentration, swaying slightly on her feet. After a moment she spoke, her voice devoid of its usual kindness and warmth. *"A silver axe. Obsidian eyes. The smell of sap and pine. Sadness."*

"A silver axe? The sign of our Order?" Aldarin pinched the bridge of his broken nose. "Sadness? More bad news."

"I'm afraid so. We have no other choice but to convene the temple Conclave, even if the bulk of our initiates are still deployed in Arelium. We need to decide what to do."

"The Conclave?" asked Jelaïa.

"The First Priestess, the first of the temple masters, and two Knights of the Order," said Ka'arka.

"So, Praedora is part of the Conclave. Who are the other members?"

"Sir Manfeld is the first of the masters. He led our expedition to Arelium. The two knights are elected every five years, one to represent the scriers, the other to represent the, um, purebloods as it were. Sir Aldarin and Sir Caddox are the current representatives."

"That despicable man," growled Aldarin. "Let us hope he has mellowed with age."

"He certainly has not," said Praedora sadly. "But you have, Aldarin, so maybe that will be enough. I will send word to Sir Caddox, urging him to meet with us as soon as possible. We cannot do much more until the Conclave convenes."

"Then I will take my leave," said Aldarin, bending low to kiss the priestess's hand. She placed her other hand on his head affectionately.

"Very well. Take Ka'arka with you and try not to get into trouble. Jelaïa, you will stay here with us. Aldarin has told me of your awakening. It is time for me to teach you how to master the fires of Brachyura."

CHAPTER 11

THE MORLAKIAN PIT

"How can we keep hiding things from them? It is not the same since the Pact. There is a distance between us. They no longer understand my motives. They question my every decision. And they are right to do so, for I have become what I despise the most: a falsifier, a deceiver, a teller of lies."

KRIARI, FIRST OF THE TWELVE, 123 AT

᪥

THE BLOODY TRAIL north was easy enough to follow. Reed, no longer needing to travel lying down, sat up front next to Jeffson. After about an hour of riding, they came across the first body, an elderly man face down in the dirt, his back and legs covered in claw marks. Further up the trail lay the corpse of a woman, her tunic torn to shreds, both legs broken.

"Why are they doing this?" said Avor, his face clouded

with anger. "Why take prisoners only to kill them later on? It makes no sense."

"It is therein that your error lies, lad," Vohanen replied soberly. "These creatures do not follow any sense of logic. Maybe these poor people couldn't keep the pace, or they angered their captors, or maybe one of the greylings just got bored. Push it from your mind, we can do nothing for them now save avenge their deaths."

"Aye, they will pay for this," rumbled Taleck. "I will eviscerate a dozen of their number for each body we find."

The path took them up a steep incline and, as they crested the rise, the Pit came into view at the bottom of the ravine below, a dark and ugly stain amidst the green and brown. It was almost identical to the place where Reed had spent the last twenty years; a rough, oval-shaped crater gouged out of the earth, surrounded by a crenellated wall twelve feet high and dotted with squat stone watchtowers, unlit signal fires on their flat roofs. The only way up to the ramparts was via a set of stairs cut into the inner side of the wall. Below the stairs, a wooden stockade protected four long buildings: barracks, stables, and other utilities. Reed's heart leapt as he saw a flash of crimson on the flag flying from one of the towers: the rising sun motif of the Old Guard.

"Come here, lad!" called Vohanen. "Your eyes are sharper than mine. Any movement?" The young knight raised his hand above his eyes to shield them from the glare of the setting sun and focused on the distant walls.

"Nothing, Father. Neither friend nor foe."

"Strange. Let us proceed with caution."

Jeffson cracked the reins and the weary shire horse plodded steadily on down the steep path into the ravine. The sun continued its inexorable descent towards the western horizon. It would be getting dark soon. Not the best time to be out near the Pit.

The gate to the stockade was wide open. The travellers came to a halt before the barracks and dismounted. Hundreds of overlapping clawed footprints covered the ground, further proof that the greylings must have passed this way many times. Vohanen drew his short sword.

"Lad, take the horses to the stables. Krelbe, get the cart out of the square. Find a spot nearby away from prying eyes. No need to announce our arrival. Reed, Jefferson, and I will take the barracks. Taleck, check the other buildings."

Reed grabbed his spear from the back of the cart and followed Vohanen into a thatched stone building. They were greeted with a dismal sight. The corpse of one of the Old Guard sat behind a wooden desk, his hands nailed to its surface. The man's head was tilted back almost vertical, his mouth pried open and his spear forced down his throat, impaling him to the chair below. Streaks of dried blood ran from ragged holes where his eyes had been. From the sagging skin and putrid smell, he had obviously been dead for days.

Behind the first macabre figure, three more men had been similarly mutilated, their eyes gouged out, their ruined bodies pinned to the floor with spears and swords. The room stank of faeces and rotting flesh.

Vohanen strode over to the corpse behind the desk and ripped the spear from its throat with an angry tug. "I knew this man," he said quietly, his voice simmering with rage. "Captain Ansen. Great sense of humour. He even made Krelbe laugh once, strangest thing I ever saw." He pulled the nails out of the corpse's hands and carefully laid the body down onto the floor.

"We have been complacent, Reed. Complacent and forgetful. There are many theories about why the Twelve left these lands behind, but I believe it is simply because they had nothing left to teach us. They gave us everything we needed to survive and prosper, and all we had to do was apply that knowledge. But we have let so much of what they taught us slip away. Worse than that, we have allowed distrust and prejudice to drive a wedge between us, weakening us even further."

"What do you mean?" asked Reed curiously.

Vohanen blinked as if remembering who he was talking to. "Nothing. I have already said too much. Suffice to say that while the nine Baronies have been disintegrating over petty disputes, the enemy has not been idle. We should have garrisoned more men at the Pits. Maintained the towers. Kept regular reports. I fear a time will come when we will have to face the consequences of so many years of inaction."

"Vohanen!" came a voice from outside. Taleck had returned, his hands covered in blood.

"Bodies. Lots of bodies," the one-eared veteran grunted. "Buildings are full of them. Twenty, thirty maybe. Horses too. No villagers, though, only men of the Old Guard."

"Not enough," said Reed, scratching at his beard.

"Not enough what?"

"Bodies. Even undermanned there would be at least a hundred guardsmen here. Where are the rest?"

"Let's go up to the wall while there's still a little light left," said Vohanen, eyeing the setting sun.

Jeffson looked up at the steep chiselled stone steps.

"My Lord will be staying down here," he said in a tone that offered no discussion.

They found nothing on the ramparts save for a few torn cloaks and discarded spears. The nearby towers were well-stocked with wood and barrels of supplies but little else. Vohanen stood in silence, gazing down into the blackness of the Pit as the wind ruffled the coarse fur mantle around his shoulders.

"It's too quiet," he murmured. "Where are the birds? The rodents? The greylings have stripped everything clean."

"What's that?" Avor was pointing at a dark patch on the slope of the crater, barely visible against the blackness surrounding it. Vohanen stared at the spot, waiting for his eyes to adjust.

"It's a tunnel entrance," he said slowly as realisation dawned. "Look! There's a path leading up the inner slope of the crater to the ramparts."

"A way down into the Pit? But why would the greylings need such a thing? I thought they were expert climbers?"

"They are. It can't be for them. I think we have found where they are taking their captives. Let us reconvene with Sir Reed and devise a plan."

"Is it time to tell him of our true purpose in coming here?"

The older knight watched as the last sliver of orange sun disappeared behind the ridge of the ravine. Soon darkness would reclaim the crumbling walls.

"Yes, lad," he said. "It is time to tell him everything."

∽

Vohanen bit into a crispy leg of roasted rabbit. Greasy juices dribbled from his mouth and trickled down his braided beard. The group of men had set up camp in the kitchens, the only room that didn't stink with the nauseating smell of the dead. The entrance had been barred shut, the shutters on the windows pulled tight, and a fire lit in the grate.

The Knights of Kriari had finally abandoned their rectangular tower shields, leaning them against one of the walls among racks of dried herbs and spices. Krelbe, as it turned out, was an excellent cook, mixing potatoes and carrots from Reed's cart with a brace of rabbits caught by the knights on their way down from Dirkvale.

"So, tell me how it goes again?" said Vohanen, his mouth full. "*Saw a Girl at the Town Fair?*"

"The *country* fair, Father," said Avor, throwing up his hands in exasperation. "The *country* fair. We've been singing the damn song for ten minutes, now, how can you not even remember the first line?"

"*You've* been singing it — rather badly if I may add — I've been listening."

Miraculously, a keg of ale had survived the rampant destruction and was quickly commandeered and expertly tapped by Jeffson. Reed, after pleading with his manservant for a good few minutes, managed to secure half a glass for 'medicinal purposes'. He sighed contentedly as the amber liquid wetted his dry throat. *Ah, Ferris, what I wouldn't give to share another drink with you, old friend.* He looked up to see Vohanen staring at him thoughtfully.

"We have not been entirely honest with you, Sir Reed," the tawny-haired knight said slowly.

"Honest, huh?" said Reed. "Something else you have in

common with Aldarin. I don't think he ever lied to me, and I don't think you have either. But the Knights of the Twelve are quite adept at concealing the truth by omission."

"That does indeed sound like one of our brothers," said Vohanen with a laugh. "And you are right, I have been keeping many things from you. For what a man does not know cannot cause him pain. One of the Twelve said that. Don't ask me which one." Avor passed him a tankard of ale, which he accepted with a nod.

"To wash the rabbit fat from your beard, Father," said Avor seriously, making Taleck chuckle.

Vohanen frowned and drank deeply, adding a fresh layer of froth to his already dirty beard. "No respect for your elders, lad, that's your problem." Setting the tankard aside, he squatted down, clearing a space on the dirt floor.

"It will be easier to just show you. As you have surmised, the Morlakian Pit is located at the bottom of the ravine here." He unsheathed his short sword and drew a circle in the dirt. "To the south, Fallow's End. To the north, Terris Lake." He drew a second circle, a foot above the first.

"Now, there are two things that you should know. The first is that Morlak is not flat, far from it. It's mostly uphill all the way, from the southern borders to the northern peaks. The second is that when Kriari founded his temple here, one of the last things he had us do before disappearing from these lands was … dam Terris Lake."

Reed looked down at the map, and the pieces began to slot into place. "So, if the dam was removed …"

"The ravine would be flooded."

"But that's incredible! You would completely flood

the Pit. The greylings would be annihilated. It's the perfect solution!"

"And therein lies the problem. You weren't listening. *Kriari* had our ancestors build the dam, even before there was enough water in the lake for it to be necessary. He didn't want to flood the Pit. He wanted to protect it."

"I don't understand."

"Neither do I. The reason has been lost in the eddies of time. But if Brachyura built a wall around the Pit and Kriari dammed the lake, they obviously didn't want the Pit destroyed."

Reed leant back, shaking his head in disgust. "Why would they want to protect those creatures? They massacred thousands of us. In fact, they nearly destroyed the human race entirely. Why help them?"

Vohanen only smiled sadly.

"Remember what I told you, Reed. We have forgotten much. Too much. And now that our founder's plans have been lost, it is up to us to decide how to interpret their actions with what little information we still have. I have been lobbying for years to destroy the Pit. Argued for uncountable hours with the other members of the temple Conclave. Slowly and patiently convincing the men of the Old Guard that it was the right thing to do. All I needed was a turning point, a final spark to set the fire alight.

"When our fellow knights returned from Morlak and we lost contact with the Pit, I finally had what I needed to convince the Conclave. They agreed that if Arelium did not send sufficient aid, and if we could not find any surviving members of the Old Guard, then there would be no other option but to flood the Pit. We just don't have the manpower to hold off the greylings alone.

"A contingent of fifty knights is camped near the dam as we speak. Once I send word, they will dismantle years of work in a matter of hours, and send the cold waters of Terris Lake to drown every living thing within miles."

"Every living thing?" said Reed, raising his eyebrows. "What about the missing guardsmen? The villagers? The greylings surely didn't go through all the effort of bringing them here just to kill them. That means they could still be alive."

"Maybe. In the depths of the Pit. In one of the hundred winding tunnels. Surrounded by a horde of greylings. Even if they are not dead yet, they soon will be. There are only six of us, Reed, what would you have us do? It is too late for those poor men and women. The best thing we can do for them is to fill the Pit with water and end their suffering."

Reed set down his ale and stared at his hands, rough and calloused from years of holding the wooden haft of a spear. Hands that reminded him of his father. What was it he had said? *It is through times of hardship and strife that we learn who we really are.*

"I'm not leaving them," he heard himself murmur.

"What did you say?"

"I said I'm not leaving them. I am a watcher, a protector, a guardian of the wall. I am the light against darkness, the burning sun against the cold of night, the mighty shield against the unknown." Reed recited the oath of the Old Guard and found that the words gave him strength.

"It is not for you to decide—" began Vohanen, his eyes growing hard.

"As a matter of fact, it is. I am not under your command. I was sent by the Lord Regent to determine what has happened here, and give whatever aid I can. And that is what I am going to do."

"Foolishness! You have not even fully recovered from your injuries. You will not last more than a few minutes alone down there."

"He will not be alone," Jeffson interjected. "I will accompany him. He will need someone to carry him out again after he inevitably collapses from all the exertion."

"Two of you. Two more unnecessary deaths! Fine! You are right. I cannot stop you. You have my promise I will send word of your passing back to Arelium. A pity. I was growing to like you, Reed."

"Father." Avor had been silent throughout the exchange, nursing his tankard of ale and staring into the dancing flames.

"What, lad?"

"I wish to go with them."

"Nonsense! You will do no such thing."

"Sir Reed is right, Father. There may be survivors. What are the tenets of our Order? Brotherhood, unity, cohesion. Working together. We must strive to adhere to the teachings of our temple. Can you truly, in good conscience, give the order to flood the Pit knowing there may still be people down there? Will you sleep peacefully at night, free of guilt? Will you be able to look Mother in the eye and tell her you did everything you could? For I will not."

"DAMN YOU BOY!" Vohanen bellowed, leaping to his feet and throwing the empty tankard against the far wall where it hit one of the tower shields and sent all four crashing to the ground like a line of dominoes. The big knight was quivering with anger, his shoulders heaving.

"You are a stubborn, disrespectful, snake-tongued brat, do you know that? Bringing your mother into all this. A low blow indeed. Why is it you want to risk your life for these people? People you have never met? Where does all this sense of duty come from?"

"From you, Father," Avor replied simply. "I am your son."

On hearing this, Vohanen deflated a little. He took a deep breath and glanced over at Taleck and Krelbe, who were watching the exchange with interest.

"Yes. Yes, you are," he said, and sat back down heavily. "By the Pit, have it your way, insufferable lad. Taleck! Krelbe! You leave now. Ride through the night. Give us four or five hours once you arrive at Terris Lake, then get the knights to start dismantling the dam. Son, you have first watch."

"And you, Father?"

"Doesn't look like I have any choice, does it? Your mother will whip the skin off my back if I return without you. Tomorrow, I'll follow you down into the Pit."

CHAPTER 12

THE CARVED ARCH

"My brothers and sisters all swear by the law of parsimony: the simplest explanation is often true. I cannot adhere to such a reductive way of thinking. Every trivial action can lead to a large number of complex alternatives. And all must be explored, no matter how far-fetched they may seem."

ZYGOS, SEVENTH OF THE TWELVE, 122 AT

✥

*T*HE ORDER *of Mina?* thought Praxis as he watched Derello grasp wrists with the bronze-armoured knight. He wracked his brain, trying to dredge up every last bit of information he had amassed on the Schism, the shadow war between the divergent factions of the Twelve. He had no memory of the Knights of Mina. Were they working to destroy the nine Baronies or to protect them? Or perhaps neither? Kingfisher Isle was far enough removed from the continent that they may have simply avoided taking sides altogether.

He would need to find out more, but it would not be easy. His current position as Lord Regent was too valuable to throw away on a whim. It would seem he must keep up this ludicrous charade for a while longer.

"Sir Ghelsin," he said, moving forwards to grasp the man's forearm and feeling the power beneath the articulated gauntlets. "Lord Praxis, Regent of Arelium. I have come a long way to talk with you."

The Knight of Mina shrugged. "Not sure I'm the best one to answer all your questions. My temple masters await a little further inland. If you follow me, I'll take you there." He made a sucking sound and pushed at his front teeth with his tongue, dislodging a piece of raw fish.

"We would be honoured to accompany you," said Derello hesitantly, clearly thrown by the knight's demeanour. "May my men come with us also?"

Sir Ghelsin shrugged again, making his bladed pauldrons ripple. "Do what you like. When we saw your ships, I was told to go down to the beach and bring you back. No specifics."

"And our weapons?"

The knight looked round at the honour guard and sniffed dismissively, one hand scratching at a boil on his neck. "Don't think you're much of a threat. I could probably kill you all myself if it ever came to that. You can keep 'em."

Charming, thought Praxis. A pity Sir Manfeld had stayed on the boat, it would have been quite entertaining to see his reaction to all this.

"Very well," Derello said. "One last thing. What happened here? Where are the villagers?"

"No idea," said Ghelsin. "Don't come down here much, to be honest. Haven't seen any of 'em these past few weeks. Boats are gone too. Maybe they decided to leave in light of recent events."

"Recent events?"

"You'll see. Ready to go?"

"Could you just give us a minute?"

Ghelsin nodded and wandered over to a rack of dried fish.

"Well?" said Derello in a low voice.

"Something strange is going on," said Orkam, running a hand over his shaved head. "I don't know what, but I can feel it. Intuition, I guess. Like when I was on gate duty back in Arelium. Troublemakers always have a certain look about them."

"Agreed," said Hirkuin. "Shall we return to the ship, or at least bring more men ashore?"

Derello bit down on his mauve-tinted bottom lip and fiddled with one of his jewelled earrings. "I do not wish to be seen as an aggressor, gentlemen. These are Knights of the Twelve, not some rabble of malnourished peasants. If the greylings are beginning to return to the nine Baronies, we would do well to cultivate our alliances rather than test them. It is time for a little trust. Besides, this is the most fun I've had in ages."

"I must protest," said Hirkuin heatedly.

"Duly noted, my dear Hirkuin. Now, tell your men to form up behind us. Sir Ghelsin?" The armoured knight turned round at the sound of his name, raising one thin eyebrow. "We will come with you. Please lead us to the temple of Mina."

Ghelsin nodded and set off up the wooden boardwalk. Shrubs pushed up through the sand as they moved away from the beach, then gave way to scraggly bushes, and finally sweet-scented resinous cedars, their needle-like evergreen leaves twisting in the sea breeze.

The village disappeared from sight as they pressed further into the woodlands, onwards and upwards, fallen leaves and twigs cracking under their armoured feet. The Knight of Mina led them on unerringly, despite there being no discernible path, leaping over a fallen tree trunk and skirting round the occasional big rock or knotted root.

The cedar trees ended abruptly and the travellers emerged blinking from under the leafy canopy to find that Ghelsin had led them up onto a grassy knoll overlooking the rocky southern side of Kingfisher Isle. To their left, a solitary wooden archway marked the entrance to a paved stone path descending back to the shoreline. The wide chiselled pillars supporting the arch were decorated with hundreds of detailed carvings: fish, squid, boats, and small armoured figures holding long two-handed swords.

"Our destination," said Ghelsin, pointing to the way down.

"That doesn't look like a temple," Hirkuin said brusquely. He and his men were starting to tire.

Ghelsin rubbed his nose. "I never said I was taking you to our temple. You wished to meet our temple masters; this is where they are."

"So, you brought us all the way up here just to tell us to go all the way back down again?"

"It is the only viable path," said the knight, his eyes narrowing, "And you would do well to speak to a Knight of the Twelve with a little more respect, or you and I are going to have a problem."

"I'm sure the captain meant no offence," said Derello brightly, stepping between the two men. "It has been a long and difficult journey."

"Of course," Hirkuin said slowly, raising his palms. "Apologies, Sir Knight."

Ghelsin sniffed and set off towards the gateway.

"Well, what comes up must go down, I suppose," said the Baron with forced cheerfulness. "Not much else we can do but follow him, eh?"

The paved path zigzagged down a sheer rock face, so narrow they had to walk in single file. The grey, weathered stones were covered in clumps of green moss and patches of lichen making them wet and slippery. Praxis heaved a sigh of relief when he reached the bottom unharmed. Here the path ended and, less than a hundred yards away, a long triangular spur of basalt protruded into the sea like a natural pier, its rough sides lashed by tempestuous waves. Praxis could just make out two distant figures kneeling at its apex.

Ghelsin wordlessly beckoned them forwards and the men of Kessrin picked their way through the rugged terrain until they reached the base of the spur. A particularly large wave crashed onto the rocks nearby, drenching them with ice-cold water.

Praxis was now close enough to see that the immobile figures were two Knights of Mina, kneeling before a nine-foot-tall statue of an armoured woman seated on a stone throne. It was incredibly lifelike, with curling, auburn hair framing a proud, stern face. The armour was painted in gold, which sparkled in the late afternoon light. In one hand, the statue held a metal goblet, while the other rested on the pommel of a two-handed greatsword similar in style to the one Ghelsin wore strapped to his back.

"That's ... not possible!" stammered Derello, his eyes widening in shock. "That statue. It's the woman from the stained-glass window of Kessrin!" He fought to regain his composure and Praxis saw that the man's painted mask was once more beginning to slip. "The woman who gave her name to the *Emerald Queen*. How can this be? Kessrin keep is hundreds of years old. I don't understand ..."

"Mina, Last of the Twelve, the patron of our Order," said Sir Ghelsin, bowing his head in reverence. "Come, let us pay homage."

They edged cautiously out onto the promontory. Hirkuin pulled a silver amulet from around his neck and brought it to his lips. A couple of the older soldiers uttered a prayer or fondled similar trinkets. In the hundreds of years since their disappearance, the Twelve had become more than simply gifted warriors for some; they were looked upon as gods.

The two kneeling knights stood, their faces completely covered by their visored helms, and made way for the visitors to pass. Derello reached the statue first and doffed his tricorne hat, bowing gracefully. "Lady Mina," he said respectfully.

The statue's eyes *opened*.

There was no spark of colour hidden in those deep sockets, no white sclera or pigmented cornea. Nothing but two bottomless voids as deep and as dark as the ocean depths.

Vast and unending. With a creak of armoured joints, the giant woman set down her goblet and rose ponderously from the stone throne.

Derello gave a strangled yelp and scrambled backwards. Praxis stood rooted to the spot, stunned. This was no statue but one of the Twelve in the flesh, returned to Kessrin after three hundred years. *What is this new madness? How did a simple Kessrin dagger lead us to this?*

"Little man," said Mina, Last of the Twelve, leaning on her sword and looking down at Derello's recumbent form. Her voice was cold and passionless, each word sending a chill through his veins. "Or should I say, little Baron? I have been following your progress with great interest."

Her gaze shifted to Praxis, and he felt it peel away the layers of secrets and lies wrapped around his brain, exposing his shrivelled, rotten core and the kernel of naked truth residing within. His scar burned. "Lord Regent," she said icily. "I see you have found the dagger. Give my regards to my brother, I'm sure you will see him soon." She cocked her head to one side and gave him a half-smile so like his own it made him want to scream.

Focus! he thought, grasping at the tattered remains of his psyche. *There must be a way to salvage this.*

Mina returned her soulless eyes to Derello, who had risen to his knees, his tricorne hat lost to the waves. "I thank you for coming to see me, Lord Baron, it saves me the inconvenience and effort of seeking you out. It is *time*, you see."

Derello rose unsteadily to his feet. His mascara had run down his face, his lipstick was smudged, and his immaculate gelled hair was in disarray. He stared at the armoured figure in bewilderment.

"Time? Time for what?"

"Time for the greylings to return to this land. Time for them to take back what they are owed. And we must help them, Derello. We must let the human race die."

Her words hit the group of men like a tidal wave. One of the soldiers began to laugh, almost dropping his crossbow. Another turned his head and retched, spewing bile onto the wet bedrock. Orkam was shaking his head in disbelief. Only Praxis seemed unmoved.

"Wh ... why?" Derello sputtered, looking round wildly at the others. "You fought against the greylings for years. Why aid their return? If the Twelve abandon us now, it will be the end of us!"

"It is not for you to question our motives!" said Mina sharply, raising her voice. It echoed across the sheltered creek, causing a flock of seagulls to take flight, squawking angrily. Her ivory brow furrowed. "I had hoped you would be more accommodating. We have given you more than enough time to live your lives to the fullest, to prepare for the end."

"We ... we did not know ..."

"Instructions were left. Plans were laid. All you had to do was follow them. To let the Knights of our Orders guide you." She pursed her thin lips. "Your father was just as stubborn. I thought it would be easier to deal with you, but maybe I was wrong."

Derello stood up straighter. The confusion vanished from his face. "What did you just say?"

"Your father. When I met with him five years ago, I reminded him of our obligations. He refused to comply and I had no other choice but to dispose of him. You are weaker than him, more malleable. I thought you would see reason."

"You chose to *dispose* of him?"

"I sunk his ship."

"You *sunk his ship* … You … you murdered my parents," Derello said calmly, slowly drawing his jewelled scimitar from his scabbard. "Then I must kill you."

"My Lord," Praxis cautioned.

Derello turned to him, his expression blank. "This is not your fight, Lord Regent. I thank you for all you have done up to this point, but you should return with the others to the carrack."

The woman laughed, but there was no humour in her empty eyes. "Little man, do not try my patience, we do not have time for games."

The Baron started forwards, but one of the bronze-armoured knights moved to block his path. Mina waved the knight back and set her sword down beside the throne. She removed her golden gauntlets, flexing pale fingers.

"Come then, little man. Let me teach you a lesson in humility."

Derello said nothing but sprang forwards, hoping to take her off-guard. His curved sword whistled towards the unprotected joint above her left knee. Mina's hand came down fast, faster than the eye could see, and batted the blade away. The Baron spun round, reached into his boot and, with a flick of his wrist, sent a hidden dagger spinning towards her neck. Mina shifted slightly and the dagger hit her shoulder-guard, clattering to the floor.

But Derello was already moving, using the distraction to get behind her. With an angry cry, he raised his scimitar with two hands and thrust forwards with all his strength, aiming at a small vulnerable spot on her lower back. It was not enough. With a shriek of tortured metal, the blade snapped, leaving Derello holding an inch of steel and a broken pommel. He stumbled backwards, but Mina was faster, encircling his neck with one powerful hand.

"So fragile," she said, almost regretfully. "We spent so long training you, teaching you, and you have learnt nothing. And now all I need to do is squeeze and the bloodline of del Kessrin will be no more. Come, let me show you something first."

She turned and dragged Derello to the edge of the outcrop. Raising her arm, she lifted him off the ground, suspending him above the dark, murky waters. Derello kicked and struggled, his manicured fingers scrabbling at the vice-like grip around his neck.

"Look, little one. Look into the deep."

She closed her eyes and concentrated. Beads of sweat appeared on her forehead. Her lips twisted. A distant rumbling could be heard, slowly getting louder. The craggy bluff behind them began to shake. The sea churned, bubbles rising to the surface. With a loud crack, a fissure appeared in the rock face. A large boulder broke free and plunged into the water, sending ripples running towards the shore. Waves lapped over Mina's armoured feet, but she paid them no heed.

"There, little one," she said, raising her voice above the growing din. "It comes."

Praxis could see a shape beneath the water, a round patch of darkness growing steadily closer to the surface. He drew his stilettos and saw the Baron's men were readying their own weapons. The rumbling intensified, sending more rocks plummeting into the sea.

"Please," whispered the Baron, gasping for breath. "*Please*."

With a primaeval screech of rage, after years of hiding in the silent depths, the kraken burst forth from the ocean in an explosion of white-flecked foam. It was the largest living thing Praxis had ever seen. Its bulbous dark green head was a hundred feet long, the slimy, mottled skin covered in hard ridges and throbbing pustules. Two globular eyes the colour of egg yolks protruded over a gaping maw filled with rows of serrated teeth. The kraken screeched again, and two thick tentacles coated in enormous pulsing suckers rose menacingly skywards from behind its round cranium, water dripping from their pointed tips.

One of the guards screamed, his breeches wet with urine. Dropping his scimitar, the man turned to flee. He managed only a few paces before Ghelsin stepped into his path and decapitated him with a nonchalant swing of his sword. The headless body took one final step before collapsing in a puddle of blood. The wispy-haired knight smirked and kicked the corpse off the promontory, watching without emotion as the tide caught it and pulled it under.

"Amazing, is it not?" said Mina, breathing fast, her gargantuan form shaking with effort. "We were once bitter enemies and now, after hundreds of years, I can call such a creature to me by just the strength of my will. It will be most useful in the months to come. How did Brachyura put it? Ah yes, the beginning of the end."

Praxis bit his lower lip so hard it started to bleed. The pain pulled him back from the brink of madness and reminded him who he was, a Knight of Zygos, Seventh of the Twelve; the planner, the manipulator, the administrator.

Every situation could be turned to his advantage with the right decisions.

Time slowed and his gaze took in the struggling form of Derello, his face a dark shade of purple as he fought for breath. There were two wildly divergent paths open to him. Mina obviously knew who he was. He could throw off his disguise of Lord Regent and pledge himself to her cause, leaving the Baron to his fate. Or he could retain his title a little longer, and risk his own life in an attempt to save Derello.

It was an easy decision to make.

"My Lady," he called out, surprised by the strength and calm of his voice. "Allow me to kill the Baron for you. Let me prove my loyalty by ending the bloodline of del Kessrin."

CHAPTER 13

THE VALUE OF SORROW

"My daughter, I am not very good at goodbyes, but do not mistake my lack of words for a lack of feelings. Your mother and I are so, so proud of you. You have become all we hoped you would be and more besides."

BARON LISTUS DEL ARELIUM, 426 AT

✦

"COME WITH ME," said Praedora in a commanding tone and Jelaïa, with a quick curtsy to the three blind acolytes, followed the priestess to another room further up the corridor; an empty, barren chamber with no furniture or other noticeable decorations. The entire far wall was an open balustrade, jutting out of the rugged cliff face over the Sea of Sorrow, where waves crashed against the rocks many hundred feet below.

Praedora crossed the empty room to the balcony,

motioning for Jelaïa to follow. As she left the shelter of the temple, the young Baroness was hit by the full force of the coastal winds pummelling the cliffs. She gripped the stone parapet for support as a particularly violent gust pulled at her chestnut hair like a petulant child.

"This is as good a place as any to begin," said the priestess, the wind making her own auburn hair whip around her face. "First of all, you will need this." She reached into the folds of her robes and withdrew an axe-shaped silver pendant similar to the one she herself wore.

"I am honoured, my Lady, but I do not think—"

"Wait and watch," Praedora said. She grasped the amulet in both hands and twisted the haft of the miniature axe to the right. With a click, the bottom half came free, revealing a glass vial hidden inside the hollow interior.

"When each initiate arrives at the temple, we draw a vial of their blood. And again, when they finish their training and become a fully-fledged Knight of the Twelve. This is Aldarin's blood. I do not offer you the amulet to try and entice you to join our Order. On the contrary, if you use the vial sparingly, you will be able to call on the fires of Brachyura for years without ever returning here."

Jelaïa stared avidly at the red liquid, her hand stretching out involuntarily towards the silver amulet. Praedora calmly moved the vial out of reach, dangling the silver chain over the edge of the balcony.

"There is a condition, of course. You must learn to control yourself. It has been many years since we last had someone react this strongly to the Scrying, but I will not help you if I do not believe you are able to overcome the harrowing addiction that the awakening always brings."

Jelaïa found she was only half-listening. *What does she know? She is nothing compared to the strength of my inner fire; she is as frail and dainty as a porcelain vase. If she does not hand the vial over to me, I will take it by force.*

"Now," Praedora continued smoothly. "Let me explain how our powers work. When two descendants of Brachyura share their blood, they share their emotions, memories, hopes, and fears. These feelings become raw energy, flowing from one host to the other, crackling like bottled lightning, filling every corner of our being until we have no choice but to release the pent-up force or succumb to it and risk incineration from the inside out.

"Two things determine the strength of the bond between the descendants. The first is the intensity of the negative emotions. Childhood trauma. Anger. Hate. Fear. A scarred and difficult life leads to more intense feelings, and to a deeper link between the participants.

"The second is emotional: the stronger the feelings of love and friendship, the easier it is for a bridge to form between the two minds and for the memories to intertwine. Aldarin has not had an easy life; and there is, if I am not mistaken, a great deal of respect and trust between you both. All of these things contribute to the strength of your bond."

Praedora cracked open the half of her own silver amulet and removed the vial of dark blood lodged inside.

"In all my years as a priestess, I have only reacted strongly to two Knights of the Twelve. Aldarin was the second, and Sir Manfeld the first. Manfeld was abused as a young boy by his uncle and harbours years of hate, resentment, and shame. He is also a kind, honourable, respectable man, constantly striving to uphold the teachings of Brachyura and make this temple a better place. I love him like a brother. And his blood gives me power."

Bringing the vial to her lips, Praedora allowed two drops of the sticky red liquid to land on her tongue. She swallowed and closed her eyes. Her body began to shake as the blood mingled with her own. Suddenly, with an ecstatic cry, the priestess's eyes snapped open. Her green irises had disappeared, replaced by two balls of incandescent blue fire.

Stretching out her arms, Praedora let the coalescing energy explode skywards from her fingertips, lighting up the cloud-filled sky with a sheet of bright azure light. A curtain of boiling flame filled their vision for an instant before being torn apart by the wind.

Jelaïa was speechless. She could still feel a slight tingle of warmth on her cheek. The sheer raw prowess on display was of a magnitude greater than she could ever hope to achieve. How could she have thought, even for a moment, of challenging someone like that? It would be suicide.

Praedora closed her eyes again, calming her breathing. When she opened them, her emerald gaze had returned.

"That is our power," she said. "And with it comes an insatiable hunger. I could lie and tell you that this hunger will disappear over time, or that you can learn to ignore it, but better you know the truth: if you cannot control it, the gnawing sensation in your stomach will spread to your chest, then your heart, then your mind, like an unstoppable infection. Your longing will grow stronger and stronger until it obscures all other sense of thought or purpose. Madness will follow. Madness and death."

Jelaïa nodded, looking out over the Sea of Sorrow. The wind and menacing grey clouds were agitating the dark indigo waters, pushing the swell towards the saw-toothed rocks below her. A seagull cawed overhead, fighting to reach the shelter of its nest before the inevitable storm.

"I understand," she said, her eyes never leaving the sea. "And I want to learn."

Praedora spat out a mixture of saliva and blood. "I never thought otherwise. There is a way to fight the hunger. In theory, it is very simple. Each emotion can be negated by a strong opposing emotion. Anger by calm or sadness, loneliness by friendship, chaos by serenity. It will be up to you to find how to counteract the negative emotions in Aldarin's memories with feelings of your own."

"I will try," Jelaïa replied dubiously, reaching cautiously for the silver amulet. She unscrewed the haft and shook a couple of ruby droplets into her mouth. It took only a moment for the pain to arrive. The memories began to flash before her eyes, each one piercing her mind like a white-hot needle.

A grey-haired man with a red-veined, bulbous nose and bloodshot eyes beating a young boy with a birch rod. The boy turns, anger in his eyes, and knocks the bundle of twigs away.

An empty grave, the boy shovelling the soft dirt, his hands covered in blisters. He wipes a tear from his eye.

A raging sea, dark and terrifying, under a new moon. Waves crashing against rocks hidden in the black of the night. A young man fights against the deadly currents, pulling the limp form of another. He reaches the shore, drags the figure out of the cold water, but it is too late. He cries his anguish at the uncaring sky.

And, for the second time, Jelaïa felt the power building within her, coursing through her body like molten metal, permeating every pore with liquid fire. She screamed as the burning agony reached her eyes, blocking out the sun.

"I cannot hold it!" she moaned. "*I cannot control it!*" She raised her arms to release the pain, her palms starting to glow.

Two cool hands cupped her cheeks, the fingertips pressing gently into her temples. Praedora brought her face in close, forcing Jelaïa to look into her eyes.

"Look at me!" the priestess said forcefully. "Listen to my voice."

"It's too late!"

"Jelaïa. Listen to me. *Your father is dead.*"

The words cut through the pain, dousing the burning fire. Aldarin's shattered memories of hate and loneliness were pushed aside, replaced by her own. Touring the farmsteads on horseback with her father, reading together in his private library, walking hand-in-hand through the gardens of Arelium; a thousand things that she would never do with him again. Because he was gone, and would never be coming back.

She let out a sob and sagged like a puppet with its strings cut. The blue-white flames crackling beneath her skin faded away as if they had never been there at all. Jelaïa collapsed into Praedora's arms and wept, her heart heavy with grief.

"I am so sorry," the priestess said softly, her hand gently caressing Jelaïa's hair. "As I said, it is the only way. Do you feel the hunger? The gnawing sensation in the depths of your stomach?"

Jelaïa shook her head. She felt nothing but emptiness.

"We can resist the addiction, we can control the ebb and flow of Brachyura's flame but only by countering the flood of raw emotions with our own. And nothing is more powerful than grief. If you are still willing, I can help you."

"I … I think I would like that," said Jelaïa. She breathed in the fragrant scent of honeysuckle and found her feelings of heartache start to subside.

"Very well. Now, let us leave this cold and windy balcony, and go find my fellow priestesses for a cup of verbena tea."

"Praedora?"

"Yes, my dear?"

"How do you keep your own hunger under control?"

The priestess looked at Jelaïa strangely for a moment, her face unreadable. "I … no one has ever asked me that before. I suppose there is no reason why you shouldn't know. Sir Manfeld is my cousin. And his abusive uncle? He was my father. My two siblings and I suffered greatly for a long time before we managed to escape from that Pit-spawned man. I have enough grief to last a lifetime."

Jelaïa spent the next few days sticking to Praedora like glue, using her every waking moment to learn all she could. Most of her training was centred on the fires of Brachyura. The silver axe-shaped amulet with its hidden vial of blood never left her neck. She learnt how to aim the explosion of energy, how to raise and lower the intensity of the flames, and, most importantly of all, how to use the grief of her father's death to dissipate them harmlessly.

She was helped by Niane and the other priestesses. It was from them that she discovered another unwanted effect of her newfound powers. The strain of physically containing another's raw emotion was not without consequences. If the fires of Brachyura were used too frequently, too vigorously, or too carelessly, the host risked harming their own bodies permanently. At best, burnt skin or loss of hair; at worst, blindness or death.

Two of the priestesses had been found by the Order too late, their sight already burned from them due to lack of knowledge and training. Niane, born and raised in the temple, had given up her sight by choice.

During the last Scrying, she had been visiting one of the outlying villages when the roof of the village hall collapsed, trapping dozens of people. With time running out and no other help nearby, she had called on the fires of Brachyura to burn away the fallen timber and rubble, releasing those inside. At the cost of her sight.

Jelaïa felt nothing but admiration and respect for these women who had put aside whatever dreams or ambitions they may have had to serve the temple and the Order willingly. It also made her realise that it was not what she wanted to do. She missed Arelium, her mother, and Praxis. Her place was with them, helping to rule the Barony that carried her name.

Praedora's duties were numerous and varied, and Jelaïa was able to see much more of the troglodyte temple. There were rooms of all shapes and sizes, some barely bigger than a closet, others wider and longer than the Great Hall of Arelium. These larger spaces used light wells, vertical shafts running down from the surface of the cliffs, to bring air and daylight into the enclosed rooms and courtyards below.

She saw the infirmary with its impressive store of

medicinal herbs and bandages, the Conclave meeting hall with its round stone table and four marble chairs, the stables — one of the only buildings above ground — now mostly empty of horses. And finally, the bathhouses, the big stone tubs filled with seawater using the same ingenious system of pipes and pumps as in Kessrin keep.

Every evening, the initiates gathered together in the refectory for the communal meal. Row upon row of benches and tables lit with fat wax candles filled a domed dining area with easy access to the kitchens. Most of the benches were still empty, as the force of knights sent to relieve the siege of Arelium had still not returned. Jelaïa had heard that some were still overseeing the rebuilding of her Barony, whereas others had accompanied Praxis to Kessrin.

Great piping-hot pots of stew and platters of roasted meats covered one of the tables at the far end of the hall. Jelaïa helped herself to a large portion of roast lamb and a shining yellow corn cob. Weaving her way through the tables, she found a seat opposite Praedora who was chatting animatedly with Ka'arka. The ebony knight smiled when he saw her, the wrinkles twisting the white scars on his face.

"My Lady, how goes your training? You look the part at least!"

Jelaïa looked down at the emerald-green dress she had started wearing, and the silver amulet around her neck. "I'm … not sure. Not too bad, I think?"

"Oh, don't be silly," said Praedora, giving Jelaïa's hand a playful slap. "You've made more progress over the last two days than I did during my first two years. I've never seen someone adapt so quickly. It's like you were born into it."

"Well, maybe I was. Who knows how I inherited Brachyura's blood?"

Praedora shot a sidelong glance at Ka'arka. "Yes, I wanted to talk to you about that. I believe I can shed some light on the subject. But it will have to wait. Ka'arka was telling me that Sir Caddox has arrived at the temple. We will convene the Conclave at first light tomorrow."

The Conclave! Aldarin! Jelaïa was so caught up in her training that she had left her friend to his own devices.

"Have either of you seen Aldarin?" she asked rather guiltily. "I have not seen him for days. Does he not eat with us?"

"Aldarin has something important to do," Ka'arka replied solemnly. "You will find him in the same place he has been since his arrival. Down in the smithy."

The smithy was easy enough to find; Jelaïa had only to follow the resonant banging of metal that echoed up the surrounding tunnels. As she approached, the ambient air grew hotter and hotter until she was sweating profusely. The forge itself was an enormous hearth, twenty feet wide, filled with chunks of black charcoal burning brightly.

Thick smoke escaped through a square light well positioned in the middle of the room. To the left of the forge, a pair of bellows allowed the blacksmith to regulate the flow of air to the fire. To the right stood a slack tub and wrought-iron anvil; and behind the anvil stood Aldarin, stripped to the waist, his tanned, muscular torso glistening with perspiration.

The knight had not heard her enter. He had his back to her, concentrating on the workpiece placed delicately on the horn of the anvil. He shifted, and Jelaïa smiled when she saw the gleaming pronged helmet, its broken horn restored, its shattered cheekpiece repaired. Aldarin was studying the glowing metal critically, using a planishing hammer to smooth out the last few bumps and blemishes.

Jelaïa watched him silently for a while. He seemed at peace, lost in the simple joy of his work.

"Aldarin," she said softly, and he turned round, his eyes shining.

"Jelaïa. I have finished. I am whole again." He set down his hammer and used a dry cloth hanging near the fire to wipe the perspiration from his body. He grinned. She had never seen him happier.

"You have been here the whole time?" she asked.

"Indeed. Things of such importance must not be rushed. And with the other knights gone, I had all the time I needed to work in peace. And time to think." He came to stand before her, smelling faintly of musk and sweat. "I wish to ask you something."

Jelaïa, her eyes level with his naked chest, found herself blushing once again. *Damn the Pit!* she thought. *Can I not be this close to men without becoming a human beetroot?*

"Of … of course, Aldarin," she said, concentrating on a spot behind his left shoulder.

"Have you given any thought to the future? Do you wish to stay here in the temple?"

"I was wondering the same thing earlier this evening. And I think the answer is no. This is a wondrous place, Aldarin, and I have met many kind, selfless, loving people. I can understand why the temple is so important to you. But it is not my home. Arelium is my home. And once I am confident that I can keep the fires of Brachyura under control, I wish to return there."

Aldarin nodded thoughtfully. "I had imagined as much. It is the best place for you. This is what I wanted to talk to you about. Over a hundred years ago, when our numbers were greater, each of the nine Baronies maintained a garrison of Knights of the Twelve. They formed the core of the Baron's defences, his honour guard, and the final rampart against the enemy.

"After the Schism, the tradition was lost as the Orders drew on the garrisons to bolster their own internal struggles against the fallen. In fact, I believe Morlak is one of the only places still fully manned. But the events of the last few months have led me to think that maybe it is time for the tradition to begin anew. It is time the Knights of Brachyura returned to Arelium."

He sank to one knee and bowed his head. "That is, if you will have me, my Lady."

"Oh, Aldarin, nothing would please me more!" said Jelaïa in a choked voice. "Everything is so much easier when you are by my side."

"My Lady—" the knight began, but he was interrupted by the tall, lanky initiate who had served as a reluctant guide to Jelaïa on her first day. He came tumbling into the smithy in a tangle of flailing limbs, breathing hard.

"Sir Knight, my Lady," he wheezed, winded. "Something is happening above ground. A visitor is approaching. Praedora is asking for you both."

"Armoured?" asked Aldarin.

"She didn't say, Sir Knight."

"Very well. Take Lady Jelaïa with you, I will follow shortly."

The initiate bobbed his head and set off at a jog, Jelaïa running to keep up. They emerged blinking into the upper courtyard. Behind them, visible through the stone columns, the setting sun covered the western sky with lustrous hues of dark orange and crimson, partially reflected in the green-blue waters of the Sea of Sorrow. The multitude of bright colours reminded Jelaïa of the stained-glass window in the Great Hall of Kessrin.

They passed under the open portcullis. Praedora was waiting for them on the other side, leaning against the base of the ten-foot-tall statue of Brachyura. To her left stood a knight Jelaïa had never seen before, squat and broad-shouldered with blond hair and a broken nose. With a clink of metal plate and ringed mail, Aldarin appeared, tightening the straps on his vambraces. He stopped short when he saw the blond knight.

"Sir Caddox," he said coldly.

"Scrier. I see reports of your demise were greatly exaggerated. A pity."

"Arelium could have used your help, Caddox. Where were you hiding when Sir Manfeld put out the call to arms?"

"*Hiding?*" said Sir Caddox, his eyes flashing, "I ought to—"

"Later, gentlemen, later," interrupted Praedora sharply. "I did not ask you two here for a battle of egos. Something is coming. I can feel it. A pounding in my brain, battering at my skull as if I were about to have a vision. It is getting stronger by the minute. Look to the road."

Jelaïa squinted down the path and could see that the priestess was right. A giant figure was making its way slowly up to the temple, its shadow long and slender under the setting sun. As it drew closer, she could see it was a man, dressed in a tattered red and golden tunic, his bare feet scratched and bruised from many days on the road. He looked strangely familiar, as if she had seen his shaved scalp and dark-skinned features before.

Then it hit her and she turned in horror to stare at the bronze statue towering over her.

"That is ... not possible," she whispered, falling to her knees, but the others were not listening. The three knights and the red-haired priestess were lying prostrate in the dirt before the temple, their arms stretched out before them, their foreheads pressed against the soft earth.

The colossus reached the temple. His obsidian gaze took in the statue built in his likeness, the axe motif carved into the stone gatehouse and, finally, the three prone figures. He smiled a thin smile devoid of any warmth.

"My children," intoned Brachyura in a voice as deep as the Pit. "I have returned. It is time for us to fulfil our oaths and hasten the greylings' return. It is time for us to end the world of men."

CHAPTER 14

A Familiar Sound

"It has happened again! The ambush was perfect. I had archers on either side of the gorge and cavalry hidden on the edge of the forest. The greylings were taking the bait. I only needed them to advance twenty more yards, and the trap would be sprung. Then they stopped. Turned tail and retreated into the Pit as if called there. And maybe they were."

GUANNA, SECOND OF THE TWELVE, 12 AT

⤶

"I DON'T KNOW WHY I have to wear this Pit-spawned thing," grumbled Vohanen, trying for the third time to attach a thin strip of fabric across his nose and impressive beard.

"Just a precaution," Reed replied, his voice slightly muffled by his own mask. "The fumes from the Southern Pit were toxic. Breathe in just a little and you get a cough, breathe in too much and you start to hack up blood. I can't smell any sulphur here so it may be different, but it pays to be careful."

"Well, we are not going to be down there long enough for that to matter, are we? A couple of hours, that's it. Unless you can breathe under water."

Reed sighed. The Knight of Kriari had slept badly, clearly worried about his son, and had been crotchety since breakfast.

"It is not too late for you to stay here, Father," said Avor, strapping his tower shield to his back. "Do a bit of cleaning maybe, saddle the horses, that sort of thing?"

Vohanen glared at him.

"I believe we are ready to proceed?" queried Jeffson. The round-shouldered manservant had found a padded gambeson and was adjusting what looked like spiked bronze knuckle-dusters. He flexed his palms experimentally.

"What in the Pit are those?" said Reed.

"We call them knuckle knives, my Lord," Jeffson replied with a shrug. "A souvenir of another life. I seem to remember them being quite effective at dissuading unwanted violence."

"I'm sure they are." Reed moved closer and spoke in a low voice for Jeffson's ears alone. "You do not have to come with me, you know. I will not think any the less of you."

"Dereliction of duty, my Lord?" the manservant replied with a raised eyebrow. "Why, perish the thought! I would be shunned! Never employed again! A pariah doomed to wander the nine Baronies, penniless and alone."

"By the Twelve, Jeffson, I can never tell when you are serious or not!"

"Quite, my Lord. You'll survive, I'm sure. Now, shall we

get going? As loath as I am to agree with Sir Vohanen, time is not in our favour."

"We'll follow your lead, Merad," Vohanen growled, scowling. "You seem to have the most insight into our current location."

"I'm not sure anyone has ever descended into one of the Pits before, Sir Knight. I think most of us didn't even know it was possible."

"Well, there's a first time for everything, eh, Reed? You just tell us where you want us, and we'll handle the rest."

They left the warm comfort of the kitchens behind and began the steep climb up the stone steps leading to the ramparts. Reed was out of breath by the time he reached the top but was reassured by the lack of pain in his chest and legs. Maybe the healer was not quite so useless after all.

The greyling-made path down into the Pit was clearly visible in the early morning light, dug straight into the topsoil on the upper slope of the crater.

Vohanen eyed the narrow trail warily. "Reed, you're the lightest of us. Would you mind scouting ahead a bit? Make sure it'll take our weight?"

Reed climbed over the crenellated battlements and tested the packed earth with the butt of his spear. It seemed safe enough. Motioning for the others to follow him, he moved cautiously down towards the tunnel entrance. The path was so restricted in spots that he had to press his back up against the slope, slowly edging his feet forwards inch by inch, sending loose soil tumbling hundreds of feet into the blackness below. One wrong step and Reed would suffer the same fate.

Avor came the closest to plummeting into the crater. As

he was negotiating a particularly treacherous stretch of the trail, his boot slipped on a lichen-covered rock and he lost his balance. With a yelp, he teetered backwards, his arms pinwheeling desperately. Jeffson, only a few feet behind, bounded forwards and grabbed hold of the knight's belt just as he was about to fall.

Eventually, they all reached the tunnel entrance without further mishap. Reed tugged at his mask and peered into the inky blackness but could see no further than a few yards. "What now?"

"We'll have to make some light, my Lord," Jeffson said. "We won't be of any use if we go in there blind."

"A shining beacon for the thousands of greylings lying in wait," said Vohanen sourly.

"We don't have any choice," Reed said. "One torch—"

"If I may, my Lord," Jeffson interrupted. "I would suggest rushlight?"

"Rushlight?"

"Yes. Another leftover talent from my misspent youth. Rush stalks soaked in grease and beeswax. Easy to conceal about one's person, far less likely to, ahem, attract unwanted attention than a torch or candle."

"Fascinating," said Vohanen, rolling his eyes. "Maybe we should climb back up to the wall, oh, and back down the other side, head out into the valley, cut down some reeds, dry them out, find some bacon fat in the kitchens, wait a few days for it to dry, then come back up here?"

"I took the liberty of bringing some with me, my Lord," Jeffson continued evenly. "If we use them sparingly, there should easily be enough for our expedition."

Vohanen snorted in disbelief, muttering something

about thieves and crooks, but grudgingly accepted one of the thin straw-coloured stalks.

Jeffson lit the dry tips with his tinderbox. The rushlights began to glow dimly, giving off just enough light to see a couple of feet into the tunnel. "Better, I suppose," admitted Vohanen. "But still not quite enough."

"One final piece of advice, my Lords," said Jeffson, pointedly ignoring Vohanen. "We must allow our eyes to adjust. When I was … working at night, we found it useful to close our eyes and massage the eyelids gently for a few minutes; it helps speed up the pupil's transition from light to dark."

"It certainly can't hurt," said Reed. He leant his spear against the tunnel wall and attached the rushlight to the silver wolf's head clipped to his vermilion cloak, then began to use his palms to apply gentle pressure to his eyes. When he opened them a few minutes later, he could see even further down the tunnel.

"Excellent, Jeffson, you are a man of many surprises," he said. "I will speak most highly of you to Lady Jelaïa when we return!"

"Please don't, my Lord, she'll want to give me a knighthood or some other useless title and I'll be trapped into spending all my time in court or at one of those exhausting jousting tournaments. A cursed gift if ever there was one."

"But *I* was knighted by Baron del Arelium!"

"Precisely, my Lord. *Precisely*."

Reed shook his head and took a few hesitant steps into the darkness. After a few paces, he saw something dark spattered on the dirt floor. He bent down to bring his rushlight closer.

"Dried blood. Red, not black. Definitely human. Should lead us right to them."

Avor nodded and drew his short sword, gesturing to his father to do the same. They pressed on. The tunnel was sloping steadily downwards, leading them deeper and deeper underground. The air was stale and dusty — and stank of something foul. Whenever the path divided, they searched for splashes of red blood.

Moments later, Jeffson stopped suddenly, his head cocked to one side as if listening for something.

"What is it?" Reed asked, his voice sounding unnaturally loud in the silence of the tunnel.

The manservant was frowning. "Can you hear that, my Lord?" he said softly. "I thought I heard laughter. A small child, laughing."

Reed shook his head. "I'm sorry, I heard nothing. The wind playing tricks, perhaps."

"Perhaps," Jeffson replied, sounding unconvinced. He started moving again.

Reed began to lose track of time; every passageway looked the same. He imagined the cold waters from Terris Lake rushing down the tunnel to meet them, sweeping up every living creature in its path and battering them against the tunnel walls until their lungs were filled with dirty fluid. Death by drowning. One of his worst fears.

"Where are the enemy?" said Avor, his voice a low murmur. "No sign of them but for a few footprints."

"Asleep, hopefully," Reed whispered back through his mask. "If they really are nocturnal, they should be resting during the day. Let us hope our luck holds for a while longer."

After a time, they began to hear a faint sound of chittering. Avor and Vohanen doused their rushlights and took up their shields. The spots of blood became more frequent and, as the chittering grew louder, a dim pinprick of light appeared ahead.

"What do they need light for?" Vohanen asked. "I thought they could see in the dark?"

"I fear the light is not for them," Reed replied nervously, his mouth dry. "I think we have found our prisoners."

They crept closer and nearly ran into two greylings stationed near what seemed to be the entrance to a larger cavern. The grey-skinned creatures had their backs to the group of men, focused on something happening in the open space beyond. Avor and Vohanen, moving surprisingly silently for such big men, quickly cut the sentries' throats before they could cry out, then quietly lowered their dead bodies to the ground.

"Nowhere to hide the dead," Jeffson said, pulling the straps of his knuckle knives tight. "We have no choice but to continue and hope they will not be found."

Reed stifled a cough and passed through the mouth of the tunnel into a scene from his worst nightmare. The cavern floor was covered in shrieking, cavorting greylings, hundreds of the little bald, yellow-eyed creatures, jumping and yelling excitedly. In the centre of the room, two bonfires illuminated a large rectangular cage made of wood, sinew, and broken bones. Human prisoners were packed tightly inside, several of them pressed painfully against the bars. Some were dressed in the leather surcoats and vermilion cloaks of the Old Guard, others in dirty tunics or dresses: the captured villagers from Fallow's End. Reed could hear their groans, screams, and cries for help over the chittering and grunting of the enemy.

But it was what sat against the far wall of the cavern that made Reed want to turn and run. A new type of greyling, larger even than the threshers, close to twenty feet long. It was immensely fat, with a sinuous, slug-like body covered in warts and weeping sores. It had two ridiculously spindly, clawed arms and no legs at all, the bottom part of its body tapering down to a long, slimy tail. Two sagging, wrinkled breasts hung above its distended belly.

The thing had the same hairless, round head as its lesser brethren but no visible eyes, only two puckered sockets covered with ridged, badly scarred skin. It had a wide, flat nose like a pig's snout, the nostrils dribbling yellow-green mucus down its face. Beneath the nose, a tiny mouth filled with triangular teeth opened and shut as the creature mewed and called to the greylings before it, its head weaving back and forth, its snout sniffing and snuffling like a hound searching for a scent.

There was a commotion near the cage and Reed saw that the greylings had pulled forth a young female prisoner in a threadbare brown dress and were pulling her towards the blind monstrosity. The woman screamed and kicked, scratched and bit, but to no avail. The greylings held her tight.

The enormous creature leant forwards, its slick, shiny tail tremoring in anticipation, stringy saliva dripping from its lipless maw. With a shriek of delight, the thing's clawed arms sliced down, decapitating the woman with one clean cut. Bright red blood gushed from the headless body, splashing over the creature's head and breasts. It sank its teeth hungrily into the torn neck, sucking noisily on the ragged stump.

Once the corpse was pale and bloodless, the thing threw it aside with an angry splutter, where it was immediately set upon by a horde of greylings, cackling as they tore the mangled body to pieces. The creature was becoming more agitated now, whining in discomfort, the rolls of thick fat jiggling as it twisted and turned. Its stomach pulsed unnaturally, bulging outwards like an inflated balloon.

With a final whimpering cry, a thick flap of dark grey flesh peeled outwards and something was vomited from the thing's belly; small, long-limbed, and covered in stinking black ichor. It opened its bulging yellow eyes for the first time and shrieked with joy as it looked up at its progenitor.

Its *mother*.

The obese, pox-riddled slug was giving birth to greylings.

It was all too much for Reed, who lifted his mask and retched violently, spattering the cavern floor with the remains of last night's meal. A hundred malevolent eyes turned towards the sound. The slug creature raised its head and let out an ear-splitting shriek, so loud and piercing that Reed thought his ears would burst. He clamped his hands over them as the high-pitched sound made his very bones vibrate.

Then, in a flash, he remembered.

He had heard the noise before, twice in fact. Once when the greylings attacked the Southern Pit, and again when they emerged from under the ruined gatehouse during the siege of Arelium. And each time the greylings had responded to the call.

The thing was not only their mother. It was their *leader*.

Vohanen was the first to react. "Lad, shieldwall!" he roared, bringing his ram's head shield up in front of him. Avor hurried forwards and set his shield beside that of his father with a clang.

"Reed, Jeffson, protect our flanks. We are going to try and reach the prisoners."

The cage was only twenty yards away but at least fifty greylings stood between the Knights of Kriari and their goal, milling around uncertainly.

"Forward!" Vohanen cried, and the two men began to advance at a steady pace. They reached the first of the greylings. Avor glanced across at his father then nodded. With an angry cry, the two hefty wooden shields were simultaneously thrust forwards into the mass of greylings. Two of the creatures were caught by the heavy metal bosses and crumpled to the ground, their fragile skulls caved in. The others were pushed back.

Reed saw with astonishment that Vohanen now held his sword in his left hand and his shield in his right, allowing it to overlap perfectly with Avor's, protecting them both. Greyling claws left thin furrows in the wood as the attackers tried to scratch their way through, but the planks were thick and hardened with resin, built to resist all but the strongest of blows.

Howling in frustration, the greylings tried to get around the shieldwall, only to be dispatched by the short, stabbing blades that Avor and Vohanen wielded with great precision. Reed and Jeffson were a few paces behind the two knights, spear and knuckle knives at the ready.

The cage was getting closer, less than ten yards away. A greyling ducked under Avor's sword and leapt at Jeffson. The manservant coolly side-stepped the clumsy charge and delivered two quick jabs to the thing's jaw, snapping the bone with a loud crack. A second creature scampered in from behind. Reed whirled and thrust his spear forwards, taking the greyling in the throat. He winced as he felt a twinge of pain in his chest, just below the ribs.

"They are beginning to surround us!" he shouted above the shrieks and screams. They must have killed thirty or forty of the creatures, but many more remained.

"Nearly there!" said Vohanen, his left arm slick with black ichor. The bloated birther was still wailing incoherently, twisting its flabby body in an effort to shift its vast bulk.

"We're at the cage!" Avor began slashing at the ropes and sinew holding the structure together, his sword catching the light of the nearby bonfire as it rose and fell.

"Back, get back, give me room!" he yelled in frustration as the prisoners pushed forwards eagerly, grimy hands pulling at his shield and boots.

"BACK!" bellowed Vohanen, swaying to avoid a greyling's claws, his return swing slicing the thing open from chest to groin. He ripped off his mask and let it drop to the floor. "Back or we leave you here!"

The last few words had the desired effect and the prisoners retreated in panic. With a final grunt of exertion, Avor cut through the last knot of sinew and part of the cage collapsed.

Reed saw movement at the far end of the cavern. Three, no four threshers stomped out of one of the side tunnels, eight-foot-high monsters wielding a mixture of crude clubs, axes, and swords. *Damn the Pit!*

"Vohanen, we have to leave now!" Reed said, tapping the

knight on the shoulder and pointing at the distant threshers. "I've fought them before. Your shields won't hold!"

The big knight nodded, making the beads in his plaited beard jingle, and began pulling the dazed soldiers and villagers from the cage.

"Hurry, hurry!"

The threshers were getting closer, pushing and growling at the smaller greylings to make a path through them.

Avor cried out in agony and Reed saw that one of the attackers had managed to crawl under the knight's tower shield and rake its claws across his unprotected legs. Bright scarlet blood welled up from an inch-wide gash in his thigh. Gritting his teeth, Avor brained the greyling with the pommel of his sword and tied his mask around the wound in a makeshift tourniquet.

The cage was nearly empty now, only a few stragglers remained. A heavy-set, bearded man stumbled out of the prison, his arm around a frail-looking woman. His bleary eyes focused with some difficulty on Reed.

"Sir Knight, please, listen to me," he croaked, barely audible over the sounds of metal on claw. "You must help her, you must get her out. Get her out or the Barony is lost." He pushed the woman forwards and Reed caught her just before she fell. She looked up at him through a tangle of long black hair with wide, frightened eyes. One blue, one green.

There was no mistaking who she was.

Lady Syrella, the White Rose, Baroness of Morlak.

CHAPTER 15

THE INNER WOLF

"The voice of my bonny, she's calling to me. Down, down, under the sea.

I thought she was dead, but she still speaks to me. Down, down, under the sea.

Her sunken blue eyes are the last thing I'll see. Down, down, under the sea.

When I leave you behind, will you still think of me? Down, down, under the sea."

OLD SAILOR'S SEA SHANTY, 421 AT

❧

"AN INTERESTING PROPOSAL," said Mina, her black eyes never leaving the weakly struggling del Kessrin. "You remind me of my brother, always looking to balance the scales. You may approach."

She released her iron grip and Derello tumbled to the ground, coughing and spluttering, five ugly bruises forming where Mina had pressed her fingers into his neck. He lay there panting, breathing in great gulps of air to fill his empty lungs.

Praxis drew his stiletto and moved to join them, sparing a furtive glance at Orkam as he passed. The bald captain was staring steadfastly ahead, refusing to meet his gaze. *By the Twelve, I hope I am doing the right thing,* he thought, ducking under the crossed blades of the two bronze-armoured knights.

"Lord Regent," said Mina, inclining her head in mock respect. "He is all yours." She glanced down at the kraken thrashing its tentacles in the water below and closed her eyes for a brief instant, muttering something under her breath. With a deafening screech, the squid-like monster plunged beneath the waves, leaving behind a bubbling circle of white, frothy foam.

Praxis held out his hand to the kneeling Baron and, after a moment's hesitation, Derello accepted, allowing himself to be pulled to his feet. Both men were soaked to the bone from the waves that battered the rocks. The Baron's make-up was a distant memory and without it he looked young and vulnerable.

"I am so sorry for all of this," Praxis murmured, still holding the other man's hand. "But I just can't see any other way."

"I understand," Derello whispered back hoarsely, his face red and blotchy. "You must do what you think is right."

"Exactly. Oh, and Derello, one more thing?"

"Yes?"

"RUN!" Praxis screamed and he swung the Baron back towards the shoreline, sending him tumbling down the rocky outcrop to crash into the backs of the two knights. All three figures collapsed in a tangled knot of metal. Praxis, without missing a beat, spun back towards the golden-armoured demi-god and slashed wildly at her still-outstretched arm, scoring a thin crimson line along her massive hand from thumb to forefinger. Mina looked down in surprise at her bloody palm, a confused expression on her face.

"To arms! The Baron is in need of aid! For Kessrin!" Praxis shouted, turning his back on Mina and charging down the spur.

Derello was wrestling with one of the visored knights, a fight he was sure to lose. The second knight had recovered his two-handed sword and was removing the sheath, intent on cleaving the Baron in two. Praxis rammed into him from behind. As they fell, he tugged open the bronze-armoured knight's visor and stabbed him repeatedly in the face with his long dagger. His opponent tried to shake him off, but Praxis held on tight, his weapon rising and falling, cutting and slicing, transforming the eyes, nose, and mouth of his opponent into an unrecognisable slab of bloody meat. The knight gave a choked gasp through ruined lips and was still.

Praxis paused to take stock of the situation. Close to the shore, the Baron's honour guard were trading blows with Ghelsin. The sallow, hook-nosed knight was bleeding from a dozen small cuts. Two dead guardsmen lay sprawled at his feet.

To his left, Hirkuin and Orkam had come to the Baron's aid. The Arelian's spear and the Kessrin's scimitar worked well in tandem. The Knight of Mina had dropped his sword when Derello had bowled him over. Now weaponless, he was trying to close the gap with his assailants but couldn't get inside the spear's long reach or the scimitar's wide swings.

Then there was the problem of the visor: excellent protection, terrible visibility. The Baron, all but forgotten by the bronze-clad knight, crept up out of his field of vision, leapt onto his back and hammered a curved dagger into the small space between the armoured gorget and helmet. With a savage twist, the dagger was pulled free, ripping through the jugular in a spray of blood.

"MY CHILDREN!" came a titanic voice, full of rage, boiling like the thunder of a thousand storm clouds. "YOU ARE KILLING MY CHILDREN!"

Mina stepped down from the throne, her visage twisted into an animalistic snarl. She held the seven-foot-long sword in one hand, blood from her wound seeping into the pommel. She was both beautiful and terrifying, primal and god-like. They could not stand against her.

"Back to the ships!" Praxis shouted.

"NO! She killed my parents!" Derello almost screamed.

"And she is about to kill you! Stop acting like a spoiled brat and more like a Baron. We have to leave now!" Praxis signalled to Orkam and the squat guard captain began half-dragging, half-carrying the Baron towards the cliff face.

"I think not," Sir Ghelsin said, moving to block their way off the rocky outcrop. His face was a mutilated ruin. A lucky cut from a scimitar had opened his left cheek to the bone, another had removed half his ear. His dirty bronze armour and bladed pauldrons were streaked with blood. Behind him lay the mangled remains of the Kessrin honour guard. He raised his gory two-handed sword and kissed the crosspiece in mock salute.

"I will avenge my fallen brothers, Lady Mina," Ghelsin vowed, holding the sword vertically above his head in a traditional duellist stance.

Damn the Pit, we were so close to making it out of here alive!

Praxis tried to devise a viable exit strategy, but he could see none. Before them an armed Knight of the Twelve, behind them a furious demi-god. He had never felt so trapped. Time to admit he had made the wrong choice. He had played the game, and he had lost.

"Orkam, Hirkuin, leave Ghelsin to me," he said, drawing his second stiletto. "I'll buy you all the time I can. Get the Baron back to the ships. Kessrin must learn of what transpired here."

"And what makes you think I will let you do that?" said Ghelsin with a sneer. "You will all die here. I will take great pleasure in removing your eyes from your still-warm corpses to offer them as tribute to my—"

There was a piercing whistling sound and the knight's head and upper body disappeared in an explosion of red matter and shattered bone.

"What in the Pit?" Praxis exclaimed, wiping spots of blood from his face.

"Reinforcements!" yelled Orkam gleefully, pointing at something behind Praxis, out in the water. He turned to see the *Emerald Queen* come into view, the wind in her sails. There was a flash from amidships and with another mournful whistling, a six-foot-long steel-tipped bolt took Mina, Last of the Twelve, in the shoulder, punching her off her feet.

"Yes!" cried Hirkuin, hammering his fist into the air.

"That won't be enough to stop her," said Praxis wearily.

"Annoy her, maybe, but not stop her. We need to get to that carrack."

The *Emerald Queen* slowed. A rowboat rocked dangerously as it was lowered into the choppy waters.

"Swimming it is then!" said Derello and waded into the swell, shivering at the cold. Praxis followed, grimacing. He knew he would have the worst of it. Derello and Hirkuin were excellent swimmers, and Orkam had spent years as a sailor before joining the town guard. His own training as a Knight of Zygos had included learning how to swim, but that was a long, long time ago.

He forced himself to concentrate on the distant shape of the bobbing wooden boat, moving slowly towards it, fighting against the current that was pulling him back to the shore. He heard a cry of rage somewhere behind him but didn't dare look back.

The crest of a wave battered his face and he went under, swallowing a mouthful of brine. He surfaced, coughing, and was hit by another. The undertow spun him around and he lost all sense of direction.

Calm. He thought. *A serene mind is an ordered mind. An ordered mind is a sane mind.*

He opened his eyes but could only see murky water. Which way was up? His lungs began to burn. Fighting a wave of panic, he moved towards what he thought looked like the lightest part of the icy gloom.

His chest was on fire now, his heart pounding like a hammer, his head throbbing. He could feel himself weakening, his feeble strokes not strong enough to bring him closer to the surface. *So, this is how it ends,* he thought miserably as his vision began to blur, *the Lord Regent of Arelium drowned off the coast of an insignificant isle in the middle of nowhere.*

A gauntleted hand plunged into the cold water inches from his face and grabbed hold of one of his leather shoulder straps. With a powerful jolt, Praxis was heaved from the water and deposited on the bottom boards of the rowboat. He felt his stomach clench, and vomited a dirty-brown stream of seawater. He rolled onto his back, panting and shivering. Sir Manfeld was looking down at him with a worried expression, his snowy-white moustache wet and bedraggled.

"Methinks you may have overestimated your swimming skills, my Lord," he said disapprovingly. "It was imprudent to attempt such a distance in your current state of fatigue."

With a lurch, the rowboat banked hard to port, taking the survivors back towards the *Emerald Queen*, the four Knights of Brachyura assigned to rowing duties setting a brisk pace. Derello, Orkam, and Hirkuin sat huddled together in the stern under a sheepskin. A hundred yards away on the rocky spur, Mina, Last of the Twelve, tall and unmoving, fixed them with her empty stare.

"What is she doing?" said Praxis, combing back his damp hair. He could still taste the salt in his mouth.

"I do not know," Sir Manfeld replied. "She removed the ballista bolt without any trouble. We tried a couple more salvos, but she dodged them easily. It will be much harder to hit her now that she is aware of our presence."

They reached the carrack and one of the sailors lowered a knotted rope. Praxis climbed over the gunwale to find that the lower deck was packed with blue-uniformed Kessrin crossbowmen and silver-armoured Knights of the Twelve. The tarpaulin covers had been removed from the

eight ballistae and the four bow-like siege weapons on the
starboard side were aimed at the golden figure on the distant
promontory.

"Where are the *Sapphire Night* and *Latent Folly*?"
snapped Derello, strapping on a dark blue boiled leather
breastplate. Praxis could see that the young Baron was still
angry, furious even, his movements clipped and precise. It
seemed the painted mask would remain unworn.

If Sir Manfeld was surprised at the Baron's sudden
change in demeanour, he didn't show it. "We thought it prudent to divide our forces in case you returned to the fishing
village," he said, as more sailors heaved the rowboat out of
the water.

"Then let us re-join them now and retreat to Kessrin to
plan our next move."

The order was given to raise anchor and the helmsman
spun the wheel, turning the *Emerald Queen* back towards the
northern beachhead.

"We have no choice but to beat windward," said
Hirkuin, as teams of sailors began hauling on the braces and
trimming the sails in an attempt to harness every gust of
available wind. "If you no longer need me, my Lord, I will
go and supervise the tacking manoeuvres."

"Stay a moment," said Derello harshly. He had requisitioned a curved scimitar and was replacing his lost throwing
daggers. "I have a few things to ask Sir Manfeld. Like why
ten of my best men were brutally murdered by Knights of
the Twelve."

Of course! Praxis thought. *He doesn't know! The Schism!
The shadow war that followed! He doesn't know!*

Sir Manfeld shifted uneasily on his feet. "I am not sure this is the right time, my Lord—"

"I think it is the perfect time, Sir Knight. I will not tolerate traitors or manipulators. I suggest you phrase your answer well, for if I do not like your reply, or if I suspect but a modicum of untruth, I will have you and your men thrown off my ship."

The atmosphere suddenly changed at his words, the men stationed on the lower deck dispersing and subtly forming into two separate groups; Kessrin on one side, knights on the other.

Sir Manfeld stroked his moustache in contemplation. "I swore never to tell you this until you were ready, my Lord. And, in all honesty, I thought you never would be, treating the title of Baron like a game and spending more time perfecting your wardrobe than ruling Kessrin. But it seems you have changed. Or simply come out of hiding."

"The Knights of Mina killed my parents, Sir Knight. Sunk their ship without reason or provocation. You are right, the time for games is over."

The old knight's shoulders sagged. He looked haggard, as if his years had finally caught up with him.

"We were betrayed, my Lord," he said in a small voice. "Mithuna, Zygos, Mina, and others. The more zealous of our Orders. They claimed that the time of Man was at an end, that the greylings would soon return and we should let them reclaim the nine Baronies."

Praxis listened silently, the words a twisted echo of his own speech to the dying Baron of Arelium.

"We could not believe Brachyura would want such a thing. Why spend years upon years helping and teaching us how to survive, to build, and to fight, if we are fated to become extinct? Why not have simply left the human race to succumb to the greylings four hundred years ago? We argued. Callous words. And when words failed us, we turned to our fists, then to our blades. We call it the Schism, the great rift between the Knights of the Twelve, and the beginning of our decline."

The carrack had rounded the northern peninsula and the golden yellow sands were in sight. The *Sapphire Night* and *Latent Folly* were still at anchor, close to the shore. With a flashing of coloured flags, the boatswain signalled to the two caravels that it was time to depart.

"The infighting lasted for years," Sir Manfeld continued. "I think it only stopped because both sides had become too weak to carry on. I suppose you could say we were victorious, but it was a Pyrrhic victory.

"We chased the fallen knights from their temples and destroyed what we could, burning the wood and shattering the stone in an attempt to remove all traces of their existence. It is our greatest shame, the reason behind the Schism hidden even from our own initiates."

He looked up, tears shining in his eyes. "You must believe me when I tell you I did not know that the Order of Mina was in exile here. And I certainly did not know that Mina herself had returned. If I had, I would never have let you set foot upon those accursed shores without the Knights of Brachyura. And now I must carry the death of your men on my conscience. Their blood is on my hands. You are right to hold me accountable. I will accept any punishment you see fit."

He fell silent. Derello tugged pensively at an emerald earring and looked out over the waves.

"You *are* to blame, Sir Manfeld. But so am I. If I had believed in myself enough to assume my own strength of character instead of creating a flimsy persona, if I had spent more time investigating my parents' disappearance instead of courting young women, if I had confronted the Barony's problems rather than avoiding them, things may have been different. We have been caught in a trap of our own making, victims of distrust and hubris."

The Baron wiped a blood-stained hand against his sodden green breeches and held it out for the knight to shake it.

"I propose an oath. Let us swear that we will no longer hide things from one another. No more secrets?"

"No more secrets, on my honour," said Sir Manfeld gravely, filled with newfound energy. He grasped Derello's wrist with his gauntlet.

"And so, Lord Regent," said the Baron, turning to Praxis, arm extended. "Now you see me as I am. Remember the parable of the two wolves? Well, the second wolf has won, the painted mask has fallen, and there will be no more smoke and mirrors. Will you take this oath with us? An alliance of trust? An end to secrets?"

Praxis opened his mouth to reply, and the kraken erupted out of the boiling water behind him with a screech of ancient, immeasurable fury.

CHAPTER 16

THE FORGOTTEN PACT

"These incessant attacks continue to drain our resources and tire our men. And they are not the only ones to feel such fatigue. I am growing weak. They do not know it, but I nearly collapsed from exhaustion after the battle of Hellin Pass. And still, the enemy come. We have killed thousands. Hundreds of thousands. Massacred entire armies. And yet, still, they come."

BRACHYURA, FOURTH OF THE TWELVE, 122 AT

*I*MUST HAVE MISHEARD, Jelaïa thought as the echo of Brachyura's powerful voice grew fainter. *End the world of men? What in the Pit is going on?*

Praedora was the first on her feet, enthralled, her eyes sparkling with undisguised adoration. "My Lord! My Saviour! You have returned to us! After all this time! They told us you were dead, but I knew it could not be true. You simply left us to grow and flourish, like a gardener tending to his flowers. And now you have returned! I am Praedora, First Priestess. May I have the honour of presenting my friends and companions: Lady Jelaïa del Arelium, Sir Caddox, and Sir Aldarin."

"Rise, my children," intoned Brachyura, gesturing with one enormous hand. "I am pleased to see my temple still standing after all these years. It is the one place I can still call home." He strode over to the bronze statue carved in his image, tracing the curved metal lines of the cloak and armour. "And it is the only place I would entrust to keep my most valuable treasures."

Jelaïa followed the giant's gaze and her mouth dropped open. Something was happening to the parts of the statue he had touched; it was as if the metal was *melting*. Liquid bronze began to run down the sides like coppery waterfalls, forming a rapidly spreading puddle at the statue's base. And what had been hidden in plain sight for over three hundred years was slowly revealed.

A suit of burnished silver armour, as dazzling and as radiant as the brightest star. It was a masterwork of craftsmanship, covered in figural gilded etching. The gold-leaf decorations culminated in an embossed symbol of an axe and tower worked into the top left corner of the ornate breastplate. There was no helm, only a riveted bevor to protect the lower face and neck.

One ridged gauntlet was holding a six-foot-long battle-axe, its two crescent-shaped blades shaped to mimic the curve of a butterfly's wings. As the statue continued to melt, the axe fell free and Brachyura caught it deftly in his right hand before it hit the ground. His grip tightened around the hardwood haft and something vaguely resembling a smile flitted briefly across his broad features.

"'Tis most agreeable to hold her once again. We have seen much, she and I. And now the end is nigh, I will need her once again."

He reluctantly set the weapon down against the base of the statue and kneeled in order to work more pieces of armour free from the bronze sarcophagus. Soon the pauldrons, cuisses, greaves, vambraces, gauntlets, tassets, breastplate, and sabatons were stacked in a neat pile next to the butterfly-shaped axe.

Jelaïa and the others watched in silence, none of them daring to interrupt the dark-skinned giant. Aldarin seemed particularly anxious, wrestling with some inner struggle.

"The stage is set," said Brachyura, rising to his feet. He looked west towards the setting sun, now reduced to a thin sanguine slash on the horizon. "I am weary from days of travel and lack of sustenance. We will stay here tonight, and tomorrow, with a heavy heart, I will don my armour and take up my axe. I will cease to be Brachyura the Builder and become Brachyura the Fighter."

"And what do you wish of us, Lord?" said Praedora. Her rapt expression had shifted to one of bewilderment.

"The Pits are emptying, as was agreed. You have read the instructions. Tomorrow we march at full strength for Kessrin."

"What instructions, Lord?" the priestess said. "I do not understand."

"The scrolls I left. The plans. The nature of the Pact with the greylings. They were to be preciously guarded. Where are they?"

Praedora's face grew ashen. "The Pact ... no ... that can't be right. We didn't believe them. We persecuted them, drove them away. We called them traitors ... what have we done?"

The giant frowned in annoyance. "You speak in riddles, child. Of whom do you speak?"

"The other Orders. They ... told us of this 'Pact'. Sixty years ago. At a great assembly of the twelve factions, the largest meeting of our Orders since the disappearance of the Twelve. There was talk of age-old documents unearthed from the depths of the temple archives. Documents containing a great secret, a monumental falsehood perpetrated for years by our forefathers, a generation-spanning deception devised by the Twelve and hidden from all but a chosen few.

"The First Priestess of Zygos had brought these scrolls to share their contents with all present. My predecessor, Viara, was one of the many to hear her speak. In her final days, weak and frail on her deathbed, she passed on to me all she could remember. The first three written words hammered into my brain like rusty nails. '*We have lost*'."

She wiped a tear from her eye and took a deep, shuddering breath. Brachyura, stone-faced, nodded at her to continue.

"In the years following the great victory at the Battle of the Northern Plains, the Twelve scoured the nine Baronies clean of greylings. They burned them out of their forest dens, led expeditions deep into the underground caves, systematically eliminating any traces they could find.

"And yet it was not enough. Like a chronic disease, the greylings always returned, sometimes only a handful emerging from the earth, more rarely a larger swarm of creatures numbering thousands, such as the host defeated by Brachyura at Hellin Pass.

"And so things may have remained, the greyling threat constant and unstoppable. However, something happened. Mithuna, Third of the Twelve, made a startling discovery. The greylings, after a hundred years, were starting to learn the language of man.

"Only the larger creatures we call threshers possessed the intelligence to comprehend our words fully, but it was enough. And it opened the door to a new possibility, one that up until then would have been inconceivable: *peace*.

"The Twelve slowed their methodical eradication of the enemy and began to take prisoners, sending them back underground with oral and written messages. And one day, they received a reply. The Twelve came together for what would be the last time, near one of the Pits, and ventured down into the crater. It is not written what they saw down there—"

"Desolation," interrupted Brachyura sadly, his colourless eyes downcast. "Desolation and destruction. The death of all living things." He looked as if he was about to say more, then fell silent.

"The scrolls tell us that the Twelve saw defeat. Something they could not escape from. And so, they made a Pact, a Treaty of Peace. For the next three hundred years, the greylings would remain underground, ceding the surface to the race of men. In exchange, there would be no more raids, no more blocking of tunnels or closing the six Pits, no more unprovoked attacks. And, most importantly, the Twelve would be cast out, some imprisoned, some exiled, all forbidden any contact with the nine Baronies.

"Once the tercentennial was over, the greylings would be allowed to return to the surface, reclaiming what they believed to be their rightful place. And the Twelve swore to assist them. If they did not, whatever destructive force they bore witness to under the earth would be released."

She let out a sob and bowed her head, her grey-streaked red hair falling across her face. Aldarin was staring at her, shaking his head as if refusing to believe what he had just heard.

"So, the Schism, the fallen, the years of infighting, it all was born from this ... falsehood?" he said incredulously. "Brother turning on brother, our homes destroyed, the defence of the Baronies left to fester and rot ... how could we have let this happen? It is not the others who have betrayed the trust of our forefathers. It is us. *We* are the traitors. *We* are the fallen!"

"I'm so, so sorry, Aldarin," Praedora replied in a cracked voice, laying a hand on his arm. "I wanted to tell you many, many times. But I swore an oath, like those before me. It was not a secret to be shared. The risk was too great. All it would take was a moment's lapse in vigilance and the nine Baronies would collapse into panic and chaos. Such a burden is too heavy to share with others. It is the responsibility of the First Priestess alone."

"And now you know," said Brachyura solemnly. "Oaths have been taken. Promises have been made. Our fate is written in stone, and there is no changing it. I take no joy in what must be done, but the Pact has allowed humans three hundred years of peace. We could do nothing more."

"But, Lord—" Aldarin began.

"Enough, child," Brachyura cautioned, his voice low

and dangerous. "Do not test my patience. I do not ask for your understanding or your consent, only your obedience." He turned towards the gatehouse.

Aldarin moved to block his path.

"Lord," he said, his voice thick with emotion. "Wait. I cannot begin to describe what it means to me to see you in the flesh. I have tried for nearly twenty years to follow the path you had set out for us before your disappearance. I was broken, broken and lost inside my grief for a long time after my mother died. Your teachings gave me a sense of purpose, your temple gave me a new home, and new friends."

Brachyura narrowed his jet-black eyes. Aldarin shifted uncomfortably under his gaze but found the strength to continue.

"When I look back on what I have done, do you know what I am the most proud of, Lord? Not that I have helped others, but that I have taught them to help *themselves*. To build their own walls, to fight their own battles. We have given them strength and independence. Courage and resourceful-ness. By working together, we are capable of so many great things. You are a builder, a creator! I cannot believe you wish to destroy so much culture, so much history."

"I do not wish to harm you, child. Out of my way."

"Listen to him, Aldarin," pleaded Caddox, speaking for the first time. "You border on heresy."

"I cannot. The men and women of this realm should not have their future decided for them."

"Out. Of. My. *Way.*"

Aldarin forced himself to look into his progenitor's eyes, fixing those two cavities of absolute blackness. He felt them engulfing him, pushing down on him like a physical force, crushing his spirit, reminding him of his insignificance.

Who was he to question one of the Twelve? He was nothing, an insect standing before a living god, an infant before an ageless behemoth. His stomach cramped painfully. All he need do was look away. Look away and step aside.

Then, somewhere deep inside him, small and flickering like a candle in an ocean of blackness, he found a dim glimmer of hope. He grasped at it, drew upon it, feeling it grow and push back against the dark.

Inch by trembling inch, never breaking eye contact, he brought his hand up over his shoulder and seized the handle of his axe. With a final Herculean effort, he drew it forth. The last of the sun's rays caught the name engraved on the axe in silver by Aldarin's own hand, making it shine. The name '*Brachyura*'.

Aldarin felt a great weight lift from his shoulders. He found he was no longer afraid. He raised his axe before him in a warrior's salute and uttered a single word, the culmination of twenty years defending those who could not defend themselves.

"*No.*"

Brachyura's hand moved forwards in a blur and suddenly Aldarin was flying backwards, his armoured form crashing into the stone wall of the gatehouse ten feet away. He rose groggily to his feet.

"Stop this foolishness, child."

Jelaïa cried out, turning to Praedora and Caddox who still hadn't moved. "Help him!" she shouted. The priestess said nothing, her emerald eyes overflowing with tears. Caddox winced and looked away.

Aldarin again moved to stand between Brachyura and the gatehouse. A thin line of blood trickled from his nose. He lifted his axe.

A fist larger than his head slipped through his guard and hit him twice in the solar plexus, winding him. A low sweeping kick knocked him off his feet. He planted his axe vertically in the ground, using it as a crutch to pull himself up, but Brachyura jerked the weapon out of his hand and threw it casually out of reach.

"Why do you not fight me, little one?" Brachyura asked, his brow wrinkled in confusion.

Aldarin wiped the blood from his face. "I do not need to fight you to make you see reason, Lord."

The colossus sighed, his makeshift gold and crimson tunic flapping in the wind. "It will not work. I have made my decision." A lightning-fast punch took Aldarin in the ribs, breaking the bone with an audible crack. He screamed in agony.

"Help him!" yelled Jelaïa, tugging on Praedora's robes. "He is suffering. Help him!" Praedora's hair was a mess, her eyes wild and unfocused. "No, no, no, no," she mumbled distractedly. "We mustn't, we mustn't."

With a moan of frustration, Jelaïa rounded on Caddox. "And you! Fearless Knight of the Twelve. You shudder and cower like a mewling kitten! I do not know you, but I know Aldarin and, if you are half the man he is, you must feel in your heart that what he is doing is right!"

Caddox's pale face became flushed with anger. "Damn you, woman! Damn you to the Pit! I am no coward!" He yanked his battle-axe from its metal-ringed sheath and charged at the ten-foot figure, aiming a powerful overhead swing at the giant's unprotected back. At the last moment, Brachyura spun around, both hands raised, and with a thunderous clap caught the descending axe blade between his palms. Caddox swore and pulled hard on his trapped weapon, but the blade remained stuck fast.

"You begin to try my patience," Brachyura said, scowling. He let go of the axe and caught hold of Caddox's wrist. "You must be disciplined." One hard squeeze was all it took to crack the small, fragile bones and the wounded knight sank to the ground, cradling his broken hand.

"Lord," came a tired voice. Aldarin was upright, his hand pressed to his side, his face a mask of blood. He managed a crooked smile. "We are not done."

"ENOUGH!" boomed Brachyura, loud enough to make Jelaïa's ears ring. He picked up Aldarin by his breastplate and threw him to the ground, placing his bare foot on the knight's chest to prevent him from moving. "I do not understand. Why do you continue this? We cannot change what has been decided."

He pressed down gently with his foot on Aldarin's broken ribs, soliciting a scream.

"Stop it! Just stop it!" said Jelaïa, running forwards. "Leave him alone. I will not see you hurt him again!"

"I ... This is not your fight, Lady Baroness. I have no quarrel with you."

"That is what you do not understand. You still see us as we were when you left: bickering children, unpredictable and divided. Much has changed. This man has saved my life. He has saved my lands. He has comforted me while I grieved, pulled me up when I faltered. He is a part of my life. When he is joyful, I share his joy. And when he is in pain, I share his pain. I ... *love him*, don't you see? I love him and you *will not touch him*."

And snapping open the silver axe talisman hanging around her neck, she downed its contents in a single gulp.

A wave of energy engulfed her. Incandescent blue flames exploded from her fingertips, striking Brachyura in the chest and sending him hurtling backwards.

Jelaïa fought to control the pain that wracked her body. Her eyes felt like burning coals. Brachyura struggled to rise and Jelaïa hit him again, setting his tunic on fire. He collapsed. *I can't hold on much longer,* she thought, feeling the hunger begin to gnaw at her insides.

She saw with horror that Brachyura was on his feet. With a growl, he tore the smouldering fabric from his upper body, leaving him bare-chested, a large circular burn-mark stark against his dark skin. Jelaïa began to panic. Calling on her last reserves of energy, she sent a continuous stream of fire from her outstretched fingers, but this time Brachyura raised his own enormous hand in reply, and blocked the conflagration.

No! thought Jelaïa, and poured more and more power into her fingertips. A sickly smell of burning flesh filled the air as Brachyura's hand blackened and sizzled from the heat. He took one shuddering step forwards, then another. He was only a few feet away. Jelaïa felt her vision waver.

Then, a second blinding ball of blue-white fire slammed into the giant's side, knocking him to his knees.

Praedora stood there, her face a mask of fury, her eyes burning with azure flames, her fiery red hair trailing out behind her. She was as pure and as terrible as any god, her shining radiance eclipsing even one of the Twelve.

"How *dare* you!" she shouted. "How *dare* you come into our lives! Degrade us. Torture us. I do not know who you are, but you are *not* Brachyura. You are not the person who told us to treat others with respect, to strive to better ourselves, to lend our strength to the less fortunate.

"You are a bitter, resentful old man, broken by the weight of your years. In your long exile, you have lost the most important thing of all. You have lost your hope. You are still bigger than us, stronger than us, but you will never beat us.

"For if we, your descendants, will not bow to you, do you really think you will convince the others? The desert dwellers of Da'arra? The hardy mountain men of Morlak? The seafarers of Kessrin? We will fight you every step of the way. You will have no choice but to kill us all. We are survivors! We are warriors! And we will not give in meekly to our fate."

She closed her hand into a fist and the bright blue light faded away. "No more games, Lord. No more threats. We will not be moved. Now, either help us or destroy us, the choice is yours."

"I will help you," said Brachyura, so softly Jelaïa thought she had misheard.

"Sorry?"

"I will help you," repeated the burnt, scarred demi-god, tears as black as tar streaming down his cheeks.

"A good choice," said Jelaïa. Her eyes were still aching, her vision blurred and tinged with blue. The sound of roaring water filled her ears as the blood rushed to her head.

She smiled faintly and passed out.

CHAPTER 17

FOND FAREWELLS

"This looks like a good spot, not too wide, not too deep. We'll dig trenches upstream to divert the flow of the river, and use rocks for the foundations. The tree-trunks from Dirkvale will serve to brace the foundations and anchor the supports. Mud and leaves to fill in the gaps. If all goes well, it will keep the lake water from flowing down into the ravine for a long, long time."

KRIARI, FIRST OF THE TWELVE, 123 AT

∽

"LADY SYRELLA?" SAID Reed. The woman nodded, on the verge of exhaustion. "She needs water," the bearded man added, concerned. "We've been down here for what seems like weeks."

"Later!" Reed snapped and hauled the Baroness over his shoulder, ignoring the pain in his chest. She was as light as a feather. He made for the exit of the cavern as fast as he dared.

Jeffson was already there, handing out rushlights and giving directions back to the surface.

"Vohanen, Avor, we're leaving!" he shouted over his shoulder. He risked a glance back. The two Knights of Kriari were struggling. Avor's wound was bleeding through his bandaged leg, making him limp. His father had an arm around his waist and was half-dragging him along, his tower shield strapped to his back. And behind them, the threshers were gaining.

"By the Pit!" swore Reed, reaching the tunnel. "Jeffson, I need you!"

"My Lord?" his manservant answered calmly, as if they were simply going out for an afternoon stroll. Reed gently lowered Syrella. She had fallen unconscious. "Come take the Baroness from me, get her to the surface. It is paramount that she makes it out alive. Can I count on you?"

"The Baroness? Of course." Jeffson threaded his rushlight through the pocket of his padded gambeson, cradled the limp body in his arms, and hurried to catch up with the other prisoners.

Vohanen was now only a scant few yards away, sweat pouring down his face, his arm wrapped tightly around Avor. The younger knight was looking dangerously pale. He had lost a lot of blood, leaving a smeared trail of crimson between the shattered cage and the tunnel mouth. The threshers had nearly caught them.

Reed hefted his spear in one hand, testing its balance. The Old Guard had no archers; they had neither the men to form a large enough unit, nor the funds to supply them. But the great thing about the Old Guard's weapon of choice, the spear, was its versatility. It could be used in an offensive formation to protect an advance, in a spearwall to defend against attack or, if needed, as a ranged weapon to assail the enemy from afar. Guardsmen were trained in all of these tactics, and while Reed had never been the best man on the practice field, he was far from the worst.

He scanned the advancing threshers, searching for a viable target. The brute closest to the retreating knights was the greatest threat but armoured, his hulking torso protected by a sheet of rusted metal. That would mean aiming for the head. The second thresher was bare-chested but partially obscured behind the first. A more difficult throw. Then Reed looked to the rear of the cavern and smiled. Maybe there was another way.

The sharpened metal tip of the thrown spear took the brood mother directly between its two sagging breasts, puncturing through the soft flesh with ease and driving several inches into the rock on the other side, pinning its body to the wall. The creature wailed in pain as black ichor began to spew forth from the gaping wound in its chest. It tried desperately to remove the shaft of wood, but its feeble thrashings only tore the flesh open further, hastening its demise. It raised its bulb-shaped head one last time and let out a cacophonic screech.

Reed clamped his hands over his ears. The threshers had halted their pursuit and turned back to the brood mother, grunting nervously. The few remaining greylings scampered up to the dying creature, howling and whimpering. Vohanen and Avor used the distraction to put some distance between them and their pursuers, hobbling past Reed into the tunnel.

"Just a scratch," Vohanen was repeating to his son over and over. "Just a scratch, you'll see. We'll fix you up good and proper." Reed lit another rushlight and followed them into the blackness.

Suddenly Avor pulled up short, leaning against the wall of rock. He was breathing hard, his face as white as snow in the light of the flame. "Enough, Father," he wheezed. "Enough." He coughed into his glove and Reed could see blood mixed with the spittle.

"What are you blathering about, lad, we're nearly out. Just through the tunnel and up the slope, eh?"

"We've lost too much time, Father. The dam will soon burst, the tunnels will be flooded."

"Nonsense, we have plenty of time!"

"Not if the threshers catch us. Not if we have to fight every step of the way."

"Then I will stay, hold them off as long as I can, give you and Reed a chance to get out."

Avor shook his head sadly. "You don't understand. Look at me. I am already dead. Let me at least go to my ancestors with sword and shield in hand. Let me face death honourably, on my own terms."

"NO!" shouted Vohanen, punching the tunnel wall, his eyes brimming with tears. "I cannot do this, Avor! I cannot leave you here. What will I tell your mother?"

Avor put his hand on his father's arm and held his gaze. "You will tell her I died bravely, Father. She will understand."

A tear rolled down the old knight's cheek, running into his braided beard.

"Damn you, Avor! Damn you!" He searched the dying man's eyes for some sign of weakness or hesitation but could find none. "If this is what you want, then I will not stop you.

But I will miss you, my first, my eldest, my brightest. I will miss you more than you will ever know."

He put his arms around his son and held him close. A howling sound echoed back down the tunnel. The threshers were on the move.

"We must go," said Reed softly.

Vohanen nodded and let go. He unbuckled his embossed ram's head tower shield with trembling hands and helped Avor fit his failing grip around the handle. "It was always my plan to give this to you one day, Son. I guess now is the time."

"Thank you, Father. For this … and for everything."

Avor positioned himself in the middle of the tunnel and set down the massive rectangular shield, blocking the way completely.

Vohanen gave his shoulder one last squeeze. "Goodbye, Son. May the Twelve be with you."

"Father?" Avor said without looking round.

"Yes, Son?"

"You called me Avor."

"Yes, Son, I did. Farewell."

Vohanen and Reed left the Knight of Kriari standing proud and alone, their last and only protection against the approaching greyling tide. After a few minutes, they heard a strong masculine voice echo up out of the darkness.

"*I saw a girl at the country fair, prettiest I could see,*

Saw a girl at the country fair, her name was Marjorie,

Saw a girl at the country fair, but she didn't want to dance with me,

But she whisked me off for a tumble in the loft and next year we were three."

The song carried on for two more verses, then abruptly cut off.

Vohanen bowed his head.

⚘

They caught up with the others as they were climbing the steep incline out of the Pit and onto the walls. Vohanen walked in a dazed stupor, cutting himself on sharp rocks, slipping and sliding on the loose scree. Twice Reed had to pull him back from the edge of the crater. "Your son did not save your life so you could throw it away like this!" he shouted angrily after the second near-accident. "Focus!"

Vohanen gave him a sullen look but began to move up the slope more carefully.

Jeffson, still holding the limp form of the Baroness, frowned when he saw Avor was missing. He craned his neck to look down towards the tunnel entrance. Reed caught his eye and made a sharp chopping gesture with his left hand. Jeffson's frown fell, and he shook his head sadly.

The prisoners gathered in the courtyard. The stout, bearded man was organising the rationing of what little remained in the garrison kitchens, while a thin, gaunt-faced officer of the Old Guard was pumping fresh water from the well.

"Captain Quinne," said the bearded man, wiping a dirty hand on his tunic and holding it out for Reed to grasp wrists. "I'm in charge of her Lady's honour guard. Or at least, I was."

"Merad Reed, Old Guard."

"Aye, I recognised the cloak. Thank you for saving our lives, Reed."

"We're not safe, yet. We've sent men to destroy the dam near Terris Lake. The whole valley is soon to be flooded. We need to get people moving to higher ground."

Quinne's eyes widened at this, but he quickly regained his composure and saluted smartly with a "Yes, Sir!". Reed smiled ruefully and removed the sweat-soaked mask from his face, relishing the feeling of fresh air on his itchy beard.

"Cart is still here, my Lord. Horses too." Jeffson was looping the collar of the harness over the shire horse's neck while it munched contentedly on a sack of grain.

"Good. Let's pack as many of the prisoners as we can inside the wagon. Throw out the unnecessary baggage if you have to. Injured first, then women and children if there's still enough space. Get Quinne to help you. When you're ready, head back up to the ridge where we were yesterday. It should be safe enough."

Brushing back his salt-and-pepper hair, Reed jumped up onto a nearby crate to address the crowd looking at him uncertainly; cold, tired, and miserable.

"Men and women of Fallow's End! Watchmen of the Old Guard! I am Captain Merad Reed, a survivor like you. I know you are still coming to terms with what has happened. That you have seen loved ones, friends, and fellow soldiers killed. I share in your suffering. I have lost much to these despicable creatures, but vengeance is at hand! The Knights of Kriari are working as we speak to let loose the icy waters of Terris Lake. Let us move to higher ground so that we may witness first-hand the destruction of the Pit!"

There were a few scattered cheers, but most of the prisoners were too exhausted to care. With a click of his tongue, Jeffson sent the shire horse plodding forwards and those not able to find a spot on the back of the cart shuffled after him on foot.

Reed caught a glimpse of Syrella as the cart passed him by. The Baroness was awake, sitting next to an older woman who was dabbing at her face with a damp cloth. She saw Reed looking at her and flashed him a weak smile.

Reed found himself near the rear of the group, walking beside the lean, grey-haired Old Guard officer who had been manning the pump. He was armed with a basket-hilted sword and carried a large canvas bag over one shoulder.

"Storemaster Dunwich, at your service, Sir," he said. "Apologies for not saluting, this Pit-spawned bag is killing my back. I fear if I move my arm, I'll topple over." He looked further up the line of travellers, running his tongue over dirty yellow teeth. "Ah-hah!" he exclaimed. "Perkale, Ronjin! I see you up there, larking about. Don't think I've forgotten about you two. C'mon over here, double time."

The two guardsmen he was speaking to had the good sense to look embarrassed. They were obviously new recruits, one suffering from a severe case of adolescent acne, the other trying to grow a pencil-thin moustache. They reminded Reed of the poor young guardsmen he had tried to lead to safety when the greylings first attacked the Southern Pit. It felt like years ago, but it was only a few months.

"Weren't doin' nuffin' Sir, honest!" said spotty-faced Perkale, wringing his hands.

"I'm sure you weren't. Take this bag from me, would you, it's giving me gyp. Go share out the contents among the surviving watchmen."

Reed peered over the storemaster's shoulder. The bag

was full of supplies: a dozen or so standard-issue spears, three grey uniforms, and a vermilion cloak.

Dunwich caught him looking. "One of these is for you," he said, pulling out a leather surcoat. "Not proper for an officer to be out of uniform."

"Th … thank you," stammered Reed. He looked down at his dark blue shirt, the same one he had been wearing for days. It was spattered with mud from the road and greyling blood. One sleeve had been torn open. With a shrug, he unclasped his cloak then removed the shirt, letting it fall by the wayside. The white bandages underneath were stained red. Reed slipped the leather surcoat over his head and immediately felt comfortable. The fabric was tight in just the right places, loose just where he expected it to be. He buckled his cloak and looked down proudly at the crimson sun embroidered on his breast.

"Don't mention it," said Dunwich. "Seems like it's the least I can do, seeing as you saved us all from certain death and all. What about a weapon? You can have the officer's sword I found if you like? Or a spear? There are plenty of spears!"

"A spear. Definitely. Thank you. I wouldn't know what to do with a sabre like that."

"Easy," said the storemaster, pulling a spear from the bag. "Just stick 'em with the pointy end. Works well enough, as long as you don't forget which end is which. Bit like a spear, really. What happened to the one you had, anyway?"

"I left it buried in the chest of that nightmarish slug-thing."

"Aye, I bet you did," said Dunwich, shaking his head

incredulously. "You have that look about you, Reed. Like you could take on the world."

The storemaster shooed the recruits away to share out the rest of the weapons and the two veteran guardsmen passed the time swapping stories about the Pit. Reed learnt that Dunwich had stashed the bag of weapons under some loose floorboards in the barracks "just in case". It sounded like something a storemaster would do. Reed talked about how Dunwich's Southern Pit counterpart was resourceful enough to cook up some rat stew when supplies were running low.

As for the attack on the wall itself, it had happened in a similar fashion to what Reed had experienced all those weeks ago. A small number of greyling scouts had climbed the ramparts, using the element of surprise to separate and eliminate the men on watch. They had been pushed back, at great cost, but had returned the following night, managing to get over the wall and into the outbuildings on the other side, massacring the reserve guard while they slept. Again, thanks to the courage and resilience of the Old Guard, they were defeated.

What none of the defenders had realised, of course, was that the attacks were a diversion to draw attention away from the sides of the crater. For two nights, the greylings had worked on the narrow pathway leading from the tunnel mouth up the slope to the wall. By the time the Old Guard had understood what they were doing, it was too late. On the third night, threshers emerged from the caverns and it was over. Any who stood against them died. The handful of survivors were herded down into the Pit, soon to be joined by the villagers of Fallow's End.

"The perpetual darkness was the worst of it," Dunwich was saying as they climbed steadily up above the ravine. "They only lit the fires when that big slug came down to murder one of us. Probably just did it so we could see what was happening. It was like they enjoyed watching us suffer. I could see the hate in their eyes. I wonder why they despise us so much?"

Reed grunted noncommittally. The pain in his chest was worsening, each laboured breath felt like someone was prodding his injured lung with a poker. He almost cried out with relief when they finally reached the top.

Vohanen was standing on the very edge of the ridge overlooking the ravine, gazing north. "Won't be long now," he said. "Look."

Reed followed the knight's pointing finger and saw a great flock of birds wheeling and soaring on the horizon. "They have been driven from their homes," he said sorrowfully. He could hear a faint roaring noise now, barely a whisper but growing steadily louder.

"It is coming, Reed," the Knight of Kriari said, his eyes red and raw. "It is coming to bury my son. My only regret is that I will not be able to hear his killers scream."

A twenty-foot-high tidal wave, hundreds of yards wide, burst over the far ridge and cascaded down towards the Pit; a great and terrifying waterfall of unstoppable force. The wall of water hit the bottom of the ravine like the cavalry charge of a thousand horses, obliterating everything that stood in its path.

Trees were uprooted, boulders pushed aside, animals crushed and drowned. No one spoke, they only watched in silence as the relentless deluge reached the wall surrounding the Pit. For a brief instant, the time-worn stone and mortar of the Old Guard wall resisted, a testimony to the skill and ingenuity of Brachyura, then the first of the fissures appeared, soon joined by others until finally, with a sound like rolling thunder, a section of the wall crumbled into the crater.

Vohanen began to weep quietly as the ice-cold water poured eagerly through the gap it had made and down into the Pit. Reed placed his hand on the old knight's shoulder and the two of them watched quietly as the crater was rapidly flooded. Jeffson approached, and with him Lady Syrella. Some colour had returned to her cheeks, and she had washed her face and hair.

"Sir Knight, Sir Reed," she said, curtsying gracefully. *She really is quite stunning,* thought Reed absently as the flow of water down into the ravine began to slow.

"My Lady," he said. He bowed in return, eliciting a twinge of protest from his injured ribs.

"I apologise for the interruption, my Lords. But it is paramount that I speak to you with all haste. For I have been betrayed, my Barony stolen from me, imprisoned and left to die in that terrible place. And once the enemy learns of what has happened here, they will return to finish their mission."

The tower flying the colours of the Old Guard split down the middle and toppled into the crater, the flag disappearing from sight. Another Pit lost. Another chapter of the Old Guard destroyed.

Reed sighed and tore his eyes away from the desolate valley. "Then what you need, my Lady, is an army. And I think I know just where to find one."

CHAPTER 18

RETREAT AND REGROUP

"So, think of the ballista like a large crossbow. See the two coiled ropes in the middle? When we pull back the bow, those coils of rope twist and compress. Once the bolt is loaded, all I need to do is strike the release lever here and I can hit anything within a couple of hundred yards with the speed of a loosed arrow. Those steel tips will rip through anything: flesh, armour, wood, or stone. Once all our ships are armed with a few of these, we will be unstoppable."

HIRKUIN, CAPTAIN OF THE KESSRIN GUARD, 418 AT

❧

"BALLISTAE!" SHOUTED HIRKUIN, pushing Derello out of the way as one of the kraken's pointed tentacles, slick with seawater and covered in clenching suckers, hurtled down with sickening velocity, smacking into the deck inches from where the Baron had been standing. A second tentacle followed the first, tearing a great rip in one of the sails on the mainmast.

The *Emerald Queen* rocked dangerously, pulled violently to port by the extra weight. A crossbowman lost his footing and fell screaming into the churning swell. The ballistae teams were struggling to load the six-foot-long bolts into the slider, fighting to keep their balance.

"By the Twelve, where are the caravels?" said Orkam. The smaller boats were still hundreds of yards away, turned against the wind. They would not arrive in time.

"We have to do something about those tentacles!" Praxis yelled over the creaking of strained wood and the cries of panic. Drawing his last remaining stiletto, he set upon the nearest tentacle, slashing at the dark green skin. It was soft and rubbery, and his blade skittered uselessly across the surface.

"Manfeld!" Praxis cried, hating to have to ask the knight for help. "A little assistance if you would!"

The Knight of Brachyura had donned his pronged helm and unsheathed his double-bladed axe. "Stand back!" he cautioned, and aimed an overhead blow at one of the pulsing circular suckers. The axe bit deep, cleaving the protuberance nearly in two. Thick dark blue blood gushed from the wound, covering his silver gauntlets.

"My brothers! With me! We must free the ship!" He began hacking at another of the suckers, and was soon joined by three more knights. Behind him, Hirkuin had organised a group of crossbowmen and they sent a flight of bolts buzzing towards the thing's exposed face. Only one of them penetrated, hitting an enormous pustule on the kraken's ovoid cranium. The rest pattered harmlessly off its mottled skin.

With an angry screech, the kraken finally released its grip on the ship, bleeding from a dozen wounds. The injured appendage thrashed violently, catching one of the knights and sending him sailing into the mainmast. He hit the mast hard with a crunch of broken bones. The second tentacle came down again, pulverising one of the ballistae into splinters and crushing the two sailors loading it.

"Ballista one, ready to fire!" a haggard sailor cried. A flailing tentacle ripped his head from his shoulders. Hirkuin jogged across the deck, dodging an unattached knot of rigging as it whistled overhead.

"Release! Release!" he said desperately, reaching the siege weapon and hammering down on the lever. With a twang, the taut bowstring sent the bolt rocketing forwards, boring into the raging sea monster.

"Reload! Reload!"

The tentacles were battering the deck now, rising and falling like a pair of drummer's mallets as the kraken vented its pain and rage. Sailors ran for shelter beneath the sails and masts as the planking split and cracked. Those who were not fast enough were crushed to death or sent tumbling into the Sea of Sorrow.

Another ballista fired but, in their haste, the artillery crew had failed to compensate for the ship's roll and the shot went wild. The kraken lashed out in retaliation and the ballista was ripped from its base, the wreckage obliterating two of the crew members before falling over the side.

A questing tentacle managed to catch a Knight of the Twelve by the waist and hauled him up into the air. The hapless man was dragged slowly and inexorably off the ship before being deposited struggling into the kraken's gaping maw. The razor-sharp teeth clamped down, easily cutting through the plate armour, and the flesh and bone beneath. The knight's lower body disappeared into the thing's gullet, his head and torso lost to the sea.

"Get the men below decks," said Derello calmly. He was the eye of the storm, serene and composed in the middle of the chaos, standing with his arms crossed and his eyes fixed on the writhing kraken.

"My Lord?" said Hirkuin.

"Just do it, Captain. They have suffered enough." His roaming eyes found Praxis huddled down behind the gunwale.

"Lord Regent! I believe it is time to consolidate our alliance, what say you?"

"What do you have in mind?"

"We are going about this the wrong way. We don't need to kill it, we just need to stop it from coming after us. There are two port-side ballistae left. I think we should try and blind it."

"Sounds just like the sort of stupid thing you would recommend, Derello," said Praxis sourly. "Tell me what to do."

"You take the one closest to the prow. The bow arms are already primed and ready, you just need to release the bolt. And you're not on solid land, Praxis, so you'll have to adjust for pitch and roll, do you understand? Aim for the left eye, I'll take the right!"

Damn the Pit! fumed Praxis. *I'm starting to regret saving this man's life.* He took up position behind the ballista and forced himself to slow his breathing. He swivelled the weapon towards the creature's globular eye and closed his ears to the pandemonium, focusing only on the rocking of the boat.

Back and forth, back and forth, back and … *Now!* He pulled the lever and the bolt was propelled from the bow, puncturing the orbit in a spray of gelatinous goo. Derello fired his own bolt almost simultaneously, piercing the kraken's right eye and rendering it blind. The monster let out a wretched howl and plunged under the surface of the sea in a fountain of white foam.

"An excellent shot, Lord Regent!" grinned the Baron, slapping him on the shoulder. "Now let us see to the wounded and get away from this Pit-spawned place."

Hirkuin, Orkam, and Sir Manfeld emerged from the ship's hold, battered and bruised, but otherwise unharmed. Sailors were dispatched up the masts to survey the extent of the damage to sails and rigging, while Sir Manfeld assembled a group of Kessrin to clear the debris from the lower decks and attend to the wounded.

"We're lucky," said Hirkuin, his round face marred by a purple bruise on his left cheek. "Apart from a ripped sail and some loose rigging, the *Emerald Queen* is still seaworthy. She's not just a pretty lady but as sturdy as an ox underneath all that gold leaf."

"Then let us return to Kessrin," said the Baron. "I don't know about the rest of you, but I could do with a hot bath and a jug of wine! We'll regroup, reinforce, and return to Kingfisher Isle with ten carracks and a thousand men. And I will burn this place to the ground."

꙳

The *Emerald Queen* made the return trip alone. Derello thought it prudent to leave the *Sapphire Night* and *Latent Folly* to keep watch while they were away. True to his word, as soon as the wounded carrack had limped into port, the Baron ordered his nobles to muster their ships before heading straight to the bathhouse, waving away the crowd of administrators bombarding him with questions.

Sir Manfeld and Orkam returned to the Arelian camp outside the town gates. Praxis, after a quick wash and change of clothes, wandered through the corridors of the keep, making a mental note of anything that might prove useful in the future.

Compared to the great keep of Arelium, which was simply designed and utilitarian, the Kessrin stronghold was a sprawling maze of passageways and stairs. Navigation was made even more difficult by the verticality of the towers and the sky bridges linking them. Each tower had only one or two bridges meaning that Praxis was constantly forced down or up the central staircases to cross from one tower to another.

The more he explored, the more he understood the logic behind what he had first thought to be random architecture. The Great Hall, kitchens, servant quarters, and barracks were located close together on the ground floor, all near to the open courtyard allowing access to the four peripheral towers. The more important locations, such as the treasury, arsenal, town archives, and reliquary, were situated in the towers themselves, often on the higher levels, hidden from sight.

The central tower contained only the Baron's living quarters, Lady Arkile's chambers, the bathhouses, and guest accommodation. There were no sky bridges linked to the central structure; the only way to reach the top was to pass through the Great Hall and climb the stairs behind. It was a highly defendable position. With a well-stocked larder and a handful of men, the Baron could hold out for days.

Finally, after an hour or two of exploring, Praxis ascended the spiral steps leading to the sky bridge where the assassin had met his untimely fate at the hands of Aldarin. He realised uneasily that he felt a flicker of trepidation. Why? He hadn't known the man, had never met with him face-to-face, and had been particularly careful not to reveal anything to compromise his façade.

He pushed open the heavy door and stepped out onto the stone walkway, the wind whipping through his black hair. The paving slabs had been scrubbed clean, and if not for a small patch of dried blood Praxis would have wondered if he was in the right place. He looked out over the town, down towards the Bay of Doves. A pair of carracks were pulling into the bay, one bedecked in violet and purple, the other a motley shade of green. The first evidence of the vassals answering Derello's call to arms. From this height, they looked no bigger than toy boats, frail and brittle.

He tapped his fingers idly on the stone ramparts, wondering again if he had done the right thing. How would he justify to the temple masters why he had sided with the Kessrin Baron over the Knights of Mina? And Mina herself! He could try and plan some elaborate explanation in the hopes of smoothing any ruffled feathers, but the truth was he had acted on instinct. Pure and simple. And contrary to everything he had been taught. Instinct was fickle, unpredictable, untrustworthy; anathema to the ordered principles of Zygos.

And, of course, there was another reason; one he was loath to admit. *Power.* While he was Lord Regent, he could call upon the full might of Arelium. He was the *de facto* ruler of a Barony that was hundreds of miles long and home to tens of thousands. He had renewed alliances with the Knights of Brachyura and the Barony of Kessrin. Never had an initiate of Zygos accomplished so much. He would be a fool to simply throw it all away to satisfy a bunch of crotchety old men who had spent the last fifty years hidden away, bemoaning the loss of their temple, and their false persecution at the hands of their brothers.

When the time was right, when Zygos walked the earth once more, he would bow before him and hand over the keys to Arelium on a silver platter. But until that day, he intended to hold on to that power for himself.

His gaze shifted south. Somewhere further down the coastline was the temple of Brachyura and Jelaïa del Arelium. Quite why she had decided to go there was something he hadn't yet figured out, but as long as she stayed put, he would leave her alone. And if ever she returned to Arelium? Then there would be no more surrogates, no more proxies. He would deal with her himself.

Praxis turned his back on the Bay of Doves and headed for the Great Hall of Kessrin; and the Council of War.

It was strange standing before the enormous stained-glass window again. On the surface, nothing had changed; the proud-faced woman he now knew to be Mina still stabbing down into the domed head of the squirming kraken. But looking more closely, Praxis could see the cruelty in those painted eyes. The self-assured smile of victory now seemed to be tinged with a hint of sadism. He shuddered, remembering her gaze boring into his very soul.

The gaggle of chattering vassals seated on the wooden stools and benches of the hall were paying the glass image no mind. All eyes were fixed on the Baron, his painted mask thrown aside, his inner wolf revealed. Praxis had to admit that the transformation was astonishing. Derello had abandoned all make-up and jewellery save for a single ivory stud in his right ear. His hair was still oiled but slicked back hurriedly behind his ears instead of expertly styled in the latest fashion. His once-twinkling eyes were hard and cold, his lips pulled together in a grim smile.

The wide-sleeved shirt and pantaloons were gone, replaced by leather trousers and a coat of chainmail, belted at the waist. A scimitar hung at his side, two throwing daggers poked out of his boots, and two more were in sheaths strapped to the underside of his leather vambraces.

Lady Arkile stood a few paces behind him in her simple black dress, hands clasped primly in front of her.

The Baron raised one hand, calling for silence.

"Thank you, my friends, for answering my call with such celerity and efficiency. I wish—"

"Are you all right, my Lord?" one of the nobles interrupted. He was a portly, overweight, middle-aged man dressed in purple breeches and a dark pink waistcoat. At least three chins battled for dominance under two fat, worm-like lips.

"What do you mean, Lord Bansworth?" said Derello, giving the man his full attention.

"Well … I mean … it's just that you seem different, my Lord. A little pale, maybe. Perhaps with winter approaching, you have caught a bit of a chill? I have an excellent healer I can recommend. Perhaps if his Lordship would like to retire to his chambers, I can send him to you?"

"I have never liked you, Lord Bansworth."

The obese noble's face turned the colour of his waistcoat. "Well, I don't think—"

"Exactly, Bansworth. You don't think. You are a conniving, sleazy, pot-bellied pig who has done everything possible over the last five years to undermine my grip on the Barony whilst consolidating your own.

"Now, to answer your question, I am feeling fine, thank you. I agree I owe you an explanation so listen closely as I will say this only once. After my parents died, I was so weak, so plagued with loneliness and self-doubt that the only way I could be Baron was to create a fiction, a contorted image of who I really was. That version of me is dead. Dead and buried on the shores of Kingfisher Isle. The man you see before you is my true self."

"Of course, my Lord," Bansworth burbled, bowing as low as his ample stomach allowed. "We are simply glad to see you returned safely to us."

"Oh, and Bansworth?"

"Yes, my Lord?"

"If you *ever* interrupt me again, I will have your lips cut off for me to use them as bait the next time I go fishing. I hope we understand each other."

"Yes, my Lord," the noble replied, his chins trembling as he sank back into his seat.

"Excellent. Now, there is no easy way to say this: the

Barony of Kessrin is in grave peril. Kingfisher Isle is now home to one of the Twelve, called Mina, and her Knights. This would normally be joyous news, except she has betrayed us, betrayed Kessrin, and the entire human race. She has allied herself with a kraken and wishes to deliver us to the greylings."

The Great Hall erupted into chaos, nobles rising to their feet shouting, knocking over stools and glasses. Lady Arkile, pale-faced, looked like she was hearing the news for the first time. Derello waited patiently for the noise to die down and for the nobles to retake their seats before continuing.

"We were sorely equipped to deal with her treachery. A great many of our fellow Kessrin were killed and the *Emerald Queen* damaged. This is why I have called you here. These are *our* lands. *Our* people. We are the masters of the sea, the undisputed captains of the western coasts. And now we are being challenged. My decision is already made. I will take the ships I own and I will sail in force back to Kingfisher Isle to scour every inch of that island clean from the taint of Mina and her acolytes. Lord Regent, do I still have your support in this?"

"Arelium stands with Kessrin," said Praxis with his crooked half-smile.

"And Kessrin thanks you," Derello replied formally. "As for my loyal vassals: I am your Baron, but I will not force you to do this. You can choose to come with me, to set aside petty squabbles, to band together and bring justice to the filth that murdered my parents, or you can return to the comfort of your fiefdoms. So, what will it be?"

Lord Bansworth rose ponderously from his chair. "It is a simple choice, my Lord. I will sail with you. My ships and men are yours to command."

The man to his left stood and gave his allegiance, then another, and another, until all the noble houses of Kessrin were on their feet.

"For Kessrin!" Bansworth warbled, and the cry was soon echoed by the others.

That was very well done, thought Praxis, glancing over at Lady Arkile who was watching Derello with admiration. *But then again, he had a good teacher.*

Hirkuin appeared from one of the side doors, his ginger moustache carefully groomed. He threaded his way through the crowd of nobles and bent to whisper something in the Baron's ear. Derello frowned and beckoned Praxis over.

"My Lord?"

"Troubling news, Praxis. Lady Arkile? Would you continue for a few moments without me, please? Hirkuin, Praxis, let us go up to one of my private balconies."

A passageway at the far side of the hall led them up to the second floor and out onto a spacious balcony enclosed by a columned parapet overlooking the Bay of Doves.

"Show me, Hirkuin."

The captain pointed at a distant speck on the horizon, long and thin, topped with a blue triangle.

"It's the *Latent Folly,* my Lord," said Hirkuin gravely. "It's at full sail, running before the wind. No sign of the *Sapphire Night.*"

Derello nodded and went back inside, returning moments later with a bronze eyeglass. "They might just be close enough to tell us something." He closed one eye and squinted down the length of the tube.

"Yes, I see them. Signal flags in the crow's nest. Repeating the same message over and over again. Let's see if

I remember …" He knitted his brow in concentration, his lips moving soundlessly.

The eyeglass slipped from his hand and fell to the floor, the lens cracking as it hit the stone.

"Oh no," Derello murmured. "May the Twelve come to our aid."

"What is it?" said Praxis impatiently. "What do they say?"

"The *Sapphire Night* is sunk. All hands lost. Mina has raised three more krakens. And she is bringing them here. She is going to attack Kessrin."

CHAPTER 19

THE CONCLAVE

"What did you call me? A dirty scrier? And all four of you purebloods needed to come over here to tell me that, did you? Fair enough, fair enough. Oh! Hey, wait a minute! Who's that over there? Aldarin! Leno! Torkin! Gellan! Prine! My fellow scriers! Come join us! I'm lonely here all by myself! Now, how about we start again ... What did you call me?"

KA'ARKA, KNIGHT OF THE TWELVE, 409 AT

A HAND. THIN, ELEGANT *fingers. Ashen skin.*
A glowing ember. The ember becomes a spark. The spark becomes a flame.
The hand is burning now, the flesh shrivelling, the fingers bending, curling inwards like claws.

Jelaïa awoke, drenched in sweat. She opened her eyes but could see nothing, only darkness.

I am blind! she thought. *I failed to control the fires of Brachyura and now I am blind!*

A long, sinuous body, covered in ivory scales.

A round reptilian eye with a vertically elongated pupil.

Row upon row of sharp, triangular teeth.

"No!" cried Jelaïa, and her eyes snapped open. She was in her guest quarters, lying on the rock-hard mattress. A few feet away, she could make out the unmistakable silhouette of Aldarin, dressed in a simple blue tunic, his massive frame squeezed into a creaky wooden armchair.

He was fast asleep, his head tilted back so that his chin was pointing at the ceiling, his mouth agape, a thin trickle of spittle hanging from his jaw. It was then that she realised she could see. A bit blurry and unfocussed — but, by the Twelve, she could see!

She let out a yelp of delight. Aldarin awoke with a start and his chair tipped forwards, depositing the groggy knight unceremoniously onto the floor.

"Oh, Aldarin, I'm so sorry," she said, trying to hide a smile and failing miserably. "It's just, I thought I had lost my sight, just like the other priestesses."

"I have had better awakenings," he replied reproachfully, rubbing his eyes with his knuckles. "I am starting to see a pattern of pain and injury when you are around. First, I jump off a collapsing building into a pigsty. Next, I am stabbed by a Knight of Mithuna. Then, having survived all that, my ribcage is nearly crushed by a returning member of the Twelve, and *finally*, I crack my skull open on the cold stone floor of my own temple."

He rubbed his aching head. "I feel that the last one

was probably the worst. It's bleeding, isn't it? I can feel it. Fractured, probably."

"Why, Aldarin," Jelaïa said in mock surprise. "If I didn't know you better, I would think you were attempting to make a joke!"

Aldarin drew himself up to his full height, squared his shoulders, and looked at her sternly. "I would never do that, my Lady, it would be most improper for a Knight of the Twelve."

"Didn't you say you wanted to be my protector and never leave my side?"

"Yes, I suppose I did. I believe that makes me what Praedora would call a 'glutton for punishment'. And you, my Lady, how are you feeling?"

"Empty and exhausted, like a candle burnt down to a stub." She looked at her hands. They were red, raw, and itching, as if she had spent too much time in the sun. "Though all things considered, I think I got off lightly. And yourself?"

"A cracked rib and a dozen more bumps and bruises. My patron does not pull his punches. Thank the Twelve he did not use his axe."

"I do not think that was ever his intention. How did you know he would not kill you? How did you know he would stop?"

Aldarin looked at her quizzically. "I did not, my Lady."

"Then you are a fool," she said, grinning. "A stubborn fool, and you may have just saved us all. What now?"

"Caddox is still in the infirmary. His hand is badly broken. It will be a while before he holds an axe again. Brachyura is still sleeping in what he tells us are his chambers, built by his own hand over three hundred years ago.

I must admit I am having difficulty adjusting to all of this. I think, despite recent events, we should proceed with our initial plan to assemble the Conclave."

"Agreed," said Jelaïa. "And perhaps you would allow me to participate, as a representative of Arelium?"

"I'm sure that could be arranged. But first — breakfast! I have not eaten in an age!"

"An excellent idea. Just give me a few minutes to freshen up."

"Yes, my Lady."

"Aldarin?"

"Yes, my Lady?"

"By freshen up I mean get undressed. Would you mind waiting for me outside?"

Aldarin coughed, mumbled some apology under his breath, and fled the room. Jelaïa closed the door behind him with a smile, and began her search for something suitable to wear.

⋙

Breakfast was fresh oats, warm, golden-crusted bread rolls, thick syrupy pancakes, and the last few bowls of hand-picked blackberries before winter set in. Aldarin attacked the feast with gusto, his plate overflowing with food. Jelaïa watched him idly, one finger twirling round a loose lock of chestnut hair.

Ka'arka, his ebony skin wet and glistening from the shower, sat down on one of the benches opposite them. "So," he said, turning to Jelaïa with a mischievous smile. "What did I miss?"

"Leave her alone, Ka," said Aldarin through a mouthful of pancake. "Don't pretend you didn't go running to Praedora as soon as you had the chance. You're the worst rumour-monger I know."

"True, but there's nothing better than hearing it first-hand," the other knight replied cheerfully, stealing a couple of blackberries from Jelaïa's plate and popping them into his mouth. "Did you really set him on fire? He can't have been very pleased about that."

"I ... It's all a bit of a blur, to be honest," she said. She was starting to remember the things she had said before drawing on the fires of Brachyura. What had she said about Aldarin? That she loved him? Had he heard? She risked a furtive glance sideways, but Aldarin was paying her no heed, absorbed by the mountain of food piled onto his plate.

"Jelaïa! Aldarin!" came a commanding tone from the refectory entrance. Praedora was standing there in her emerald dress, her red-grey hair pulled tight into a stiff bun. "It is time. I have asked Brachyura to meet us in the Conclave chambers."

"Can it not wait, my Lady? I have barely finished my first plate," said Aldarin unhappily.

"Well, you should have got here earlier. Unless you want to explain to Brachyura why you are late?"

Aldarin shot up so fast his plate rattled. "No, my Lady. I think not." They walked briskly along the torchlit tunnels, catching up with Caddox as he was about to enter the Conclave chambers. His hand had been bound tightly and smelt faintly of herbs and lemon.

"Scrier. My Lady," he said, inclining his head. "Ready to enter the belly of the beast?"

"Caddox?" said Praedora sharply.

"Yes, my Lady?"

"I think Sir Aldarin has earned the right to be called by his name and title, don't you?"

"Ahem … Fair enough. Apologies, Sir Aldarin."

"I take no offence, Sir Caddox. Scrier is fine. We should never forget where we come from, don't you think? Shall we proceed?"

The Conclave chamber was sparsely decorated, with four high-backed chairs arranged around a circular stone table. A light well was positioned directly over the table, bathing it in pale sunlight filtering down from the surface. Brachyura stood behind one of the chairs, his imposing form far too big to squeeze into the seat. He was dressed in a dark blue padded gambeson, and lifted his hand in greeting as they entered.

That's the hand he used to block my stream of fire, Jelaïa thought. *I saw him burn. It should be charred to a crisp, not clean and smooth as if nothing had happened. Does he really heal that fast?*

"Welcome, all," the giant said in his resonant baritone. "Please be seated. I would like to begin by apologising once more for my behaviour yesterday. You were right, Lady Jelaïa, in my time away I had forgotten what makes us human. And though it pains me to break the Pact, you have convinced me that we should not simply step back and let the greylings take these lands without a fight."

"I thank you, Lord," Jelaïa replied, curtsying.

"And, Lady Praedora," Brachyura continued. "Please convey my thanks to whoever made these wonderful clothes. They are perfect."

"That would be Grandmother Maevlin, Lord. One of the best seamstresses we have, even if she is a bit of a gossiper."

"She asked me if I alone built this entire place in a year and a day with my bare hands. A stupid question, of course. That would have been quite impractical. I had a shovel."

"Um, yes, quite. Shall we move on? Before your arrival, Lord, we were planning to discuss the repeated visions plaguing the priestesses of the temple."

"As you wish. I am not here to lead you, Priestess, but to guide you. I will abide by whatever decisions you make. Tell me of these visions."

"The first is as follows: *Crater. Darkness. Scratching claws. Golden sands. Forgotten depths. Misery.*"

"The Southern Desert, methinks."

"Agreed. Ka'arka is from there. I was thinking of sending him to investigate. Is a chapter of the Old Guard stationed there?"

"No, alas. It was discussed, but the shifting sands made any long-lasting construction impossible. The Pit is isolated, deep in the desert. I think it unlikely that the greylings will choose to emerge from there in great strength. The sun is painful to their eyes and skin; and in that desolate place, there is no shade, no respite, nowhere to hide. When the Pit was first discovered, we left instructions with the nomads to watch for any unusual activity."

"It could be somewhere else entirely," said Caddox gruffly. "Sand is found in many places. It could be a beach, a quarry, or simply a metaphor, an image within an image."

"It's possible," Praedora admitted, "but as we don't have any other leads, I maintain we should let Ka'arka go. If we had not agreed to send Aldarin, Arelium would have fallen to the greylings. All in favour?"

"Aye," said Aldarin immediately. Caddox nodded.

"Very well. The next one we believe concerns Morlak: *Water. Snow. An unlit tunnel. A crimson sun. A bloody rose.* The sun is the emblem of the Old Guard, and the only Pit near water and snow is the one south of Terris Lake."

"I will go to Morlak," said Caddox. "I'm not much use to you here as a fighter, but I can still serve as a diplomat."

"Perfect," Praedora said, shifting in her chair. Jelaïa could see she was tired. "My own vision was obviously fore-telling the return of Brachyura, so there is only one left to elucidate: *A bird with broken wings. A headless serpent. An ashen hand.*"

"I ... I saw part of this one also," said Jelaïa tentatively. "Last night. Not the bird but a serpent and a burning hand. It was slightly different. The serpent had its head. I could see its eyes."

"The visions only give us glimpses of what *may* come to pass," said Brachyura thoughtfully. "If you no longer see the bird, then whatever event it portrayed has already happened."

"As we discussed previously, the serpent is surely Kessrin," Aldarin said. "Either the Barony or the Baron him-self. We left them in a state of relative calm a week ago; is there any cause for concern?"

"I vote we wait," Caddox replied. "Kessrin has never welcomed us with open arms, even less so now that fop is ruling the Barony. We owe them nothing. Let them come to us."

"I disagree," said Aldarin. "It is not because others act in a certain way that we should do the same. Kessrin is a firm ally of the Order of Brachyura, as Arelium was. Let us gather what knights we have left and ride there with all haste."

Praedora was shaking her head. "I admire your generosity, Aldarin, but we are already spread too thinly. Sir Manfeld is still in Kessrin with a contingent of knights. I'm sure he is well-equipped enough to deal with any threat to the Baron's life."

"It is pleasing to see you act in concert, my children," Brachyura said. "It seems that the nine Baronies are very different from how I left them. If it is agreeable to you, Lady Praedora, I would like to hear more about what has happened in my absence."

"Of course, Lord. Let us first bid farewell to Ka'arka and Caddox, then we will take all the time we need."

Jelaïa and the First Priestess stood on the gatehouse roof, looking down on Aldarin giving some last-minute advice to Ka'arka. The ebony knight was dressed for travel, his plate armour covered by a dark brown riding cloak. He was holding the reins of a chestnut warhorse, its saddlebags filled to bursting with equipment and supplies. Aldarin laughed at something the other knight said, a deep, throaty sound easily carried by the wind to the women above.

"They seem to know each other well," Jelaïa said, with a hint of jealousy. "It is rare to see Aldarin laugh like that."

"They've been friends for a long time," Praedora replied. "The first few years can be difficult for a temple initiate, even more so for those chosen by the Scrying. I am loath to admit it, but despite all our Order has done to protect and defend the less fortunate, despite all our teachings on the value of generosity and selflessness, we are still incapable of eradicating the rampant sectarianism within our own temple. The scriers are often poorly treated. I do what I can to protect them from the worst of it, but they all end up occupying a bed in the infirmary at one time or another."

"So, after suffering violence at the hands of his father for years, Aldarin finally managed to escape only for it to continue here?" Jelaïa said, disturbed.

"As I said, it was difficult. Things got better when he met Ka'arka. It was easy to pick on a single scared child, but two angry ones were a different story altogether. Especially when they fought back. After a while, they started hanging around the infirmary, talking to the other scriers, inviting them to join them. There must have been a band of twenty or thirty of them by the end. But Ka'arka was the first."

"And Caddox?"

"Sir Caddox is a brave man. A true Knight of Brachyura, willing to give his life for others without a second thought. There is arrogance in him, though. He believes that the Order should be beholden to no one, not even the Barons. And he is against the Scrying, convinced that it is polluting the bloodline and weakening future descendants."

"And yet he came to Aldarin's aid."

"Yes," said Praedora with a smile. "You were right to goad him. As I said, he is a brave and steadfast man, and I think his principles of honour and loyalty take precedence over his personal feelings towards Aldarin."

"I have yet to thank him for that. His distraction allowed us time to act."

"There is something else I was meaning to talk to you about. Something you said."

Oh no, thought Jelaïa. Down below, Ka'arka and Aldarin were grasping wrists. With a final laugh, Ka'arka donned his pronged helm and mounted his warhorse.

"You said you loved him," said Praedora softly. "Did you mean it?"

"I don't know," Jelaïa confessed. "I feel safe when he is with me. I feel alone when he is gone. I feel afraid when I know he is in danger, and I feel happy when I know he is well. He is a good friend ... my best friend."

"Love can come in many forms," said Praedora, putting her arm around Jelaïa's shoulders. "There is the love between a man and a woman, between father and daughter, between sister and brother, between one friend and another ... love is strange and fascinating, easy to recognise but impossible to explain. And having known Aldarin for twenty years, I am sure he loves you too."

"It's just that—" Jelaïa began before a white-hot pain exploded in her skull. She screamed and fell to her knees.

"Aldarin!" Praedora cried down to the big knight. "Go and get Brachyura, quickly now!" He frowned and ran towards the stairs leading into the temple.

"Jelaïa, listen to my voice. You are having a vision. Tell me what you see."

"It hurts," Jelaïa moaned, clutching at her head with both hands.

"I know, child, I know," said Praedora soothingly. "Concentrate on my voice. What do you see?"

The pounding of booted feet heralded the arrival of Aldarin and Brachyura.

"A woman," Jelaïa said, her face screwed up in concentration. "Clad in golden armour, her eyes as black as death. She holds a shining greatsword in one fist. A scaled sea-serpent, white as winter snow, its body covered with a thousand cuts. The woman's foot is pinning the creature to the floor. It thrashes and writhes but cannot escape."

Jelaïa coughed. Blood began to seep from her ears and nose.

"The sword falls. It cleaves through the serpent's neck. The light leaves its eyes. The woman raises her head. She sees me. She is laughing. Make her stop! Praedora, *make her stop!*"

"Hush, child", the priestess said, kneeling to gather the trembling woman in her arms. "It is over now. The pain will subside."

"Mina," said Brachyura gravely, his visage troubled. "Last of the Twelve. If she has returned with the Knights of her Order, then I fear Sir Manfeld will not be enough to hold them. Prepare the boats. We must go to his aid. We must travel to Kessrin."

CHAPTER 20

AN UNEXPECTED FACE

"Perception. Perception is key. The best lie is not a lie at all, only a series of misconstrued truths. Consequently, a falsehood should not be described or explained, only presented as fact. If the illusion is convincing enough, the victim will simply accept it as reality without ever questioning its veracity."

MITHUNA, THIRD OF THE TWELVE, 72 AT

෴

"MORLAK IS A mountainous, inhospitable place," said Syrella, brushing a stray lock of hair from her green and blue eyes. She was sitting on a rotten tree stump opposite Reed and Vohanen, appearing stately and dignified despite the heavy bags under her eyes and her torn purple dress. All around them, Morlakians were relaxing in the grass under the warm afternoon sun, talking and laughing, relishing their newfound freedom.

"We are hardy but few, scattered sparsely throughout the Barony. My subjects live mostly in remote hamlets and secluded villages tucked away high in the mountains. It is not unusual to hear from some of these places only once a year, sometimes even less. It has never been a problem, until now."

Reed struggled to concentrate, his eyes drifting to her long, pale neck and smooth, dainty hands that moved back and forth when she talked.

"Sir Reed?"

"Yes? Oh, sorry. Please go on."

"We received a report from the Morlakian Pit. It seemed official, stamped with the seal of the Old Guard. It was a summons, a request for aid. The missive did not go into great detail, only saying that the Barony was under imminent threat and that the Guard Commander wished to meet with the Baroness del Morlak to discuss how best to counter it.

"I decided to go — against the advice of my steward I may add. The Old Guard have always been staunch allies, never complaining or asking for more than was needed to maintain the walls. I believed meeting with them was necessary to reassure them of our continued trust and friendship.

"I left Morlak with twenty men and a handful of mounted nobles, thinking they would be more than enough to dissuade any attacks along the road. We were ambushed while passing through the woodlands outside Fallow's End."

"Greylings," said Reed grimly. "They must be desperate indeed to attack during the day. How many were they?"

"What? No, my Lord, our assailants were as human as you or me. It all started with a terrible buzzing sound, then the noble in front of me dropped from his horse, a black-fletched arrow protruding from his neck. Within seconds, another flight of shafts followed, and half our group was cut down without ever seeing the face of the enemy. The remaining nobles lowered their lances and charged off the path into the woods. None of them returned. It was then that a female voice called out of the trees. She told us that we were surrounded by archers, arrows nocked to their bows. She gave us two minutes to lower our weapons and lie down on the ground or they would open fire."

"By the Pit," cursed Reed. "What did you do?"

"We complied. What else could we do? My men had spears and leather breastplates; they would have been slaughtered like cattle. So I lay down on my stomach, my face pressed into the mud. I heard booted feet behind me and a canvas sack was pulled down roughly over my head. We were herded north, walking for hours, maybe even days. I could see nothing. Hear nothing. Our captors never spoke, never so much as a whisper.

"At last, we arrived at our destination. We were forced to our knees. I began to smell something, a nauseous mix of urine and dead flesh. There were chittering sounds, low and bestial like a pack of rodents. A pattering of feet. One of my men cried out, a scream that was suddenly cut off. Something wet and sticky spattered onto my dress and canvas hood. Then we were moving again, pulled and shoved up what felt like a set of stone stairs then down a narrow slope dug into the earth. At that moment, I realised where we were. Our captors had traded us to greylings and we were being led down into the Pit."

She shuddered, and Reed started to reach out to take

her hand before stopping himself just in time. *What are you doing?* he admonished himself. *This is the Baroness of Morlak you are talking to, not some damsel in distress!*

"We were left to rot in the same cage you freed us from," Syrella continued. "Packed in with the surviving Old Guard. As time wore on, I lost more men to that enormous slug-like creature, or to the sadistic games of the greylings. The situation seemed hopeless. We spent most of our days in the dark, blind and weaponless. There was no hope of escape. I tried to keep the men in good spirits, but it became increasingly difficult as our numbers dwindled. After a time, the cage was filled with more prisoners, villagers from Fallow's End. I kept telling myself that help would come. We have fifty Knights of Kriari stationed in Morlak, more than enough to mount a rescue expedition down into the Pit. But they never came."

"And why would they?" said Vohanen irritably. "You sent them away. You sent them home!"

"What are you talking about, Sir Knight? Whyever would I do such a thing?"

"No idea, but when I tried to talk to you about it, you damn near bit my head off. Wouldn't even let me into Morlak keep to discuss the matter with you."

"You must be mistaken, Sir Knight. The last time we met was three years ago, when you rode down from the temple of Kriari with reinforcements for the Morlak garrison. When do you claim you met with me?"

"I couldn't say exactly; about a week ago, two at the most."

"Sir Vohanen. I left Morlak over *three* weeks ago. I do not know to whom you spoke, but it was definitely not me."

"Then you have an imposter ruling Morlak in your

stead, my Lady," said Vohanen, breathing out heavily. "For the lady I saw on those ramparts was a perfect copy, from her voice to her mannerisms to her face. And if she has successfully taken your place, she now has the entire military might of Morlak at her disposal."

"Most troubling," said Syrella, gnawing at her bottom lip.

"You do not seem especially surprised, my Lady?" asked Reed.

"I have been Baroness for fifteen years, Sir Reed. There are many who are envious of my position, and many who have tried to take it from me. It is the nature of the conspirators that worries me more. If the same group are behind my imprisonment beneath the Pit and the arrival of this … imposter, then whoever currently rules the Barony of Morlak is in league with the greylings."

"'Tis a troubling thought indeed," said Vohanen. "And a problem that must be addressed. If we can return you safely to the keep, it should be easy enough to put an end to this deception."

"Yes, *if* we can get to Morlak in one piece," Syrella replied. "You are forgetting that we were ambushed on the way to the Pit. That means our attackers knew who we were, when we were travelling, and our destination. What if they have eyes on us still? Do we have enough men to escort me south?"

"I do not wish to insult my brave fellow watchmen, but they are tired, malnourished, and under-equipped," said Reed. "And Vohanen, no matter how skilled and courageous, is but one man. I was wondering, Sir Knight, what your plans are now?"

"We had agreed that once the Pit was flooded, I would regroup with the others at Terris Lake before heading back north to the temple."

"I surmised as much. The lake is only a day's ride from here, correct? Do you think your fellow knights would agree to serve as an escort to the Baroness?"

Vohanen smiled for the first time since the death of his son. "I always did like you Reed, not much of a looker but a damn fine thinker!"

"Don't be so harsh on the man, Sir Knight," said Syrella, her eyes twinkling. "I'm sure most women would agree he's a bit of both. Thank you for saving my life, Captain." And leaning forwards, she kissed a surprised Reed on the cheek. "Scratchy beard, though. You should do something about that. Now, if you would excuse me, I need to prepare for our departure."

It was decided that the villagers would take the cart south, back to Fallow's End. A few of the Old Guard volunteered to accompany them, the remainder would follow Vohanen, Quinne, Syrella, Jeffson, and Reed north to Terris Lake. They had two warhorses; big, sturdy beasts used to carrying hundreds of pounds of armoured knight. Syrella and her handmaiden rode the smaller of the two, the other was loaded with the last of the food and supplies from Reed's cart.

Perkale and Ronjin, the young recruits, took their new roles as the Baroness's bodyguards very seriously. They flanked her stallion, their eyes constantly scanning the sides of the road, spears at the ready. The first night was uneventful, and Reed awoke the following morning well-rested and in good spirits, despite the lingering pain in his ribs.

Sleep had brought no peace to Vohanen. The veteran knight was sitting apart from the others, staring blankly into space. Reed wondered if he would ever regain the carefree, joyful demeanour he had once had or whether that part of him had died along with his son.

Jeffson walked nonchalantly over to the knight and sat down next to him without waiting to be asked. The round-shouldered manservant leaned in close and began speaking in a quiet murmur. After a short time, he got up and left, leaving Vohanen with a bemused smile on his face.

Reed went looking for his manservant and found him scrubbing one of the big iron pots they had used to cook the rabbit stew in the night before. "Everything all right, Jeffson?"

"My Lord?"

"I saw you talking to Vohanen. Whatever you said to him helped, I think."

"I simply gave him some advice on how to deal with loss, my Lord, nothing more."

"I see. You never fail to impress me with your near-encyclopaedic knowledge, Jeffson. I shudder to imagine the number of books you must have read. Where did you find this useful nugget of information?"

"My Lord is too kind," said Jeffson, a strange look in his eye. "Unfortunately, there are no books that come close to describing the pain one feels when losing a child. It is something that has to be experienced first-hand to be understood."

"But that means … Jeffson, were you a father? I'm … so sorry. I didn't know."

The manservant turned away, and Reed could not see his face. "No, my Lord. And you never thought to ask. Now, if you will excuse me, I must go and see to the horses."

Reed watched him leave, his mouth agape. *This man has done so much for me, and yet I know so little about him,* he thought. *Once all this is over, I should take the time to find out more.*

The convoy got slowly underway, Dunwich shouting at his men to fall into formation. The winding path north took them through a series of gullies bordered by low-lying hills, empty of vegetation save for a few skeletal trees, their leaves long since lost to the winds of autumn. A bird called out from somewhere up in the branches.

"Sounds like a nuthatch, if I'm not mistaken," said Vohanen, walking beside Reed. He seemed calmer and more composed than when Reed had spoken to him last.

"Apologies, Sir Knight, I have absolutely no idea. After spending twenty years on a wall in the middle of nowhere, the only bird cries I can help you with are those of buzzards, sparrowhawks, and the occasional vulture."

"Well, in that case, let's just assume I'm right. Strange to hear it out here though, nuthatches rarely leave the forest."

The bird called out again, closer and more insistent. Reed felt a tingling sensation in his gut, as if it were trying to tell him something.

"Stop! Everyone stop!" he shouted. "Something's wrong!"

An arrow arced down from above, missing the Baroness by less than an inch. Her handmaiden behind her was less fortunate. The arrow took her through the eye and she tumbled from the saddle, dead before she hit the ground. The warhorse reared, throwing Syrella from its back.

"To the Baroness!" Reed yelled to Vohanen, and the two men sprinted towards her fallen form. Another arrow flashed past them, and Ronjin fell squirming. Vohanen ripped his tower shield from his back and set it down between Syrella and the hidden archer. An instant later, a black-fletched shaft hammered into the wood with a metallic thunk.

"Where are they?" said the Baroness, struggling to her knees. "How did they find us so quickly?"

"I don't know, my Lady," Reed replied. He risked raising his head above the shield and scanned the ridgeline but could see nothing more than a few dark, blurred shapes. He hunkered back down just as another arrow sped towards the shield, ricocheting off the metal rim where his head had been moments before.

"The only logical explanation is that we have been betrayed," he said grimly. "Jeffson! Get over here!" The balding, middle-aged man ran over to them with a strange, almost crab-like, gait, zig-zagging back and forth, his body low to the ground.

"My Lord?" he said, barely out of breath.

"Jeffson, Vohanen, you are the only two I know and trust. You need to get the Baroness out of here. Quinne, Dunwich, and I will provide a distraction. Wait for us at Terris Lake until tomorrow if you can. If we do not join you by then, well, then we are not coming."

"I must protest—" Jeffson began, just as Vohanen was starting to voice his own complaints.

"Quiet, both of you!" said Reed sharply. "It wasn't a

request. My wound has been bleeding again; I think I tore the stitches open when we were down in the Pit. There is no way I would survive hours on a galloping horse over rough terrain. This is the only solution. Now stop arguing and get going."

He turned to leave, but Vohanen grasped his arm. "Reed," he said earnestly. "I will do as you ask. But hear this. I give you my oath, as a Knight of Kriari, I will not abandon you. If you do not return to us, I will seek you out, wherever you might be. And if you have passed from this world, I swear before the Twelve I will wreak untold havoc on those responsible."

Reed, not knowing what to say, only nodded. Vohanen vaulted onto the agitated warhorse, rubbing its neck to soothe the beast. Reed helped the Baroness up behind the Knight of the Twelve. "It looks like I am once more in your debt, my Lord," she said, laying a cool hand against Reed's cheek. "Let us hope that when we meet again, it will be under better circumstances."

"May the Twelve be with you, my Lady," Reed replied, taking her hand in his and giving it a gentle squeeze. "Vohanen! Go!"

With a kick to its flanks, the horse shot forwards, steel-shod hooves churning the dirt covering the bottom of the gully into mud. Moments later, the second horse whisked by, Jeffson crouched low in the saddle.

With his friends gone, Reed turned back to the ambush. Three guardsmen were down, the others spread out across the gully, using what little cover they could find. One of the men, Perkale, had not managed to get both his legs behind a fallen boulder, and a black arrow had punched straight through his calf.

"Dunwich! Quinne!" Reed cried. "We're sitting ducks here. They can simply wait and pick us off one by one. We have to take the fight to them. On my order!"

He waited, patiently, spear in one sweaty hand, watching the ridge. A shadowy figure rose from the grass, sending an arrow down into the valley. *Got you!* Reed thought.

"Men of the Old Guard! On me!" he screamed, running out of the gully and up the hill towards the spot where he had last seen the hidden archer, his vermilion cloak streaming out behind him, his injured lung pushed to its limits.

A dark, hooded shape sprang out of the grass and, without thinking, Reed turned and thrust his spear forwards with all his might. It felt like he had just stabbed a wall. The wooden shaft bent then split in two. Reed, caught off-balance, tottered forwards, nearly running into his opponent. The figure laughed and gave him a shove that knocked him off his feet. Turning, it drew back the hood of its night-blue cloak. A cadaveric, chalk-white face criss-crossed with ugly purple veins looked down at him. Beneath the cloak, the man was wearing plate mail armour caked with dirt and rust.

A Knight of the Twelve.

Three more armoured forms appeared from beyond the ridgeline, flanking a fourth with a longbow slung across its back. The Old Guard charged valiantly into their midst, but they never stood a chance. Within moments it was over. Only Quinne and Dunwich remained standing, ringed by a circle of steel.

"Enough!" called a voice, and the attackers lowered their weapons. "Bring them to me!" Reed was pulled to his feet by the pale-faced knight and dragged forwards to stand beside the others.

The newcomer was clearly female, her body slim and voluptuous. She was dressed in a blue cloak similar to that of her companions, the hood drawn up close around her face.

"You have led us on a merry chase, my friends," she said, her voice low and husky. She looked at each of them in turn. "I almost thought we'd lost your trail for a moment there. Thank you, Quinne, for your invaluable assistance."

"What?" snarled Dunwich, wheeling on the Baroness's guard captain. "You Pit-spawned son of a whore!" He tried to launch himself at the traitor, but one of the knights pushed him back into the dirt.

"Maybe," said Quinne with a sad smile. "I never knew my mother. But with the coin I've earned today, I don't think that really matters." And, still smiling, he bent over Dunwich and cut his throat, spilling the storemaster's lifeblood down his grey leather surcoat.

"No!" cried Reed angrily, struggling to free himself from the vice-like grip of the hand clamped on his shoulder. It was like trying to move a mountain.

"The only problem," the woman continued as if nothing had happened, "is that you haven't fulfilled your part of the bargain, Quinne. The Baroness was to remain imprisoned in the bowels of the Pit until Morlak fell to the greylings. Your orders were to stay down there with her as long as we deemed necessary. Only then would you be paid. And yet, for the second time, you have let her slip through your fingers."

The colour drained from Quinne's bearded face and he

began to tremble. "Apo … apologies, my Lady. You are right, of course. It will not happen again."

"No, it won't," the woman replied and nodded at one of the knights, who stepped forwards and, with a fluid gesture, beheaded the babbling captain.

Reed ignored his aching lung and pounding heart. He tore his gaze away from the corpses littering the barren slope and forced himself to stand up straight. "I hope at least you will have the courage to remove your hood," he said, staring at his captor defiantly, "so that I may look you in the eye as I die."

The woman let out a peal of laughter. "Why, Reed! Whyever would I want to kill you? We have so much catching up to do! Have you still not worked out who I am?"

She pulled back her hood and Reed looked up into the beautiful, smiling face of Verona, the silk trader's daughter.

CHAPTER 21

DANGEROUS TIDES

"I'm sure you have heard of the Battle of Torc in 313 AT? My ancestor played a prominent role in defending the Barony against a particularly audacious fleet of pirate ships. There were no ballistae back then, of course; sea battles all came down to a ferocious combat of wits between captains. And I'm proud to say that my great-grandfather sent those despicable raiders scurrying back to their cove with their tails between their legs. He was the greatest naval commander of our illustrious family. Until now."

LORD TAILE BANSWORTH, 426 AT

᪣

"THREE KRAKENS!" SAID Praxis incredulously. "We barely managed to escape one of those things, how in the Pit are we going to stop three of them?"

"With three times the ships," Derello replied. He was already running from the balcony. "Let's just hope that magnanimous display of unity we saw earlier wasn't just for show." He raced down the stairs, taking them two at a time, and rushed into the Great Hall. Food and drink had been laid out on the tables, still largely uneaten. The Baron's vassals were talking quietly among themselves, blithely unaware of the impending threat.

"My friends, we are under attack!" Derello cried, leaping onto one of the benches. "Our great city is in danger. Do your oaths of fealty still hold true? Will you follow me into battle?"

"Of course, my Lord," answered Bansworth quickly, his wavering voice the first of a dozen murmured affirmations.

"Then let us prepare!" said the Baron, clearing a space on the table in front of him. "Mina is impatient to die, my friends! Instead of waiting for us to come to her, she is quite generously bringing her krakens here, saving us the trip! We will have to accommodate her as best we can!" There were a few soft chuckles and Praxis felt the tension draining from the group of nobles.

Good, he thought. *Very good.*

"Lady Arkile," the Baron said. "Any news from Talth or Morlak?" The steward shook her head.

"Then we must assume we stand alone. Gather round. Let us say this table is the Bay of Doves, and this plate of fruit our beloved town of Kessrin. Praxis, pass me that bowl of candied dates, would you? Thank you. Right, these dates represent our ships. Hirkuin, what is our current naval strength?"

"Seven carracks, my Lord, plus an assortment of caravels and other smaller craft. I am not sure we should deploy them all."

"Agreed. We'll hold the caravels in reserve. The carracks need to get out into the bay straight away. Sir Bansworth?"

"My Lord?"

"I believe you have some military experience?"

The man drew himself up proudly, his chins waggling. "Why yes, my Lord. My lineage is filled with some of the great naval commanders of Kessrin. In fact, 'twas in 313 AT that my—"

"No need for the history lesson, Bansworth. I'll need Hirkuin on the walls so I'm placing you in command of the Kessrin fleet. Don't make me regret it. Find a couple of capable men and get those ships in the water."

"Y … yes, my Lord."

"Now, Bansworth!" The vassal bowed hurriedly and spun on his heel, nearly tripping over his cloak as he bolted from the hall.

Derello added the dates to the table. "A good first line of defence. Any other day I would have said it would be enough, but today I am not so sure. We should plan for the eventuality that they manage to break through. Hirkuin, how fares the *Emerald Queen*?"

"In poor shape, I'm afraid, my Lord. Apart from the visible damage to her decks and sails, she has a punctured hull. We're patching her up. She can float, but it will be a while before she is battleworthy again."

"Very well. I want her stripped down to the bare minimum, empty her hold. And remove the ballistae as well."

"My Lord?" Hirkuin asked, stroking his foxtail moustache.

"I may still have a use for her, but let us hope it does not come to that. What of the town itself?"

"The walls have protected us from the sea spray and the coastal winds, but they won't stop a kraken. The masonry on the seaward side is badly eroded and the gates have not been closed in years."

"We can still man the ramparts, yes?"

"There are a good number of ballistae emplacements," Hirkuin agreed. "They have been unused for a long time, but we still check them regularly. It is more the lack of manpower that worries me. I fear we no longer have the soldiers to crew the weapons, man the walls, and fill the ships."

"I have already thought of that. Praxis, you have helped the Barony of Kessrin innumerable times in the past. Can I call on Arelium once more? Will you lend your strength to the defence of Kessrin?"

"Of course, my Lord," said Praxis with his winning half-smile.

"I knew I could count on you. Have your men brought into the city. We'll put archers on the walls and train up some of the spearmen as artillery crews. Have Sir Manfeld disperse his remaining knights among the men of the ramparts, it will be good for morale. Oh, and let's get him to look at the gates too. He's a Knight of Brachyura; he should know a thing or two about defensive engineering."

"There is still the matter of your loyal subjects, my Lord," said Lady Arkile blandly. "Unless you wish to leave them to die."

"Right, right, thank you, Lady Arkile, astute as always. We need to clear the docks as best we can."

The matronly steward said nothing but pursed her lips disapprovingly.

"What? I am aware that there are over a hundred vessels

out there. Listus del Arelium used boats to take the women and children to relative safety, I don't see why we shouldn't do the same. Of course, it will take a prodigious feat of planning and organisation to get them all away in time. If only I had a trusted advisor who is extremely proficient at that sort of thing."

Lady Arkile stared daggers at him.

"Don't look at me like that, I'm sure you are up to the task. The remaining nobles here will lend you their assistance."

Arkile gave a long-suffering sigh. "The barges and other shallow-keeled boats can travel inland up the River Stahl," she said. "But what of the bigger boats? The estuary is too shallow."

"Then they'll have to stay," Derello said. "I won't send them out into the open sea, it will be a massacre. Right! You have your orders! Let's get to work. For Kessrin!"

"For Kessrin!" came the reply, and the nobles of Kessrin went to war, leaving behind a plate of bruised fruit and seven forlorn-looking dates.

Praxis watched as the men of Arelium took up their positions along the ramparts. He had returned to the Baron's private balcony, its clear, panoramic view of the Bay of Doves the perfect spot to survey the preparations.

The docks had been emptied, leaving the entanglement of berths and jetties eerily silent. A long trail of boats of all shapes and sizes led inland as the fishermen and traders fled the incoming assault. Those who could not escape turned to the shelter of the town itself, flowing through the open gates, trusting the ancient city walls to keep them safe.

A flash of silver near one of the gatehouses signalled the arrival of Sir Manfeld with a group of knights. The aged veteran had assured the Baron that he could get the gates closed with a barrel of oil and plenty of elbow grease.

On the western horizon, the krakens had yet to appear. The seven carracks patrolled the bay, smaller in size than the *Emerald Queen* but impressive nonetheless. Each carrack belonged to one of the Kessrin noble families, and proudly displayed their heraldry and colours on their sails, figureheads, and occasionally even on their painted hulls. The largest and most extravagant of them all belonged to Sir Bansworth, a glittering pink and purple vessel named *Summer Dream*.

The Baron had done well. In fact, Praxis could not have done better himself. The young del Kessrin had come a long way.

A faint cry of triumph floated up from the walls below as Sir Manfeld and his comrades got the heavy, metal-banded doors of the last gate moving, swinging them slowly shut with a creak of rusty hinges. All five gates were now closed.

A flicker of movement on the horizon caught his eye, and he saw three large circular depressions flecked with white foam approaching at speed. A mismatched chorus of ship's bells rang out across the water, the defending carracks' sails swinging round as they turned to meet the incoming krakens.

Derello arrived, panting, his chain-mail clinking. "They are here. I have an eyeglass for you." He passed over one of the thin bronze tubes. "We are committed now. I always thought Bansworth was a competent sailor despite his complete lack of fashion sense. Let us hope I was right."

"Why are they lowering sails?" Praxis asked, squinting down his eyeglass.

"They're not. Just adjusting trim. The winds are strong out in the bay; they need to reduce speed to maintain manoeuvrability. Do not think a ship is like a man or a horse, able to turn at will with a spin of the wheel. Every captain must take into account wind direction, strength, and angle. There are no last-minute decisions."

The first kraken emerged from the deep, its dark green bulbous head crusted with algae and barnacles. Three of the ships swerved to meet it, ballistae firing. The monster dived under the waves before the bolts could reach it, then resurfaced with a shriek, lashing out with its tentacles at the closest ship. One scraped a thin line of mucus along the ship's hull, the other smacked into the mainmast, splitting the wood and sending the mast crashing down onto the deck like a fallen tree.

The other two krakens surfaced next to the first, dangerously close to the remaining ships.

"Damn the Pit!" swore Derello. "Mina's trying to pick them off one by one. Bansworth shouldn't have split formation. He's too far upwind."

The second half of the fleet, led by the *Summer Dream*, were frantically angling back towards the shore, but they had been caught unawares by a sudden change in wind direction that cut their speed considerably. The mast-less ship had now slowed to a halt, water fountaining up from a leak somewhere below decks, leaving only two ships to fend off the trio of krakens. Both of the ships fired and the closest kraken reeled backwards, peppered with bolts. Dark blue blood floated like a slick of oil on the water's surface.

One of the krakens surged forwards, its two tentacles latching around a ship's bow in a deadly embrace. The second creature appeared behind it and wrapped its tentacles around the ship's stern.

And then the two krakens *pulled*.

For a moment, the mighty carrack resisted them, and then, with a crack that echoed throughout the bay, the ship broke into two pieces and vanished beneath the waves.

The last of the Kessrin ships did not survive for long. Surrounded by three krakens, it managed to let loose a final salvo of bolts before being pulled apart. The screams of the unfortunate sailors and the triumphant shrieks of the sea monsters could be heard by all stationed on the town walls.

"Impossible!" shouted Derello, slamming his hand down on the stone parapet in frustration. "How do they manage to act in concert like that? Is it possible she could be controlling all three of them at the same time? We have underestimated her, Praxis."

He beckoned to one of the blue-uniformed servants waiting discreetly to one side. "Tell Hirkuin to prepare the *Emerald Queen*. We'll launch it as soon as the occasion presents itself." The man bowed and rushed off.

"Look, Derello," said Praxis, pointing. "We have managed to wound one of them at least." The kraken that had been hit at point-blank range by a salvo of bolts was moving listlessly, one tentacle trailing limply behind it.

"Hah! You're right! We have four ships left; Bansworth can still turn this around." The remaining carracks bore down on the krakens, gathering speed, their kaleidoscope of flags fluttering in the wind. The sea creatures screeched and wailed, pounding at the waves with their tentacles, then turned and charged at the approaching ships.

"What are they doing?" Derello said, raising the eyeglass to his left eye. "What new folly is this? They'll be torn to pieces!" The krakens suddenly dived, vanishing in a splash of foam.

"Pull the ships back," Praxis whispered, swallowing dryly. He could feel an ache in the bottom of his gut telling him that something wasn't right.

"I can't, I have no way of signalling to them."

The first kraken exploded out of the water directly under the starboard side of the leading ship, causing it to veer dangerously off course. Almost simultaneously, the other monster came up behind the carrack positioned to the rear of the first, pushing it forwards. The second ship rammed into the first at high speed, cutting through its hull and embedding its figurehead into the foremast. The third ship tried desperately to turn away, but it was going too fast and it slammed into the two dead-locked carracks in front of it.

Praxis watched in horror as wooden masts splintered and rigging was torn free. Yellow, green, and white sails intertwined as the ships tangled together. Small figures jumped overboard into the cold waters of the Bay of Doves. The two surviving krakens circled the wreck lazily, a long-limbed tentacle occasionally whipping out to bludgeon an artillery crew or group of sailors.

The *Summer Dream* was now the only seaworthy vessel remaining, having narrowly avoided the shipwreck by turning hard to starboard.

"Turn, by the Twelve, turn! You useless sack of lard!"

Derello said, gripping the parapet until his knuckles turned white. "Kessrin are dying down there!"

But this ship didn't change course, running instead for the open sea, leaving the crumbling fleet to its fate.

"Bansworth!" Derello yelled furiously, spittle forming at the corner of his mouth. "You coward! *You traitor!* Once I am done with Mina, I will be coming for you!" He signalled to another messenger.

"Tell Hirkuin to send the *Emerald Queen* into the wreck. Fire when ready." He threw the eyeglass down in disgust and began pacing madly. "We can salvage this, Praxis. I'll have to give up the *Queen* to do it, but we can fight back. And where is Mina? If she is controlling them, she must be close by. If we can take her out, maybe the krakens will retreat."

The Baron's flagship had left the docks, some of its sails still torn, limping slowly towards the wrecked carracks three hundred yards away. Its hull was black and sticky with tar. One of the krakens was still circling, its tentacles plucking sailors from the water and depositing them into its gaping maw. The second kraken had moved closer to the boats, swiping its limbs back and forth across the decks, crushing and maiming the men still on board.

The *Emerald Queen* reached its destination, and the second kraken turned to meet it with a defiant shriek, tentacles raised menacingly. A light appeared on the wall below Praxis and he peered down to see Hirkuin helping the crew load a strange-looking bolt into one of the ballistae, its metal tip replaced with a wad of oil-soaked rags set alight. The grizzled captain sighted carefully down the slider and released the lever, sending the bolt humming forwards like a miniature comet, trailing fire and smoke.

The bolt hit the deck of the *Emerald Queen* just as the kraken's tentacles came down. The sticky tar covering the wooden surface caught fire in a shower of sparks, and in minutes the ship was ablaze from bow to stern, red and yellow tongues crawling hungrily up its masts and sails.

The foremast collapsed onto a flailing tentacle, pinning it to the deck. The kraken howled in pain as its rubbery flesh and pulsating suckers began to burn, turning the dark green skin black. It thrashed and pulled at the trapped appendage to no avail, the flames slowly advancing up its wounded tentacle towards its head. With a final terrified bellow, the creature managed to tear the tentacle free and plunge beneath the waves.

The fire continued unabated, spreading to the shipwreck, and soon the Bay of Doves was bathed in the light of an enormous conflagration, belching grey smoke into the afternoon sky.

"Victory," said Praxis tersely. "But a hollow one. It will take years to rebuild the shattered fleet." The bay was filling with smoke, covering the agitated sea like low-hanging clouds.

"The last kraken is still out there, just beyond range," said Derello wearily. "I don't think it poses a serious enough threat to the town. Let us regroup in the Great Hall."

"Wait!" said Praxis. He could sense a faint thrumming sound, on the very edge of his hearing. He placed his palm on the stone parapet and felt the stone vibrating. He frowned. "What—"

A fourth kraken emerged from the murky water of the bay, fifty yards from the wall, pushing up through the labyrinth of piers and jetties. It was bigger than the others, its

voluminous body covered in a multitude of throbbing pustules. On the creature's back stood Mina, Last of the Twelve,
her proud face contorted into a snarl of fury, her long hair
and armour drenched with seawater.

The kraken screamed and one of the pustules erupted.
Two spindly arms tipped with sharp claws appeared followed
by a grey-skinned, hairless head and malevolent yellow eyes.
The thing chittered angrily as hundreds more pustules burst,
vomiting forth a horde of ichor-covered creatures.

Greylings, ready to assault the wall.

CHAPTER 22

THE CERULEAN FLAME

"Jeli, did you see that Dancing Bear at the Fair? It was held only by a thin rope tied to its leg. A fully-grown bear is easily strong enough to break the rope at any time, but it doesn't. Do you know why? Because when it was much younger and smaller, the rope was enough to hold it. And so, it adopted the belief that escape was not possible, and never tried again. Do not let past failures hold you back. We all grow and change, Jeli, and what seems impossible today may yet be achieved tomorrow."

BARON LISTUS DEL ARELIUM, 423 AT

"CAN WE NOT go any faster?" Jelaïa said as the skiff skipped over the waves, heading north along the coast towards Kessrin. Aldarin glowered at her from his seat by the tiller, his plate armour spattered with spray from the sea. "Just be thankful there is enough wind to fill the sail, otherwise I would be making you row."

A few yards ahead of them, Brachyura and Praedora were cutting through the water in their own craft. The giant looking almost comical, crouched near the boat's single mast, adjusting his posture every now and then so that his weight would not tip them over. He had donned his plate armour for the first time since his return from the Pit, and it fit him like a second skin, the oiled plates sliding smoothly with the movements of his body. The gorget now hid his mouth and lower face, and he wore his butterfly axe strapped to his back in the same style as his temple's initiates.

Praedora sat at the skiff's prow in her emerald dress and cloak, staring north towards their destination, her bare hands fondling the axe-shaped amulet filled with Sir Manfeld's blood. She never talked about her relationship with the scarred old knight, but Jelaïa knew that it must be deep and devoted to allow her to access the fires of Brachyura.

Jelaïa's own vial had been refilled by Aldarin moments before setting off. She glanced back at him, his helm placed between his legs, his shoulders hunched against the wind, cold and miserable. She had still not found the courage to talk about what had been said on the clifftop above the temple, her declaration of love. Maybe now was the time?

"Aldarin?" she said, moving closer to him. "Is everything all right? You seem unhappy."

"I will let you into a confidence, my Lady," the sodden knight said. "You would think that after years living by the sea, where it became such an integral part of our lives, we would grow to admire it, or at the very least respect it. I do not. I *hate* it. The sea has broken my bones and scarred my face. It has taken friends from me, fellow initiates who did not deserve such a fate, all in the name of Brachyura.

"We were forced by the temple masters to swim against the current, to swim at night, to compete against each other in tests of speed and endurance. It was ostensibly to harden our bodies against the cold, and strengthen our muscles, but for the weaker among us it was a death sentence."

Jelaïa nodded and patted his leg. *Definitely not the time,* she thought.

"I ... saw one of the incidents of which you speak when I was, um, training in the temple," she said. "You were pulling a younger boy from the water."

"Indeed. 'Twas one of our many tests. He had to reach the shore unaided. He was pulled under by the current and hit his head on a rock. I tried to save him, but it was too late. And do you know what happened next? I was caned by one of the masters for not respecting the conditions of the trial."

Aldarin raised his head and fixed his eyes on the huge shape of Brachyura in the boat ahead. "I do not know if this was part of the teachings he laid out for us, but I intend to broach the subject with him when all of this is done."

Jelaïa pulled her blue Kessrin riding cloak closer to her body and rubbed her stiff hands together. Praedora had advised her not to wear gloves despite the cold: wielding the fires of Brachyura was dangerous enough without the risk of burning leather.

She watched the coastline whisk by. The cliffs to her right had given way to marshlands, the same mosquito-infested marshlands that she had travelled through with Aldarin what seemed like a lifetime ago.

They were making good time; Brachyura had been

right to recommend they take the boats. Of course, for him there had been no other choice, even the strongest warhorse would be hard-pressed to carry him more than a few feet. They had briefly discussed riding overland to Kessrin and leaving Brachyura to travel by sea alone, but not knowing what awaited them when they arrived made the plan far too hazardous.

Fewer than fifty knights remained in the temple, most of them older teachers or young recruits. Many had volunteered to accompany them to Kessrin, but Brachyura had refused to leave the temple unguarded. The four of them would have to be enough.

They were approaching the entrance to the bay, the sky overhead covered with menacing dark clouds. As the skiffs drew closer, Jelaïa saw that the clouds were actually great plumes of acrid smoke billowing up from a burning mass of wrecked ships. Beyond the inferno, two nightmarish creatures were attacking the ash-grey walls of Kessrin, pummelling the stone with long, suckered tentacles. As Jelaïa watched, one of the tentacles wrapped around a wall-mounted ballista and ripped it from its supports, scattering the red-uniformed crew.

The monsters were not alone. Greylings in their hundreds were climbing the walls, their claws digging into mortar already weakened by the harsh elements. Arrows hissed down from the ramparts causing dozens to lose their grip, but this would not be enough to stop all of them from reaching the battlements.

Aldarin said nothing, only pulled hard on the tiller to send the skiff speeding towards the ruined docks just as Brachyura did the same. The faces of the men on the walls were visible now, the blue shirts and breeches of the Kessrin mixing with the red livery of Arelium and the gleaming silver of the Knights of the Twelve. The first of the greylings had gained the walls, leaping onto the embattled defenders, dirty claws raking unprotected legs and arms.

A pincer-helmed knight charged to meet them, decapitating three of the creatures with a wide swing of his axe. A greyling jumped onto his back but was quickly impaled on a Kessrin scimitar. The knight's victory was short-lived, however, as a snaking tentacle rose and fell, knocking the man off the wall.

"We have to do something about those tentacles!" Jelaïa shouted at Aldarin over the cacophony. He nodded grimly, locked his helmet in place, and angled the boat closer to the shore.

It was then that they saw the armoured woman. She was enormous, almost as tall as Brachyura, clad in golden plate. One of the Twelve, without a doubt. The giant stood with her back to them before one of the five barred gates leading into the city, her hands pressed flat against the wooden planks. A ballista bolt whistled towards her, and she batted it out of the air before it could reach her, frowning irritably.

"What is she doing?" Jelaïa asked. Then, as she watched, the woman planted her feet and *pushed*, leaning forwards to apply more pressure, arm muscles bunching beneath her armour. The ten-foot-high wooden door buckled, hinges screaming with protest, before crashing open, one side ripped free of its frame.

The woman made to pass through the ruined gate, then stopped suddenly and turned, her coal-black eyes scanning the bay before landing on the colossal form of Brachyura.

She smiled mischievously and mimed an elaborate bow. They were only a few yards from the shore now, but it would not be enough to catch her. She turned on her heel and vanished into the town.

Aldarin and Jelaïa jumped ashore and met with Praedora and Brachyura before the gate. "Mina, Last of the Twelve," the giant was saying. "I must hurry after her, she has always been brash and unpredictable. I fear she will cause untold havoc if not stopped."

"Go then, Lord," said Praedora. "We will deal with matters here."

"I will aid in the consolidation of the gate, at least," Brachyura said, striding towards the broken door. They passed under the wall and onto a cobbled street leading up to Kessrin keep, its five slim towers rising overhead like grey fingers reaching for the sun. A handful of blue-clothed corpses marked the passage of Mina.

"Bring me that cart," the giant said, pointing to an empty flat-bottomed wagon with four spoked wheels. He bent and lifted the fallen half of the double gate with a grunt of effort, pushing it back into place beside its partner. Aldarin wheeled the wagon as close to the gates as he could.

"We need to turn it if we want the gate to hold," said Brachyura. "Aldarin, child, lift the front wheel. I will see to the back." The cart was flipped onto its side and pushed up against the doors.

"It will hold the greylings for a while, but a couple of strong hits from one of those krakens will be enough to push it open again. You will have to silence them quickly. Good luck."

"May the Twelve be with you," said Jelaïa, realising how

stupid the blessing sounded when addressing one of the Twelve themselves.

"And with you, little one, and with you. And thank you for making me see that nothing is written in stone." He inclined his head respectfully and started up the slope, his long strides soon carrying him round a bend and out of sight.

A crack from overhead made Aldarin leap aside as another broken ballista plummeted onto the cobbles, narrowly missing the olive-skinned knight. "We have to protect the artillery!" he cried, heading for a set of stone steps leading up to the ramparts. "They are our best chance at defeating the beasts!"

Jelaïa took a deep breath, drew her dagger from its sheath on her belt, and hurried after him.

The scene atop the wall was one of pandemonium. Greylings swarmed the ramparts, biting and clawing. The remaining ballistae were silent and unmanned, their crews killed or routed. Four dark green dripping tentacles, thick as tree trunks, wavered back and forth over the skirmish, searching for new victims. Aldarin cut one greyling almost in half with an angry swing and ran forwards, only to nearly collide with Sir Manfeld. The older knight's once-pristine armour was streaked with blood and gore, a fresh claw-mark raw on his cheek.

"Aldarin?" he exclaimed in surprise. "By the Twelve, we thought you dead! We searched the castle outskirts for days!" He paused, dodging a set of claws, his return punch knocking the greyling off the wall. "Pray, tell me, where have you been all this time?"

"It is a long and sorry tale," Aldarin replied. "But I

have brought reinforcements. Brachyura has returned to us, Brother. Even now, he goes to the keep to stop Mina, Last of the Twelve. And I have two priestesses with me also." He gestured back along the wall.

Praedora was walking slowly towards them, her eyes burning with blue fire, one pale hand wreathed in flame. A greyling blocked her path, baring its teeth. With a flick of her fingers, the priestess set the creature's face alight. It collapsed, writhing, as its head began to blister and boil. Praedora stepped over the dying corpse without a second thought, Jelaïa trailing behind her, dagger clutched in one trembling fist.

Sir Manfeld's face lit up when he saw her. "Prae!" he shouted. "You have come! I have missed the sight of your face!"

"Dear Cousin!" said Praedora, the blue light fading from her eyes. She rose on tiptoes and kissed his cheek. "I have missed you too. The temple of Brachyura feels so empty without your presence."

"Has he really returned to us?" Manfeld's eyes were shining with undisguised zeal.

"He has. And I will take you to meet him. But our first priority should be to aid the beleaguered soldiers of Kessrin."

Manfeld nodded. "We were holding the krakens off at first, I think they are afraid of the ballistae. The guard captain here, Hirkuin, has excellent aim. Then, the greylings gained a foothold on the ramparts and started going after the artillery crews."

"Well, we won't achieve much by standing around here talking about it," Praedora said firmly. "It looks like there are still five working ballistae down at the far end of the wall.

Aldarin, Manfeld, work your way down to them and get them crewed and firing. If I remember correctly the little I was taught about krakens, the eyes and mouth are the most vulnerable spots. Concentrate your fire on those. Jelaïa and I will stay here and provide a distraction."

"A distraction, Prae, I don't know if—"

"I believe I spoke quite clearly, Cousin. Now get going." She waved him away and turned to Jelaïa. "Do you feel ready to use the fires of Brachyura again?"

"I think so …"

"Good. We'll take the kraken on the left. You go for one eye, I'll take the other. Remember to concentrate, focus your energies. None of that sloppy stuff I saw you use on Brachyura."

"Now wait a minute—"

"And push your hood back, let people see who you are. There are plenty of Arelians fighting here with us. It's time they saw the face of their new Baroness."

Jelaïa sighed, and lowered the hood of her dark blue riding cloak. Thin strands of chestnut hair blew around her face. Nearby, soldiers gaped at her in astonishment. A tentacle crashed onto the ramparts a few feet away, showering her with dust and loose stone.

"Focus, Jelaïa!" Praedora shouted, snapping open her amulet and wetting her tongue. Jelaïa pulled her own necklace over her head, then cursed as it slipped from her shaking hands. She bent down to retrieve it and found herself face-to-face with a chittering greyling, its body still covered in milky-white ichor from the kraken's pustule. It cocked its round head as if surprised to see her, then raised a bloody claw.

"Back!" she shouted, with a wild swing of her knife. The greyling dodged the blow, cackling, then gasped as a spear-tip burst forth from its chest, spattering Jelaïa with black blood. She looked up to see a squat, grim-faced man with a shaven pate and a pair of crossed swords embroidered on his torn crimson uniform.

"Orkam!" she cried happily. The Arelian captain grunted and pulled her to her feet. He didn't seem especially sur-prised to see her. "My Lady. I knew we would meet again. How may I be of assistance?"

"Can you get us close to that kraken?"

"Are you sure? I've spent most of my time since this all started getting my men to run *away* from it."

"Get us close and you'll see."

"As you wish, my Lady. Arelians!" he yelled "See who stands before you! Your Baroness is here and needs our help! Protective detail, now!"

A dozen grimy, sweating men with spears and steel morion helmets answered the call, forming a rough circle around the two women. Further down the wall, Jelaïa could hear faint inhuman screams as Aldarin and Manfeld fought to get to the ballistae. She reached the edge of the battle-ments and peered down at the kraken.

It was even more terrifying up close, its dark, mottled skin wet with slime, its deformed head covered in burst pustules. A few bolts had found their mark, protruding like splinters from its flesh. She shuddered, and snapped open the bottom half of her amulet.

"Spearwall!" Orkam barked, and the defensive circle transformed into a crimson wall of bristling spears.

Jelaïa let a few drops of Aldarin's blood pass her lips and

closed her eyes. She could taste the metallic, tangy liquid as it slid down her throat and set her stomach ablaze. She knew the pain was coming now, was relishing it even, but that didn't stop her doubling over when the red-hot sparks set her veins on fire.

Fight it, she thought, pushing back against the anguish. *Control it.*

She ignored the shattered memories of Aldarin piercing her skull and thought of her father. When she had been no more than five or six, he had attempted to explain to her how to play horseshoes, hammering a stake into the ground and showing her how to toss the u-shaped pieces of metal. She had been useless: one of the horseshoes had ended up in a nearby rose bush, another had nearly brained a passing gardener. It had been a perfect afternoon.

She felt the pain recede slightly, not gone but locked away behind a door. She opened her eyes. Everything was a hazy shade of blue. Flames crackled along her fingers, but there was no pain. Praedora was standing next to her, her own eyes shining like sapphires.

"Ready, Priestess?" The red-haired woman asked with a wry smile.

"Ready."

The kraken had noticed them now and it abandoned the stricken soldiers, turning towards the women with an angry screech. Jelaïa raised her arm high, iridescent light bleeding from her hand like a beacon. She focussed on the enormous round eye, blocking out the sounds of Orkam and his spear-wall as they held off the greylings, ignoring the two long tentacles heading towards her. The eye.

Only the eye.

"For Arelium," she whispered, and brought her hand scything down. Bright fire lanced from her outstretched palm; a pure, concentrated beam of light streaking down from the wall, the tip sharper than any spear, puncturing the kraken's eye like a nail striking a chicken egg. Thick goo dribbled from the burning eye socket, and the creature let out a shriek of agony, causing nearby greylings to cower in fear.

A second stream of fire hit the thing's remaining eye. Praedora swayed and gripped the stone battlement to steady herself. Tired but triumphant. The kraken thrashed wildly, the heat in both its eyes driving it mad with pain. With a plaintive cry, it retreated, returning deep under water to heal.

Jelaïa closed her eyes and let the power bleed away. Her hand was pink and itching, just like the last time she had used the fires of Brachyura, but she was otherwise unharmed. At the far end of the wall, Aldarin and Manfeld had rallied the artillery crews and were sending bolt after bolt into the lone kraken's face, pushing it slowly back. One of the eyes was already gone, while its mouth leaked dark blue blood.

Orkam joined them, threading his way around crushed ballistae and broken bodies. "I think that's the last of them," he said wearily, rubbing his shaved scalp. "What now?"

Praedora turned her gaze to the ominously silent five-pronged keep of Kessrin.

"Stay here and protect Jelaïa. I will go find Brachyura and hope he has managed to subdue Mina. Otherwise, all we have done here will count for nothing."

And, using the battlements for support, she limped weakly down the ramparts towards Aldarin and Manfeld, the thunderous cries of victory ringing in her ears.

CHAPTER 23

SHATTERED STARS

"It is a terrible thing for us to decide. But, despite all our guidance and teachings, I fear the human race is still not prepared to face what lies beneath. Even with our help, they would lose. Better give them three hundred years of peace before the end. I will sign this Pact, and I would implore you all to do the same."

ZYGOS, SEVENTH OF THE TWELVE, 123 AT

"BY THE PIT!" said Derello, watching aghast as the greylings clambered out of the burst pustules. "The wall will never hold! We have to get down there! Come with me!" He whirled round to leave.

Praxis caught his arm. "No, my Lord. It's too dangerous. Your safety is paramount. Kessrin cannot lose its second Baron in five years. We should flee, rally the nobles, seek allies in Morlak and Talth, then return here and take the city back."

"Take your hand off me, Lord Regent," said Derello icily.

"I cannot, my Lord. *Think!* Think back to what Mina said to you. She wants to end the del Kessrin bloodline, throw the Barony into chaos. Your subjects will be easy pickings for the greylings if there is no one to lead them. You must always look at the bigger picture. *Please*, Derello. If Lady Arkile were here, she would tell you I'm right."

The Baron relaxed a little but remained sombre and unsmiling. "My father taught me a good steward will always tell you what you need to hear and not what you want to hear. Listus was lucky to have you. And you saved my life on Kingfisher Isle. Very well, I will heed your counsel. I propose a compromise. I will stay here as long as the wall still stands. If it is breached, I will retreat. There is a passageway under the Great Hall that will lead us out of the city."

Praxis nodded, his mind spinning as he planned for this new eventuality. He had invested too much in Derello to let him throw his life away in some imbecilic last stand. Given a bit more time and effort, he could further insinuate himself into the man's good graces. A perfect puppet. Lady Arkile would have to go, of course. She was rather too perceptive; one slip of the tongue would be all it would take for his carefully stacked tower of cards to come tumbling down.

Below them, Mina had still not moved, standing between the krakens with her eyes closed while the great sea beasts attacked the artillery teams and their ballistae. Without the Last of the Twelve's coercion, the krakens would certainly not have such coordination and precision. Maybe if they could somehow remove Mina from the equation, they could get rid of the krakens too.

His eye was drawn to movement on the far side of the

bay. He fumbled for his eyeglass. Two sailing skiffs, approaching fast, a white axe and round tower stitched onto their pale blue sails. More Knights of the Twelve, although he didn't quite see how four more men would make much of a difference. No, wait, two men and two women. One of the men was huge, his bulky form taking up two-thirds of the boat.

"What in the Pit is that?" Derello said softly, but Praxis already knew the answer. Another of the Twelve had returned. And the gigantic battle-axe on the titan's back … it could only be Brachyura. But was he coming to save them or to finish what Mina had started?

"May the Twelve be praised!" Derello shouted exuberantly. "Now can we go down to the wall, Praxis?"

"Let us wait a little longer," Praxis replied. "Let us be sure."

The skiffs reached the shore. Brachyura and the woman in the emerald cloak disembarked, swiftly joined by the second woman and the lone knight, resplendent in his burnished armour and pincer-shaped helm. Praxis's eyes widened in recognition. He had seen that helmet before. Aldarin! Back to haunt him again! Did that mean that one of the women was Jelaïa? They were both wearing hoods obscuring their faces. *Damn! Damn the Pit!* This complicates things.

Then Mina crashed through one of the heavy wooden gates and Praxis saw his chance. "Derello! My Lord! The wall is breached! Remember your promise. We must retreat!"

"Ridiculous! We cannot lose now that we have one of the Twelve on our side!"

"On our side? Are you sure? Then why is he not attacking Mina, why is he staying with the others? Let us be prudent!"

Derello glanced down to see the hairless, dark-skinned

giant was indeed not pursuing Mina but repairing the shattered gatehouse door. The Baron rolled his tongue across his teeth indecisively.

"Fine! Fine, Praxis, you win! We'll head for the hidden passage. But, let us hope that you are wrong, for if two of the fabled Twelve are in league against us, I fear that help from Morlak and Talth will not be enough."

They returned to the Great Hall where a handful of the Baron's honour guard were keeping a watchful eye. They were better equipped than the rank and file, with metal breastplates, open helms, and greaves. One of them saluted the Baron's arrival with a "Nothing to report, Sir!"

"We are leaving," said Derello curtly. "Prepare the men. Oh, and someone go fetch Lady Arkile and her maid from her chambers; they will be coming with us."

"Lady Arkile has already left, my Lord. We saw her heading for the inner courtyard over an hour ago."

"What? Where has she run off to? One of you go and look for her."

"My Lord …" Praxis warned.

"Five minutes is all I ask. She has been the only person keeping me sane since my parents died. I owe her a few minutes, at least."

Three loud knocks came from the barred double doors at the entrance to the Great Hall. The guards made to draw their weapons, but Derello stopped them with a gesture.

"Little one?" A voice as cold and empty as the grave came from the other side of the door. "We have not finished our earlier conversation! Would you like to come out here, or shall I come to you?"

Six feet of tempered steel punched easily through the

reinforced planks. The sword blade jerked upwards, cutting through the wide bar holding the doors closed as easily as if it was paper. With nothing to block them shut, the doors swung open, revealing a behemoth in gore-spattered golden armour. Mina bent low to squeeze under the doorframe.

"Little Baron! Praxis! You came to meet me! I am so pleased. We still have so much more to discuss. Your red and blue toy soldiers are being crushed as we speak, but the townsfolk are still unharmed. Or relatively so; I had to deal with a few that tried to impede my progress to the keep." She paused briefly to stare at the coloured glass made in her image, her expression blank. "Such a pretty thing. A memory of another life. Now, shall we negotiate?"

"TAKE HER!" yelled the guard captain bravely, rushing forwards with his men. Mina's eyes narrowed. Her first stroke tore through three of her assailants. An almost lazy punch crushed another's skull. A kick broke ribs and punctured a lung. The captain came closest, raising his sword over his head for a two-handed cut. Mina knocked the weapon from his hand and drove her blade through his stomach. The man looked down at the sword protruding from his gut in astonishment, blood bubbling from his lips. His weight pulled the blade downwards and he slid off the tip to the ground.

Mina flicked her sword to remove the excess blood. The entire exchange had lasted less than a minute.

"This is ridiculous, little one," she said, her dark eyes boring into the Baron. "How many more must die before you give in to me? We can do nothing to change what must happen. The greylings have returned. The Pact must be upheld."

Derello said nothing, but his eyes flickered to the trap-door hidden under the dais. Mina looked at him curiously.

"You are thinking of escape. I was here when this place was built, little one. I know all its hidden passages. And where will you go? Do you believe there are still places you can hide? It is a touching sentiment but a false one. You sent riders to Morlak and Talth, did you not? Have they returned? They have not, and they will not. I am in contact with my brothers and sisters. Morlak is already under our control, and Talth? The Baron of Talth was stubborn and refused to comply. The greylings have taken the capital and burned their fields and villages. There is nothing left of Talth."

The Baron listened silently.

"You are right," he said finally. "I was looking to escape. But that was before I saw your self-satisfied, arrogant face. Before I saw you massacre six men for doing their duty." He drew his jewelled scimitar, the light from the stained-glass window making the steel blade shine.

"Lady Arkile told me once that everything you need to know about a man is written on his face. Every expression, every bead of sweat, every tic, every false smile. It is how I know that Lord Regent Praxis is hiding something from me, something he doesn't want me to know. And yet, it is also how I know that he truly wishes to protect me from harm."

Praxis's eyebrows creased into a frown, but he held his tongue.

"And you, Lady Mina? I remember how much it cost you to control a single kraken on Kingfisher Isle. Tell me, how have you been coping with four of the creatures? Is it not taxing your mind and body? Tiring you out?"

"Careful, little man—"

"I think it is. I think you haven't killed me yet because you are playing for time, hoping to regain your strength. And I think that maybe, just maybe, if Praxis and I work together, we may have a chance."

Mina's lips twitched. "Then come, little Baron. Let us test your theory."

"I do not think that will be necessary, Sister," came a deep, sonorous voice from the doorway.

Brachyura had arrived.

Mina spun to meet him and, for the first time, Praxis saw something akin to apprehension on her face. "Brother!" she said with forced warmth. "I thought that was you down by the docks. It has been too long!" She held out her hand to grasp wrists.

Brachyura glanced down but made no move to take it.

"Things have changed in the last three hundred years, Sister," he said. "The world is not what it once was. We were always meant to be shepherds, not kings. It was not right for us to decide their fate without their consent."

"We made a Pact," Mina said slowly, as if speaking to a child. "We took an Oath. How can you violate that now? You saw what lies under the earth. How can we defend against that? It was our only choice."

"I believe you are right. But what *we* think is of no consequence, for the choice was never ours to make. Twelve people should not arbitrate the lives of hundreds of thousands."

"*People?* We are not people, Brother. We are *gods*. And gods *can* decide. *Must* decide. I will give you one chance to turn away and leave. A gift, in memory of things past."

Brachyura smiled sadly. With a clinking of metal, he

drew his butterfly axe from the rings on his armoured back. "I do not want to hurt you, Mina."

"OATH-BREAKER!" she shouted in reply, bringing her sword round in a low, one-handed swing. Brachyura dodged backwards, and the blade thunked into one of the stone support columns. Mina tore it free in a shower of dust and mortar.

"*Traitor!*" she spat, and came at him again, attacking with a quick flurry of strikes. Brachyura blocked all but one, the tip scoring a thin groove along his left pauldron.

"Fight, Brother! *Fight!* For I will not stop until I kill you!"

She raised her two-handed sword over her head and brought it down like a hammer. Brachyura lifted his own weapon in time, but the force of the blow pushed him to his knees. Grunting, he lashed out with a foot, connecting with Mina's tibia and cracking a golden greave. He rose to his feet, axe held nearly horizontally in his left hand. With a flick of his wrist, he aimed two rapid cuts at her thigh, then two more at her ribs. Mina blocked desperately but was too slow to stop the third series of cuts that bit deep into her shoulder. Dark red blood ran slick from the wound and trickled down her arm.

"Enough, Mina," Brachyura said. "You are tiring. Lay down your sword."

"NO!" she screamed, shaking with anger. A thrust to his face was deflected by his gorget, another was pushed aside by the blade of his axe. Brachyura retaliated, the butt of his weapon thumping into her stomach. She stumbled into a pile of wooden benches.

"Mina …"

She replied by sweeping her sword in a large arc, forcing

him back against another of the columns, his giant form cracking the stone. The follow-up punch clipped his wrist and made him drop his axe. She punched again, aiming for his face. Brachyura crouched at the last moment, and her gauntleted fist smashed through the cracked column instead. The entire pillar collapsed, leaving only a jagged stump.

Brachyura left his fallen weapon and barrelled forwards, his arms wrapping around Mina's waist. With a heave of creaking joints and tortured metal, he threw her away from him, roaring angrily. The golden titan hurtled backwards through the air, sending Praxis and Derello diving for cover.

She hit the stained-glass window with the force of a charging bull.

The picture exploded and, for a moment, the thousands of coloured glass shards hung suspended in the air, catching and reflecting the sunlight, twinkling and shining like a galaxy of polychromatic stars. It was the most beautiful thing Praxis had ever seen. Then the myriad splinters dropped like a rain of deadly hailstones, covering the Great Hall with broken glass. Praxis rolled under a wooden table, pulling Derello with him.

The far wall was all but destroyed, leaving a gaping hole where the glass window had once been. Beyond it was a small square courtyard bordered with pink thrift flowers. In its centre stood a writhing marble sea serpent statue, similar to the one placed before the entrance to the Great Hall. It was the statue that had finally stopped Mina's flight, her body slamming into its ivory head, decapitating it.

The Last of the Twelve lay in the dirt, her back resting against the statue's pedestal. Her face had been lacerated by a dozen sharp pieces of glass, with more stuck in her long hair.

Blood streaked her left arm. A dark shadow blotted out the sun as Brachyura stood over her, his expression troubled.

"Believe me when I say that I did not wish things to come to this, Sister," he said sorrowfully. "Will you now listen to reason?"

Mina hacked and spat a mouthful of blood. "It seems I have no choice, *Brother*. Very well. I will release my hold on the krakens. I will withdraw to Kingfisher Isle. You will not hear from me again."

Brachyura let out a terrible sigh. "That is good to hear, Sister. Do I have your oath on this?"

"You have my oath."

Brachyura held out his arm. Mina grasped it and he pulled the injured woman to her feet.

"Now, I must regroup with my children down by the wall," he said wearily, turning back towards the Great Hall. "There may still be survivors that need my help."

"I fear not, Brother," Mina said softly, and rammed her blade through his back. The razor-sharp tip sliced through his lung and ribcage, erupting from his breastplate like a crimson serpent.

Brachyura sank to his knees, his hands grasping at the bloody blade. Mina bent low to whisper in his ear.

"Oaths mean *nothing* to an oath-breaker, Brother, they are only empty words. You should have thought of that. But then again, you always were too trusting. And now it is too late."

CHAPTER 24

THE ASHEN HAND
OF KESSRIN

"Together let us build a thing of beauty, Brother! Forget the bleak and barren fortress of Morlak, the simple, prosaic walls that ring the stronghold of Arelium. I dream of so much more! Of five great towers cut from pale grey stone, rising high above the earth like fingers reaching for the stars. It will be a symbol of both man's infinite potential and his frail mortality. It will be my ashen hand."

MINA, LAST OF THE TWELVE, 29 AT

PRAEDORA, ALDARIN, AND Manfeld arrived at the Great Hall just in time to see Mina withdraw her blade from their patron's back.

"*Lord!*" Manfeld cried out in anguish.

Brachyura lay unmoving in a rapidly-spreading pool of

his own blood. Mina limped out of the courtyard beyond the broken stained-glass window, favouring her left foot. "More yapping children," she said irritably. "It is quite infuriating. You have become more numerous than the greylings. How you found the time for such copious procreation is a mystery indeed."

"Halt, creature!" Sir Manfeld proclaimed formally. He lifted his axe and kissed the silvery 'Brachyura' engraved on the haft. "I challenge thee to a duel in the name of my Order. And I name thee mendacious and treacherous. As tradition dictates, I invoke the right to resolve our grievances by trial of combat."

"What are you doing?" Aldarin hissed. "You can't face her alone. Last time, it took four of us to even give Brachyura pause. Let us attack together!"

Manfeld turned to Aldarin and the younger knight took an involuntary step back, such was the cold fury in the temple master's eyes. "No, initiate. I am the voice of the temple. I am its leader. We will do this as custom dictates, and with honour. Prae?"

"Yes, Cousin?"

"Please note that if I fall, I wish for Aldarin to be raised to the rank of temple master, and to take my place in the Conclave."

"I don't—"

"I must do this, Prae. I can feel it in every fibre of my being. And it must be done *right*. I have never asked you for anything. Let me have this."

Praedora said nothing, only looked at him, her eyes searching his careworn face. After a moment, she nodded and moved to let him pass.

Mina watched the exchange with some amusement, leaning heavily on her sword. "If you are ready, I accept your challenge, little one. Come, meet your death."

Manfeld saluted and settled into a duelling stance, axe held out in front of him, his two hands gripping the base of the haft almost like he was holding a sword. Mina smiled and her own sword licked out, faster than a scorpion's sting, only to be knocked away. Her smile slipped and she tried again, feinting left then cutting right. Manfeld blocked both strikes almost contemptuously with the flat of his axe blade.

He went on the offensive, a series of hard, powerful strokes designed to force his enemy back. Mina retreated, looking for an opening. Sidestepping gracefully despite her wounded leg, she punched him hard in the side of the head, denting his cheek guard and tearing the helm from his head. His counterstrike sliced her left ear in half, eliciting a surprised yelp of pain.

"You are ... proficient, little knight," Mina said, breathing hard. She clutched the left side of her head as blood welled through her fingers. "And I am tired. No human has ever tested me this much before. But you will find it will take a good deal more to kill one of the Twelve."

Manfeld shook his head back and forth, blinking to try and clear his blurred vision. The blow to the head had rattled his skull. He attacked once more, but his movements were slow and sluggish, as if he was under water. Mina dodged an obvious reverse swing and elbowed the old knight in the face, breaking two of his teeth.

"By the Pit, I do not care what he said, I will not let him be battered to death like this," said Praedora, starting forwards. Aldarin blocked her path with his arm. "You heard him, my Lady. He will never forgive you if you interfere in a trial of single combat. You know what his honour means to him."

"He may never forgive me, but at least he will be alive," she replied, one hand on her silver amulet. "Now let me through, *initiate*, or I will melt that pretty helmet of yours, and the skin beneath it."

Aldarin raised his arm and let her through. Manfeld saw her approach from the corner of his eye and turned to wave her back.

"Prae, what did I say—"

Mina's two-handed sword scythed through his neck, taking his head from his shoulders. Manfeld's armoured body collapsed with a screech of metal, his arms and legs jerking spasmodically. The double-bladed battle axe fell from lifeless fingers to hit the paved floor with a clang.

Silence filled the Great Hall.

Praxis, Derello, and Aldarin looked on in horror as Manfeld's corpse twitched one last time then was still. Praedora stood a few paces away, clenching and unclenching her hands, tears rolling unchecked down her cheeks, her face a mask of grief.

Mina prodded the dead body with one giant foot. "It appears that I am the victor," she said in a toneless voice. "Now, I believe I am owed—"

"It must be terrible to never know love," Praedora interrupted softly. "There is such strength among the Twelve, yet so much weakness. Brachyura was puzzled when Jelaïa spoke to him of love. It is something you do not understand, isn't it? You call each other brother and sister, but they are simply names, used without thought or emotion; there is no deeper bond."

"Quiet, little one," said Mina, taking a threatening step towards her.

"And if you don't understand love," Praedora continued, as if she hadn't heard, "then you cannot comprehend the things love makes us do. Manfeld rescued me for love. Not a passionate love, or a romantic love, only a simple empathy between two friends. He helped me escape a troubled, violent father who used to beat me and my sisters by day and abuse us by night. We owe Sir Manfeld so much. I have strived all my life to repay my debt to him for what he did for us. And now I cannot."

"Quiet!" Mina growled, her eyes as dark and as black as the night. "I will not tell you again."

"No," said Praedora, raising a hand sheathed in burning cerulean fire. "You will not."

The blast took Mina in the chest and sent her hurtling backwards across the room, crashing through a stone column and bouncing off the far wall. She rose to one knee, coughing. Praedora stepped around the broken column, both her hands now coated in flame. A tear appeared on her cheek for an instant before evaporating in the intense heat.

"Stupid … whore …" Mina panted, steam rising from her breastplate. "The Twelve are indestructible. I … will … heal."

Praedora clapped her hands together and the armoured giant was engulfed in a pillar of radiant fire. Golden armour melted, searing through flesh and bone. Mina shrieked as her hair caught alight. The hall was filled with the rancid stench of roasting meat. Molten sludge mixed with blood and charred skin dribbled onto the paving stones. Praedora faltered but remained upright, her hands still firmly pressed together, her brow furrowed in concentration.

The blaze had reached the giant's face, scorching away the soft lips, devouring the cheeks and nose. Impossibly, Mina was still alive, moaning hoarsely and struggling to stand. With a snap, her femur broke and she pitched over backwards. Soon the hungry flames enveloped her entirely. Except for her eyes. The black, bottomless hollows were untouched, as if the fire was loath to go near them.

Praedora swayed and Aldarin rushed to catch her before she fell. She turned her head feebly in his direction and found his helmet with a trembling hand. Aldarin sighed when he looked into her eyes, already knowing what he would see. The First Priestess had gone too far. She had lost control. Her bright emerald irises were now veiled by a creamy-white liquid.

Praedora was blind.

"Aldarin," the priestess whispered. "What did she say? The Twelve are indestructible? We should check on Brachyura."

Aldarin helped her up and they headed towards the courtyard, Praedora leaning on his arm like an old woman. Praxis crawled out from under the table, followed by a shell-shocked Derello. The Baron surveyed the damage wrought in the Great Hall; the fallen columns, the shattered window, the bloody corpses of his men, and the smouldering remains of the Last of the Twelve.

"Mother, Father, you are avenged," he said in a quavering voice, before stumbling unsteadily to one of the few chairs still upright and sitting down heavily.

"Aldarin!" said Praxis, his half-smile firmly in place.

"Thank the Twelve you are safe! We looked and looked but to no avail!"

The big knight did not reply, his face hidden beneath his helm.

Does he know? thought Praxis, panicking. *How can he know?*

"Once we heard that you and Lady Jelaïa were alive and out of danger, we rushed to Kessrin as soon as we could but arrived too late! We have much to talk about, my friend."

"Later."

"Of course, of course. We can … wait. What was that?"

A damaged pillar keeled over and smashed into the dais, sending shards of stone spinning in all directions.

Derello's head snapped up. "The hall was not built to receive such punishment," he shouted as the floor began to shake. "We've lost the entire north wall and more than half of the support columns. The tower won't hold!"

Praxis grasped Praedora's other arm and, with Aldarin's help, carried the exhausted woman into the courtyard, closely followed by Derello. Brachyura still lay where he had fallen, his eyes closed. Aldarin bent close and pressed an ear to his ravaged chest. "He lives!" he said in a relieved voice. "Heartbeat weak, but he lives."

Derello wasn't listening. He was watching fissures appear in the smooth ash-grey stone of the central tower, spreading upwards and outwards from the ruined stained-glass window, splitting into smaller hairline fractures like streams from a river.

His gaze rose to the higher balconies.

"By the Twelve, there are still people up there," he murmured softly. The wall adjacent to the shattered glass window collapsed in on itself, burying the corpses of Manfeld and Mina under a mountain of rubble. The tower shifted, askew, half of its ground floor destroyed. It began to teeter precariously. Faint screams could be heard from those still inside. A window was thrown open high above them and two servants, driven mad by panic, jumped out, limbs flailing wildly as they fell.

With an ear-splitting crack that resonated around the courtyard, the tower toppled sideways like a felled tree, shedding blue tiles from its conical roof.

"Oh no," said Derello, seeing its trajectory.

The enormous pillar of stone collided with the easternmost outer tower. The noise was deafening. Chunks of rubble as big as houses rained down on the inner keep, pulverising ornate fountains, carefully pruned flowerbeds, covered columned walkways, marble statues, and stacks of crates and barrels. A large mushroom-shaped cloud of mortar and powdered grit billowed up from the wreckage, almost as high as the towers themselves, shrouding the whole area in fog.

When the dust settled, they could see that the entire north-eastern portion of the keep and the wall surrounding it had been completely demolished. What remained looked like some horrific desolate wasteland, a depressing vista of broken stone, shattered furniture, and dead bodies.

"There ... there were hundreds of people in those towers," said Derello, shaking his head in disbelief. "Buried alive. What remains? What can we do to move on from this?"

"Repair and rebuild," said Aldarin quietly. "Repair and rebuild."

৶

Jelaïa stood on the battle-worn wall of Kessrin with her eyes closed, relishing the cool sea breeze on her face. Behind her, Orkam and his men were clearing the dead from the ramparts. Hirkuin sat leaning against the battlements, filling a pipe. The ginger-haired captain had a thick bandage crusted with dried blood wrapped around his chest. He was looking up at the ruined keep, its three remaining towers pushing up through a thick cloud of dust.

The gulls had returned to the bay, diving into the water in search of fish or pecking at mussels with their sharp beaks. The bonfire of wrecked carracks had burned itself out, the fading smoke chased away by a bright yellow sun.

She could hear a commotion further down the wall. Squinting, she quickly recognised Aldarin and Praedora moving slowly along the ramparts. Jelaïa instantly knew that something was wrong. The First Priestess had her arm locked around Aldarin, and he appeared to be guiding her. But why would he be doing that, unless .... The couple drew closer and Jelaïa stifled a gasp as she looked into Praedora's white, sightless eyes.

"That bad, is it?" the priestess said, reaching out with her hands to feel Jelaïa's face.

"No ... no, my Lady. I am a little surprised, that's all."

"Do not let my blindness trouble you, Jelaïa. I have been preparing for this day for a long, long time. To be honest, I am surprised it didn't happen sooner. I've overextended myself many times in the past. I was lucky. And in any case, I do not imagine I will ever wield such power again. My link to the fires of Brachyura has been broken. I'm afraid Sir Manfeld is dead."

Jelaïa took the older woman's hands in her own and squeezed them softly.

"Oh, I'm so sorry, Praedora. I confess I did not know him well, but it was clear that the bond between you was strong."

"He was my oldest, greatest friend, and will be sorely missed. We spent nearly fifty years together, gone in a blink of an eye. Time can be such a callous companion."

"So I have heard. How fare the others?"

"Derello and Praxis are safe. Derello is coordinating the rescue teams; they are combing through the rubble as we speak. Aldarin here seems to be all right. Oh, and Brachyura is wounded, but we think he will survive. Incredibly resilient, these demi-gods."

"Praxis ... I should go see him." The prospect of seeing him again should have filled her heart with joy, but instead she felt something else there; a strange sense of unease mixed with anxiety. She pushed the thought from her mind.

"I think he would like that; he has been asking about you almost constantly. Quite a handsome man, I seem to remember."

"Yes ... well ... I mean ..."

"I'm teasing you, Jeli. Now I need to have a lie-down. We will speak again soon. Aldarin, come help a poor blind woman down from the wall."

Jelaïa watched the priestess move away, then suddenly something clicked. Her blood ran cold.

"Praedora, stop!" she called, running after her.

"Yes?"

"You called me Jeli."

"Did I, dear?"

"Nobody uses that nickname," said Jelaïa heatedly, her face flushed. "*No one*. Not my mother, not Praxis, not anybody save for my father. It was one of the things we shared between *us*, and only us. Who told you about it? Was it Praxis? Aldarin? *Tell me!*" She realised she had shouted the last part but didn't care.

"For someone so observant, it is quite stunning that you have missed something so obvious," said Praedora in a strange voice, releasing her hold on Aldarin and shooing him away. "Have you really not worked it out yet?"

"Worked what out? That you are slowly losing your mind?"

Praedora sighed and carefully lowered herself onto one of the crenels. "I told you, several times. You always hear without *listening*, Jeli. Three siblings under the yoke of a violent father. Three siblings who escaped. Three siblings who were tainted with the blood of Brachyura, three descendants of the Twelve. The eldest decided to exploit her gift. She became a priestess. The other two decided to hide it. One married a young man in a village near the Southern Pit. The youngest sold flowers for many years until she caught the eye of a dashing blond-haired nobleman, a certain Loré del Conte."

"No …" Jelaïa said, her heart beating so loudly in her chest she felt it might explode. "Del Conte's wife … is my … mother? But that would mean …"

"Yes, child," said Praedora softly, turning her sightless gaze towards her. "That would make me your aunt."

"But … why didn't you say anything?"

"It was not for me to do so. Your mother and I remained close, but she didn't want any of her children to become part of one of the Knightly Orders. I told her that I would not reveal anything to you directly, but that I would not lie to you either."

"So my father cheated on his wife," said Jelaïa bitterly, shaking her head. "He was always condoning Loré's extra-conjugal affairs. What a hypocrite! When did it start? When did Listus seduce my mother?"

"He didn't," said Praedora sadly. "Listus del Arelium loved only one woman for his entire life, and, as far as I know, only ever shared her bed."

"Then how …"

"A Barony is only as strong as its Baron, Jeli. You must know this. Listus and his wife tried for many, many years to conceive a child. They consulted healers and priestesses throughout the nine Baronies, myself among them. But it was no use. Listus was sterile. He could never have children. And so, the del Arelium bloodline was fated to disappear."

Praedora sighed.

"He confided this terrible secret to a precious few, one of them his childhood friend whom he trusted implicitly. And one day, Loré came to the Baron and offered a solution. His wife — my sister — was pregnant with her second child, less than a year after her first. Loré already had a son and didn't want any more children. What he proposed was simple: he would gift Listus the second child. All they would have to do was fake a miscarriage, and then for Listus's wife to fake her pregnancy. The Baron agreed."

"So my father is …" Jelaïa let out a sob as it hit her, and she began to weep, overcome with emotion.

"I am sorry, child. I did not intend you to find out like this, but yes, your father lives, and his name is Loré del Conte."

CHAPTER 25

PRISONER

"And so, dressed in the fleece, the wolf strolled into the pasture with the sheep. Soon a lamb was following him about and was quickly led away to slaughter."

UNKNOWN, 38 AT

◈

REED CURSED AS another stray branch hit the rough canvas bag tied over his face. He was strapped to the saddle of a russet-coloured stallion, his hands roped together behind his back. The tightly woven fabric of the bag obscured his vision completely. He had no idea where they were, or where they were going, only the identity of his captors: Nidore del Conte, a man he once thought was his friend, and Verona, a Priestess of Mithuna, Third of the Twelve.

Meeting both of them again under such strange

circumstances had been a shock. When he had seen them last, they had been walking hand-in-hand up towards Arelium keep, smiling and happy, just moments before the gatehouse had collapsed and he had nearly lost his life.

Verona had taken great pleasure in telling him what had happened next. How she had managed to lure Aldarin and Jelaïa down to the hidden pier on the outskirts of town, how she had pleaded with Jelaïa to come with them, to let them take her to safety and protect her from the greylings. And how Aldarin had twisted her words, calling her a liar and viciously attacking Nidore and herself. She had praised Nidore's bravery, lauding his strength and courage while idly running her fingers up and down the stoic archer's whipcord bicep.

Reed had not had much experience with women, but he was no fool. *Surely he cannot be falling for this,* he had thought, trying to catch Nidore's eye, but the young Lord had refused to look at him, his arms crossed defensively.

He heard a soft jingling of reins as another rider drew level with him. A faint smell of crushed flowers and strawberries. "Good day to you, Reed," Verona purred. "I hope you slept well?"

"You left me tied to a tree," he growled. "My back is on fire. Is all this really necessary?"

"I'm afraid so." Verona sounded like she was pouting. "It is best for now that you do not see the faces of my companions. They are quite shy. Perhaps this evening, if you give me your word you will not try to escape, I will allow you to sleep on the ground."

"Where are we going?"

"Ah, that I can tell you. But first, you need to hear the

rest of our tale. Where was I? Oh, yes. So, we managed to escape Aldarin's wrath — barely I might add — and found solace among other Knights of Mithuna like myself. Our Order have become outcasts, you see, shunned for doing nothing more than following the teachings of our masters."

"I don't understand."

"The Twelve, Reed. They left specific instructions to be carried out, a series of measures to be implemented at the first signs of the greylings' return. Some dissident factions refused to comply. We pleaded and begged, but they ignored us, driving us out of our temples, killing the men and women of our orders indiscriminately. My father was among those who gave his life so that we could escape."

Reed said nothing, waiting for her to continue.

"The Knights of Brachyura and some of the other Orders refused the words of the Twelve. They persecuted us. And if Nidore had not stopped him, Aldarin would have finished the job."

Lunacy, Reed thought. And yet, a tiny seed of doubt was planted in his mind. He remembered Aldarin's evasiveness whenever Reed had tried to broach the subject, his unwillingness to talk about the decline of the knights or why they had been so suspiciously absent from public affairs for the last fifty years.

"My fellow initiates of Mithuna took us in, helped us to heal and regain our lost strength," Verona said. "We decided not to return to Arelium. Listus would be of no help to us, and rumour had it that the Knights of Brachyura had arrived there in force, routing the greylings. Kessrin would be dangerous too, the town is only a day's ride from their temple, and many initiates can often be found within those grey walls. And so we decided on Morlak."

"But why—" Reed began to reply, just as a low-hanging branch thwacked into his chest, knocking the wind out of him.

"By the Pit!" he said angrily. "Is my horse blind, too?"

"Sorry," said Verona, chuckling. "I think the knight in charge of leading your horse doesn't like you very much. Yonis! A bit more respect for our esteemed guest!"

"Yes, my Lady," came the disgruntled reply.

"So. Morlak. We sent a delegation there and that haughty, pretentious Baroness turned us away like we were common beggars! Stuck-up harpy! Terribly ugly too, I can see why she has such trouble finding a suitor."

"Assuredly," said Reed, remembering the soft touch of Syrella's hand on his cheek.

"We were cast out. Me, Reed! A Priestess of the Twelve! We had to get rid of her, there was no other choice!"

"You ambushed her and left her to rot in the Pit."

"Believe me, if there had been any other path we would have taken it. I regret it terribly, but what's done is done, there's no use dwelling on the past."

"And now you are welcome in Morlak?"

"Oh yes, most welcome indeed! As you will see for yourself when we arrive!" She paused, nudging her horse closer. Reed felt a slim hand on his arm.

"You just need to decide what part of Morlak you will see. Join our cause, help us stand firm against the factions of the Twelve who wish to destroy us. Help us carry out the great plan laid down by our forefathers. I will find you a place by my side. Men for you to command. Think of a spearwall twenty yards deep. You would be unstoppable. A Lord of Morlak!"

"Or …"

"Or continue to cling to your misguided illusions, and the only part of Morlak you will see is the prison cell where you will be spending the rest of your days."

Reed almost laughed at the thinly-veiled threat but managed to compose himself. "Thank you, Verona. You have given me much to think about."

They continued southwards at a leisurely pace. Despite Verona's remonstration, the knight leading Reed's horse did not seem to be especially careful, and Reed's upper body was battered and bruised by the time they stopped to make camp.

Reed was lowered to the ground near the cooking fire and Verona, true to her word, gave orders for him to be untied.

"Turn around, face away from the fire," said a familiar voice. Reed did as he was asked and breathed a sigh of relief as the sweaty, stifling bag was removed from his head. "Don't look behind you," the voice continued. "They can become incredibly irritated if a prisoner gets to see their faces."

A bowl of stew was pressed into his hands, and Nidore sat down on a log next to him.

"I am sorry you are being treated this way, Reed," he said. "Verona assures me it is necessary."

"I'm sure she thinks so."

"I know you think I'm stupid. But I'm not. I see she is trying to manipulate me. But I don't care. She is the only one who helped me when my father nearly died. I love her. I would kill for her. In fact, I already have."

"Your black-fletched arrows. I remember you telling us how you used to train when you were younger to impress your father."

"Yes. Not that he ever cared. Or showed an inkling of love or respect towards me." He sighed. "How is he, Reed? Are his injuries healing?"

"When I last saw him, he was well. Or as well as one in his condition could be. I found him to be more … humble. More thoughtful. Praxis has been made Regent in Jelaïa's absence, and Loré is one of his advisors. The Barony has a long, difficult road ahead, but I believe that together they will be instrumental in Arelium's recovery."

Nidore nodded, tracing the lines of his palm with his thumb. "That is good to hear. Jelaïa has still not returned? I think of her often. I always felt we had a connection, but I suppose, in the end, it was nothing more than a young man's infatuation."

"The last I heard she was in Kessrin. Listen to me, Nidore. It is not too late!" said Reed earnestly. "You can still come with me, return to Arelium, return home. Your father would be pleased to see you, I am sure."

Nidore looked at him for a long time before replying. "Eat up your soup, Reed, it's getting cold," he said, and walked back to the others.

❧

Winter was fast approaching, and the night was dank and chill. Reed wrapped his cloak tightly around him, his ears alert to the slightest sound. It had been at least an hour since the fire had burned out and the last of the indistinct, huddled shapes had retired to their tents. He knew they were somewhere east of the flooded Pit, camped out in the middle of a shabby patch of grassland a couple of hundred yards away from the entrance to a pine forest.

Reed's intended escape route.

He rolled onto his stomach and crawled a few feet forwards, then glanced furtively back at the tents. No movement. An owl hooted somewhere overhead. The night sky was smudged with a smattering of thin clouds. Bright clusters of stars and a baleful crescent moon peeked out through the mist. He inched closer to the treeline, and then, gathering his courage, he stood up.

The night was silent. He crept onwards, each step taking him further from his captors. The treeline drew nearer, tantalisingly close. Less than ten yards to go. He dared not look back, his heart pounding, his breathing ragged. He crossed into the cover of the trees and let out the breath he hadn't realised he had been holding. He'd made it!

A gloved fist came whistling out of the air and pounded into the small of his back. He yelped in pain and surprise. A second punch to the thigh dropped him. Yonis stood over him, a smirk on his thin lips.

"I'm so disappointed, Reed," came a sultry voice from the darkness. "I honestly thought I had convinced you, or at least given you pause. Did you not even think about it?"

"For about ten seconds," Reed admitted, clutching at his wounded back.

"Hmm. A pity. Well, a prison cell it is then."

Yonis's fist cracked down on his skull and he spiralled into darkness.

᠁

Reed awoke to the steady drip-drip of water. His head throbbed like the Pit. It felt like he had been kicked repeatedly by an angry horse. He probed tentatively around the top of his forehead and found a large egg-shaped bruise.

"Just perfect," he muttered under his breath. He raised himself painfully onto his elbows and took in his surroundings. He was lying on a wooden bed bolted into a moss-covered wall, the stone damp and cold from rivulets of water running down the cracks in the mortar. The natural ceiling was also rough and wet: drops of water coalescing along stalactites before dripping onto a dirt floor covered with sodden straw. A set of rusty iron bars ran along the wall near his bed and a tiny slit of a window was set high above his head, well beyond reach. The corners of the cell were lost to the darkness.

The place stank; the sour smell of urine and rotten food. Oh, and rat droppings, lots and lots of rat droppings.

"You're awake."

Reed jerked sideways and pitched out of bed. "Who's there?" he said sharply, his eyes darting left and right. A hunched form detached itself from the shadows in the far corner of the cell. It was a woman, thin and malnourished, her dirty purple dress hanging loosely off her scarecrow frame. The woman raised her head and Reed saw a flash of green and blue.

"Syrella!" he cried, lurching forwards. "By the Twelve, what have they done to you?"

The Baroness pressed herself against his chest, stifling a sob. "Oh, Reed, it was awful. They got to us before we could rejoin the knights. Another ambush, further down the road. We couldn't get away."

"Vohanen? Jeffson?"

Syrella shook her head.

"Damn it!" said Reed miserably. "More pain. More loss. Every time I think I can see a small glimmer of light at the end of the tunnel, something happens and the flame is snuffed out. How do people deal with this day after day? How do they carry on after losing so much?"

"I know, Reed, I know," Syrella said soothingly, wrapping her arms around his waist.

"My parents. I … saw them in a dream. They helped me believe I could make a difference. And, by the Twelve, I have tried. But it is never enough."

"Of course you have," she replied, her full lips brushing against his chest. "You have done all you could."

"What … what are you doing, my Lady?"

"What I have wanted to do ever since I first saw you Merad. To taste your skin, to feel you under my fingers."

"*Merad?* What? No, stop, Syrella, this isn't the time or the place."

"Nonsense, there is no one here to see us, and nothing else to do." One hand slid down his thigh.

"No, stop it," said Reed forcibly, and pushed her away. She landed on her back and looked up at him, smiling.

"You are right, Verona, he is an awful bore. No fun at all." The prone form of Syrella del Morlak stretched, the features distorting and swirling. The arms grew more muscular, the long black hair fell out and new stubbly grey locks sprouted in its place. The green and blue irises burst, leaving empty eye sockets that began to fill with a dark, shining liquid.

The creature that had been impersonating the Baroness stood up. With a crack of bone, her legs continued to elongate until she was close to eight feet high, the top of her pale head brushing the ceiling. The dirty dress she was wearing was now pulled tight around her breasts and buttocks, its hem at the top of her thigh.

She gazed at Reed with eyes that instantly reminded him of his never-ending nights on the wall, staring into the depths of the Pit, a soulless, depressing darkness so empty and absolute it made him want to scream. He fought to keep calm, searching through his mind for happier memories. *A river. A hide boat. A silvery fish.*

The colossal woman stretched, her arms touching the dripping stalactites. "We have not been introduced, little one, but soon all of Morlak will know my name. I am Mithuna, Third of the Twelve, and I have returned as promised to ensure that the Pact is upheld, and that the greylings are not impeded in their return to the surface."

"*Impeded?* Is that what you think we are doing?" He found his repressed anger lurking deep inside his chest and released it, burning away any lingering doubt or fear. "You have been away too long, my Lady. We are not *impeding* them, we are *beating* them. We killed thousands during the siege of Arelium. Drowned thousands more just a few days ago. Flooded the Morlakian Pit. I don't know what you think you are doing to help the greylings, but it doesn't seem to be working too well so far."

"Careful, Reed," said Verona, coming out of the shadows

to stand on the other side of the bars. "Is this how you would speak to a god?"

Reed said nothing, a smile tugging at the corners of his mouth.

"What amuses you, little one?" the grey-haired giant asked curiously.

"It's just hit me that if you aren't Syrella then that means she is still alive. And so are Jeffson and Vohanen. They've probably linked up with the other knights by now. It's going to be difficult to kill her with a hundred Knights of Kriari protecting her, isn't it? That's probably too many to take on, even for you!"

Mithuna's arm blurred past Reed's face and battered the cell wall behind him. "If my priestess did not need you alive, I would rip your head from your shoulders here and now," she said in a low voice, simmering with rage.

"Please don't, Divine One," Verona said smoothly. "Remember the plan?"

"What plan?" Reed interjected suspiciously.

"I took an oath, you see, Reed? An unbreakable promise. I swore to end the bloodline of del Arelium. I have already failed once; I will not fail again. This time I will do things on my own terms. You are to be the bait, Merad. Just what I need to lure Aldarin and Jelaïa to Morlak, with a little help from Mithuna, of course. Or rather, the Baroness.

"And once I fulfil my oath, you will no longer be needed—" she moved closer, pressing her face against the bars and speaking in a hushed whisper, "and will see just what agonising pain can be inflicted by one of the Twelve."

Mithuna, her bottomless eyes unfeeling and pitiless, looked at Reed and smiled.

EPILOGUE

THE STONE GODDESS

"Strange, is it not, that we spent years teaching humans the meaning of hope, only to lose it ourselves? Maybe it is time for us to admit that we are not infallible. That we are not omniscient. Maybe it is time for us to listen."

KUMBHA, ELEVENTH OF THE TWELVE, 123 AT

∾

LORÉ DEL CONTE hobbled down the steps outside the Great Hall, each bending of his injured knee causing him to wince in pain. The articulated leg-brace helped, as well it should considering its exorbitant cost, but as the days grew colder, his joints grew stiffer.

"I'll be using Reed's infernal chair before long," he complained to himself, squinting at the setting sun. Since losing the use of one eye, strong light irritated him. But what bothered him the most, even more so than his eye, was the loss of his perfect smile. He had loved that smile, honed it to perfection. It was that smile that had won him the exclusive trade contract with Morlak. *Pit!* It was that smile that had won him his wife! He felt weaker without it, like a man going into battle weaponless.

He rounded the side of the keep and passed through the iron gates into the garden, his cane tapping rhythmically on the gravel path. Quite why the healer wanted to meet him here, alone, at such a late hour, was beyond him. But he owed the man his life, and a brief twilight visit to the gardens was not much in exchange.

He found the healer sitting on one of the stone benches that circled the marble fountain, the long-haired effigy locked in her eternal unmoving pose, arms raised in supplication. The healer was not alone; beside him sat another man, squat and rotund, with dirty yellow hair, a forked goatee, and wire glasses. The two men were sitting close to one another, their hands intertwined.

Loré coughed loudly to make his presence known. The healer looked round. "Ah, um, my Lord. It is good of you to come. May I present to you my, um, apprentice, Xandris, returned to us from Kessrin."

"Xandris! We finally meet," Loré said, grasping the man's free arm at the wrist. "I have heard many good things about you. The refugees swear that it's thanks to you they were cared for so well."

"Oh, I don't know about that, my Lord."

"We'll just have to see. Can't promise a reward or anything, the coffers being empty and all, but maybe I can scrounge up a title or something. Plenty of those lying around."

"My Lord is most kind."

"Well, I owe your master my life, so I spend a good deal of time trying to think of ways to repay him. I hate being in debt, you see. What is it you wanted to talk about, healer?"

"Yes. It's quite a, um, delicate matter, my Lord, which is why I chose this location."

"Well, out with it, man!"

"Indeed. It concerns my autopsy of the Baron. He was not murdered by a Kessrin dagger, my Lord. The wounds just don't add up."

"What are you talking about?"

"It was a stiletto-like blade, my Lord, not a curved one. The cut across the throat was made with the dagger, that much is true, but post mortem, that is to say after the Baron had expired. There was also some inconsistency with Praxis's testimony."

"I see, and what did Praxis do when you confronted him with all of this?"

"He … I am not sure, but I believe he, um, threatened to kill Xandris, my Lord."

"That is a grave accusation indeed, healer."

"Yes, my Lord, but one I took quite seriously. It is why I have waited so long to talk to you about all of this."

"It is certainly troubling. Anything else?"

The healer nodded. "Two more things. The first relates to the Kessrin delegation and the attack on the Baron's life. I found it strange that the weapons cache entered the keep so easily so I did a little digging. The men were never searched because someone vouched for them."

"Praxis?"

"Yes, my Lord."

"Hmmm, and the second thing?"

"The medallion he always wears, the one he said he lost during the struggle? I found it. When I searched the room again after the autopsy. Under the bed." He reached into his pocket and pulled out a set of silver scales hanging from a long chain and speckled with dried blood. "I couldn't understand why he would want to get rid of it, so I spent a couple of days in the Baron's private archives."

"Really? Who let you in there?"

"Um, you did, my Lord. I have the signed request somewhere."

"Oh, don't bother. Signing paperwork seems to be the only thing I do nowadays. I'm sure it passed across my desk at some point."

"Thank you. So, I did find something. The scales are the symbol of the Order of Zygos, Seventh of the Twelve, my Lord."

"Praxis, a Knight of the Twelve? That seems a bit far-fetched, healer."

"Maybe. Even so, I thought it important to bring these things to your attention. With Orkam and Praxis gone, and the Baroness still, um, out of sorts, you are the closest Arelium has to a ruler right now."

"Thank you for this, healer, and for everything else you have done. I was not always kind to you in the past, and for that, I apologise. Would you leave the medallion with me? I will need to think on this."

"Of course, my Lord," said the healer. He passed over the pendant and pulled Xandris off the bench. "We will leave you now. I hope you have a pleasant evening."

"Hmm," said Loré absently, absorbed by the medallion.

The two men walked away, their footsteps fading, leaving him alone. Loré sat down heavily on the bench and held the medallion up to the setting sun, spinning the silver symbol on its chain, watching how it caught the light. The garden was silent.

He paused. Silent? Where was the comforting sound of the fountain? He glanced up to see that the water had ceased to gush forth from the woman's outstretched hands. He frowned. It was only a matter of time, he supposed. Something wrong with the pipes, perhaps. This place was important to so many people. He would have to speak to the gardeners about getting it fixed.

His cheek ached from talking; the movement of his jaw always pulled on the scars, three deep grooves left by a grey-ling claw. He fished a small flask out of his jacket pocket and took a sip. The taste was strong and bitter, but the pain soon receded to a dull throb.

A splashing sound came from the fountain, like a pebble dropping into the water. He hauled himself up, using his cane for support, and limped over to peer into the pool. A marble finger, long and delicate, sat forlornly at the bottom.

By the Pit! More repairs, he thought. Another, larger splash. Part of a hand, hollow inside like a glove. He took a cautious step back as more pieces of stone fell into the fountain. Above him, a shape began to reveal itself, a female figure encased in the statue for hundreds and hundreds of years. The marble face shattered, exposing two jet-black eyes set in a lightly-tanned, smiling face. The final pieces fell away and the naked woman stepped down from the pedestal into the pool.

"Good evening, fair knight," she said in a soft, melodious

voice. "I am Kumbha, Eleventh of the Twelve. I have awoken. And so, the greylings must have returned."

Loré couldn't bring himself to speak. She was the most beautiful being he had ever seen. His remaining eye was drawn to her lustrous, curly blond hair, falling from around her face and across her breasts, reaching as far as her navel. He mumbled some apology and quickly removed his leather cloak. She accepted his offering with a smile that lit up his world.

"Are you the Baron, perchance? I placed myself here so that I would be free to join you when the time came."

"The … time?" stammered Loré, his voice cracking.

"When the greylings returned. Not all the Twelve agreed with the Pact. Some fought to stop it. We will need to find them now. We will need allies."

"The Pact? Forgive me, I'm not … sure I understand."

"Of course. I will explain. But first …" She leaned forwards and placed her hand on Loré's forehead.

Red-hot fire exploded in his brain, stronger and more painful than anything he had ever experienced. His eye socket boiled beneath his eyepatch. His leg felt like it was being torn apart. He howled in agony as his articulated brace snapped. His cheek burned, the flesh sloughing off it like melted butter.

"*End this!*" he screamed, almost fainting from the pain. His fingers pulled at the hand gripping his forehead, desperately trying to drag it away, but she held him fast. He passed out briefly, only to be jerked awake with a hoarse cry as needle-sharp points punched into his jaw. Then, suddenly, she released him and he crumpled to the ground, moaning.

"I am sorry," Kumbha said, a black tear staining her cheek. "Your wounds were grievous indeed."

Loré scrambled to his feet. "What did you do to me?" he cried. "You monster!"

Wait.

He looked down. He was standing on his own two feet, his cane lying abandoned on the gravel path. He touched his cheek and felt smooth, unblemished skin. With a trembling hand, he tore off his eye patch.

His eye. He could see.

Weeping tears of joy, he opened his mouth and ran a finger along a set of pearly-white teeth. They were all there.

Intact.

"Are you all right?" the vision of beauty said to him softly.

He looked up into her black eyes.

"I am now," he said.

And flashed a perfect smile.

End of Book Two

A BRIEF TIMELINE OF EVENTS

The calendar used throughout the nine Baronies is intrinsically linked to the Twelve, with the year of their first appearance among the scattered tribes termed 'The Arrival of the Twelve' (AT). The events described here take place in the year 426 AT.

-58 AT	A series of natural disasters, later known as the Calamity, wreaks havoc on the land and its inhabitants
00 AT	The first appearance of the Twelve among the human tribes
13 AT	An innumerable host of greylings is defeated in the Battle of the Northern Plains
14 AT	The Twelve separate, dispersing to aid the

surviving tribes and eliminate the remaining greylings

33 AT   The Old Guard is established, sworn to defend the Pits

35 AT   The Council of Baronies is created by the Twelve, who gradually concede rulership of the nine provinces to the tribal leaders

41 AT   The first founding of the great temples of the Twelve and their Orders

122 AT   The battle of Hellin Pass

123 AT   The building of the wooden dam at Terris Lake

123 AT   The last recorded appearance of one of the Twelve

313 AT   The battle of Torc

365 AT   Birth of Listus del Arelium

366 AT   The Schism divides the Knights of the Twelve into two factions, those who wish to aid the return of the greylings are cast out and named 'fallen'

370 AT   Birth of Loré del Conte

386 AT   Birth of Merad Reed

394 AT   Birth of Aldarin

404 AT   Merad Reed joins the Old Guard

404 AT   Birth of Nidore del Conte

405 AT   Birth of Jelaïa del Arelium

407 AT   The Scrying. Aldarin is accepted as an initiate at the temple of Brachyura

416 AT   Praxis begins his tenure as steward to Baron Listus

418 AT   Auguste Fernshaw is elected Mayor of Jaelem

421 AT   Derello del Kessrin becomes Baron after the death of his parents, lost at sea

426 AT   Greylings appear in great numbers at the Southern Pit and attack the town of Arelium. Listus del Arelium is killed. The greylings are finally routed by the Knights of Brachyura

THE TWELVE ORDERS

Printed in Great Britain
by Amazon